ANGELIQUE

Diary of a Contemporary Woman Continues...

LUCY PUSSETT

To Ty,
Big Love Always,
Lucy P xx

Diary of a Contemporary Woman Trilogy
Part two: Angelique by Lucy Pussett

Contact **info@lucypussett.com** for more information.

A catalogue record for this book is available from the British Library.

ISBN (Paperback): 9781916884823
ISBN (E-book): 9781916884830

Published by FreeLynx Books, Unit 71113, PO Box 7169, Poole, BH15 9EL, United Kingdom

www.lucypussett.com

This book is dedicated to anyone who has suffered discrimination, bullying and abuse solely due to their sexual orientation.

The power, the love of Angelique Santoro is here to lift you all.

Hold this book close to your heart and know you are loved.

Also by Lucy Pussett

Diary of a Contemporary Woman
(Part one, of Diary of a Contemporary Woman trilogy)

Angelique
(Part two, of Diary of a Contemporary Woman trilogy)

In addition a Spotify playlist to be enjoyed as you read Angelique on my website

www.lucypussett.com

CHAPTER ONE

JOSHUA

'Hi Joshua."

"Hey Angelique, wasn't sure if you were going to pick up."

"I gave serious consideration to letting it go to voicemail, then I decided to give you a chance at entertaining me."

"It is truly an honor to be granted such an opportunity."

"It is, no question. Had you been my mother, well…"

"Voicemail city."

"Yup. So how are you JoshUA?"

"Can't complain. All pretty much drama free, albeit a little dull and predictable."

"So, you thought you'd call me, see if I can rev up your life?"

"I thought you might be up for that bike ride I promised

you as the weather is looking more settled."

"Oh yes, that bike ride and pub lunch," I say casually, taking another long sip of my gin & tonic. "I'd totally forgotten about that."

"That's so not true, Angelique. I think you've been waiting on my call."

"Is that so? I've been spectacularly busy, not had much time for daydreaming about pretty surfer boys and the like."

Joshua laughs. "I see you've lost none of your tomboy charm."

"Fucking hope not."

"You ok, though?"

"Honestly, it's been a total shit show but I think perhaps the worst has passed."

"Happy to lend an ear if that's helpful."

"Appreciate you Joshua but it's all in hand I believe. Just time and a bit of good fortune required here on in."

"I'll fire over some dates, see if any suit your schedule and we will ride out."

"I don't have any protective gear for your Ducati."

"If you don't mind using my ex-girlfriend's jacket, lid and gloves…"

"Of course not. It's every girl's dream to use some other girl's kit. You do know how to make me feel special."

Silence on the other line.

"It's fine, JoshUA, I'm playing with you. If I have fun perhaps it'll inspire me get a bike of my own."

"And melt the hearts of men in biker cafes around the southeast."

"Well, if that's the price, they will just have to pay it," I say giggling, ending the call.

Back to drinking then. Starting to feel lightheaded, got a little buzz on now. Sean's announcement upset me, rattled me, then hearing Joshua's voice lifted me, so I'm in a bizarre place right now. I'm neither upset nor happy just half cut and floaty. It could be worse, no question.

I feel an overwhelming desire to be held. Thinking of giving my lil' sister a loving hug, smelling her familiar apple shampoo whilst daydreaming away to Wolf Alice's "Don't delete the kisses" playing in the background of this run-down bar.

It's past visiting hours at the addiction clinic and me showing up smelling of spirits is unlikely to get me many admiring looks of appreciation, right?

Text it is then. "Sup lil' sis. Hope you're doing ok. It's probably awful right about now. Just know it is going to get better. You're not in this alone. You have Martin. You have me. Don't go tiring yourself out worrying over mother. I'm all over it. Look in the mirror and smile. You got this yeah. Big love always. A XX"

Addiction divides people, doesn't it? Some are filled with empathy, kindness towards that person, seeing drug addiction like a disease, no different to Cancer. Others see addicts as scum, untrustworthy junkies. Losers, lacking self-discipline, weak people taking an easy path rather than facing their problems causing the addiction. I think the latter is how people view a person coming from a privileged, white middle class background. A loving family, spoilt with money, with security, never knowing abuse, poverty. A self-indulgent snowflake.

I have no idea what anyone thinks or feels about my sister. Moreover, I don't give a toss. She's my sister and I love her. I'm over feeling guilty about not being a perfect sibling growing up – Who the fuck is? My actions at school were not done with the goal of making her life more troublesome, that's rather an unfortunate side effect. I was a teenager, struggling at times and that's all there is to say on the subject.

Three double gin & tonics down the hatch in less than an hour? Full buzz on secured, it's time to stand up – "Whoa Angelique!!" I think, gazing down at my unsteady legs. "Right Mother dearest," I mutter under my breath, let's go see about you.

Selecting Kate Bush "Running Up That Hill" for company on my walk to the old family home, I quicken my pace. I feel like I'm gliding. Not sure if I'm walking faster than I usually do or just the perception alteration as the alcohol guides me. Twenty minutes later and I find myself staring blankly at the gorgeous castle-like front door when it suddenly opens and Mrs. Worth-Higgins appears. My heart sinks whilst a broad smile takes over my face, beautifully disguising the total loathing I have for this false bitch.

"Angelique Santoro as I live and breathe! Gosh, how long

has it been!? How are you dear?"

"I'm great, thank you. And you?"

"Well, I was doing so well and then I heard about what has happened to Catherine, to you all really and I just HAD to come and offer my support."

Translation my friends? I heard there was trouble afoot in the land of Santoro, real gold leaf gossip and got myself around here as swiftly as my short, chubby legs would carry me.

"Well, that's so kind of you, Mrs. Worth-Higgins. Don't let me keep you, I'm on a bit of a tight deadline for work today so just popping by" I say, helping her off the steps and on her way.

Mother closes the door after I've passed through somewhat aggressively. "Here we go then Angelique," I say to myself, turning around, offering an awkward embrace.

"The vultures haven't stopped circling since the news broke."

"She hasn't been your first visitor then?"

"My first visitor? No such luck. Although her expressions of concern for my well-being have been the least convincing."

"She always has been the unchallenged heavyweight queen of gossip in the neighbourhood."

"Her delight in my suffering is nothing but cruel Angelique! Backstroking her way across my pool of misery!"

You'd never know my mother was head of classics at my old school, would you? All that was missing was an exaggerated hand to forehead and a wistful gaze to the heavens.

"She always has been a bitch."

"Language Angelique! It's like you never went to a decent school. You always have had a potty mouth."

For fuck's sake.

"Sorry Mother, I'm just angry like you that you're experiencing this on top of the upset with Dad. It's a lot."

"Thank you, dear. I appreciate your support if not your language."

"Have you heard from Aveline in the States?"

"She left me a rather lovely, sweet message late last night. Bless that child, at least I have her love."

Clever Aveline, calling late enough to know Mother's sleeping medication would have done its job and her mobile would go to voicemail.

"You have my love too, Mother."

"Why yes, of course dear. I appreciate you being here."

Jesus, the irony! That sounded about as sincere as words from Mrs. Worth-Higgins, the queen of bile who just left our family home.

"Coffee?"

"Yes, please." I answer, casting an easy eye around the place. Everything looks immaculate. Mother looks immaculate. So, some things are back to normal even if the deep emotional scaring is only just starting to form.

I sit at the kitchen table, moving the large vase full of freshly cut flowers to one side maintaining eye contact with her.

"I imagine you've been in regular contact with your father."

Just couldn't help yourself could you Mother dearest? What is a passable response? No point lying because she knows I would have been and, in her eyes, there is no possible reason for one of her daughters to support him in his infidelity.

"A couple of brief conversations."

Mother's snort of derision expressed plenty. "Of course, you have."

I close my eyes for a moment to better compose myself. "It's not about taking sides. I love you both and I'm not saying it's ok, his affair. My communication with him does not mean I approve, Mother."

"Well, you'll do as you see fit. You always have."

"What's that supposed to mean?"

"Angelique Santoro. Rebel child, international sporting star, successful businesswoman. You make up your mind to do something, you just do it. To hell with the consequences."

"I'm lost. Are you suggesting me achieving things in life is a negative somehow?"

"Is it achieving something supporting the man who has ripped your poor mother's heart out!?"

Fuck my life. I can't win. I never can with her.

"That's not fair, Mother. If the shoe was on the other foot, I wouldn't turn my back on you."

If the look she gave me was anything to go by, I'd best shut my mouth...

"Do you know when Aveline returns from the states dear?"

"Not sure. Depends on how well the media and public swallow whatever golden threaded bullshit she's spinning."

Another cold stare.

Wow, honesty and just saying how things are, is not going down well today, huh. Implying my sister is like Rumpelstiltskin is hardly a new suggestion.

"I'm certain she will be back with you as swiftly as possible. I know she feels bad she can't be here just now."

"It's unfortunate timing that's all."

I muttered in agreement and focused on finishing my coffee.

"Right, well lovely to have this unscheduled visit Angelique but I really must do some prep work for class tomorrow."

"Of course, Mother. I'll see you soon."

Another awkward embrace and I'm out the door feeling about as appreciated as Mrs. Worth-Higgins.

I select Tonight Alive, "The Edge" for the brisk walk back to my flat. Has Gareth returned? Still angry or calmed down? I know it's his unbreakable love for me which made him react so aggressively to the news of my sexual assault and this makes me smile. He's my universe and everything held within it.

A cyclist with no lights on, running a red light nearly takes me out as I'm crossing the road.

"Arsehole!" I yell at him, whilst skipping out of his path.

To which he replies, "Stupid cunt!!"

Seldom I'm taken aback by anything life throws at me, but this literally makes me stand still and take a breath. Did he just yell that word at me for crossing on a pedestrian green light?! Did I just imagine this? Wow. Had I had Ralph with me, it's entirely plausible he would have been struck as he sometimes walks a couple of feet behind me playing follow my leader.

Opening the front door, I'm relieved to see Gareth cuddling Ralph on the sofa, bottle of beer in hand, a gentle energy in the living room.

"Hey, girl."

"Hey, boy."

"Everything ok?" I ask, taking my jacket off, placing myself in between my boys.

"Yeah. Sorry about storming off like that earlier, just so mad."

"Nothing to be sorry about Gareth. I was wronged, you responded accordingly."

"Still want to tear him another arsehole."

"Of course." I reply, "Got any more cold ones' in the fridge?"

"Stay sat, pet. I'll get you one."

Gareth returns, sighing as he sits down and hands me the beer.

"Czech Republic Pilsner boy? You're spoiling me."

"Award winning Czech Pilsner, to be precise."

"Ohh, look at you Mr. fancy pants." I tease, raising my bottle to meet his.

"Oh, I have news you might find interesting."

"Really? Go on."

"So, about an hour ago, I received a phone call from a headhunter."

"About what?"

"Well, apparently the Hilton is seeking a new general manager and they were wondering if I might be up for it."

"Thought you hated all things global corporate n' stuff."

"Well, I do and probably will dislike parts of the company immensely if I get the job but it's mega bucks and I was just thinking…" Gareth looks boyishly at his feet then at me.

"I was just thinking if I can earn more, perhaps I can save like you do then we can buy a proper house together."

I throw my arms around Gareth's neck and kiss his face all over.

"Yes, Yes and thrice yes, Gareth!" I squeal excitedly.

"Alright luv, was just a suggestion. Give a man some breathing space now, eh."

I jump to my feet and yell out, "Alexa, play Shut Up and Dance with Me" by Walk the Moon."

Moving to turn the volume right up to ten, I grab Gareth by the arm and yank him to his feet.

"Dance with me boy!!"

Gareth takes my hands in his and we start a silly dance grinning at one another. He spins me around and around until I'm dizzy and releases me whereby I stumble and fall into the oversized beanbag by the bay windows.

Ralph joins me, licking my face, my arms, his tail smacking into my thighs.

"It's a spaniel attack, help me!" I cry out.

Instead of offering me any kind of assistance, Gareth throws himself onto the beanbag and smothers us, planting kisses on us.

All the recent drama in my life. All the worry over family just melts away like it's nothing.

I manage to sit upright and push my hair away from my face.

"So…when's the interview?"

"Next Thursday, after my shift ends."

"Face to face or Teams?"

"All the interviews will be face to face Angelique, especially a senior leadership role for the Hilton group."

"Well, I suppose you'll be wanting some interview tips and pointers from a well-respected recruitment advisor?"

"That would be amazing. Who do you recommend?"

I roll my eyes slowly whilst shaking my head at Gareth.

"Nice. I see what you did there."

Gareth laughs. "Of course, I want your help darling. You prep me. Be a tough interviewer and fire all kinds of tricky questions at me so the real interview might feel easy."

"Yup, we shall prepare together. I feel sorry for the other candidates now." I say, picking up my phone and ordering a pizza from our favourite Italian restaurant. I crack open another beer, passing it to Gareth.

"Choose a film boy, make it a good one!!"

CHAPTER TWO

That was then, this is now.

That was then, this is now. Two years have passed since that special evening cuddled up with Gareth and Ralph. Two years gone in the blink of an eye. Time flies when you're having fun, right? I would suggest time flies whether life is fun and carefree or a total cluster fuck of crazy.

With my coaching, Gareth sailed through the four-stage interview process. It was not a very original process at the Hilton hotel group. Generic, often obvious questions flowed one after the other. Gareth said it was as if we knew what questions they would ask, what their reservations would be. Perhaps it was my eighteen years in recruitment bearing fruit, perhaps it was a spot of good fortune or perhaps it was as simple as Gareth was the best candidate for the job.

Certain cynical types were suggesting, "Oh, an openly

gay man in Brighton gets the job over far more experienced candidates! Nice spot of positive discrimination there!" Perhaps the Hilton group were seeking to engage with a manager which understood people, understood Brighton and what people really wanted from a high-end hotel. If this was the main criteria, then Gareth would have killed it.

Following his success, the local media reported with pride that it was local lad, Gareth Newman which fought off stiff international competition to become the new general manager of the Hilton hotel, on Brighton's infamous Kingsway.

The night we found out Gareth was successful, we all went out eating, dancing, and drinking until the early hours of Saturday morning. Sat on the beach with Olivia, Caitlin and all of Gareth's friends passing a joint around, huddled together for warmth, watching the sun come up, whilst listening to the sound of the waves breaking on this stony, less than perfect Brighton beach.

I'll never forget the exact moment I got the call.

It's engraved upon my memory, like burnt plastic on a cooker. Driving back from teaching my class in Brixton, thinking about how I miss seeing Kelly but how proud I was knowing she was doing so well in the Team GB squad, according to Sean.

Springsteen's "Streets of Philadelphia" was playing. I was 20 miles from London, so around 35 miles left on my journey home to Brighton.

"Angelique Santoro?" asked a woman whose voice I did not recognise.

"Yes, speaking." I replied.

"This is Detective Sergeant, Kirsty Jackson. I'm with Sussex police, calling from the Royal Sussex hospital."

"What's going on?"

"We have you down as ICE (in case of emergency) for Gareth Newman. Is this correct?"

"Yes. Absolutely. He's my flat mate, my best friend."

"I'm sorry to advise you Miss Santoro but it appears Gareth has been the victim of a violent assault."

"What?! Oh my God. What's his condition?" I asked, feeling a cold shudder over my neck, down my spine.

"I'm not at liberty to discuss details Miss Santoro but would ask you make your way safely to the hospital's A&E department and ask for me at reception when you arrive. Can you do this?" Her voice remained calm throughout, never showing any emotion. A seasoned emergency responder, a professional. This wasn't a new experience for her.

"Yes. Of course. I'll be there as fast as I can." I confirmed, trying to keep my voice steady but failing.

"Safely, Miss Santoro, is what I need from you, not fast. Safely please."

"Yes, of course officer."

I hung up the call and automatically dropped my speed, pulling into the slow lane whilst I took on board all this information.

My Gareth assaulted. Why? By whom? For what possible reason?

I gritted my teeth, dropped Nelly down two gears and booted her. I was doing over 100 mph before I changed gear again and moved into the outside lane.

"Why Gareth? What could be the reason?"

I must have asked myself this fifty times yet there was nothing obvious coming to mind.

Gareth is funny, warm, bright, and engaging. There's no way he started a fight or deserved a bloody kicking! The only person he's ever antagonistic towards is me and that's usually deliberate to amuse himself.

I couldn't find a parking space near the hospital, so I did something I never do. I just shoved Nelly up on the pavement, well half on the pavement and half on the road so someone in a wheelchair could still get past my car. Double yellow lines near the biggest hospital in Sussex? "I'm so getting a ticket, oh just fuck it!" I said out loud, locking her up and moving swiftly towards A&E.

Upon reaching reception I buzzed twice. No one appeared.

"Fuck's sake! Hello! Hello! Anyone here in accident and emergency this evening?" I yelled out with zero patience and even less charm.

A short, slightly built woman, mixed race, perhaps European Thai or Filipino appeared from a side door, smiled at me with an insincere look that suggested, go fuck yourself but said "Yes, miss. How can I assist you?"

"Angelique Santoro here, requesting you find police officer, Kirsty Jackson."

"In regard to what?"

"Sorry. Ermm. Gareth Newman. I'm his ICE contact. Kirsty Jackson said to ask for her here."

I may have been mistaken but I swear I saw a sadness in her face, in her eyes. The name meant something to her. She knew Gareth's condition or perhaps had seen him arrive in the ambulance.

Before I could ask her anything she said, "I'll take you to Detective Jackson now, she is waiting for you."

"Can I not see Gareth first?"

"No. That's not how this works Ms. Santoro." She finished abruptly, pointing at the door leading away to ITU (Intensive Care Unit.)

"Follow me."

I did as I was instructed, feeling utterly lost and helpless. Even I know ITU is bad news. You end up there if your life is in very real danger.

We passed through the double doors into a brightly lit corridor which seemed to go on forever. Those overhead lighting strips, the off-white walls, the yellow arrows on the floor seeming to hypnotize you, to lull you into a more passive state.

Outside ITU there was a small seating area, with cheap red plastic chairs where I was greeted by two police officers.

"Angelique Santoro?"

"Yes, that's me." I replied, presenting my hand to meet hers.

She shook it firmly, announcing, "This is Detective Gerald Shaw" nodding to the heavy-set man to her right. "I'm Detective Sergeant, Kirsty Jackson. I'll be taking the lead on this investigation."

"Look, I'm sorry, can someone please tell me just what the heck is going on? Why won't you let me see Gareth?"

"He's unconscious, under the closest observation Ms. Santoro."

My heart skipped a beat, my mouth suddenly dry as I repeated her words.

"He's suffered an intense assault. I can't give you more details. We all need to wait on the doctors for more information. I'm sorry."

For those of you struggling, as I was to comprehend why on earth Angelique was not being met immediately by a senior medical professional, I shall explain. In the UK and I imagine likewise across Europe and to the USA, when an emergency call is made for an ambulance due to a stabbing, a gunshot wound or severe beating, the police are notified immediately and indeed may turn up on the crime scene before the ambulance. There are two reasons for this: First, to secure the crime scene and second, to ensure it is safe for the paramedics to do their job.

Incredulous, as it will seem to you reading this, in the UK there are increasing assaults, violent abusive behavior toward ambulance staff trying to save people from further harm. Who are these people? Who the fuck attacks emergency staff whose sole purpose is to save lives, to preserve life?

So, here I was at the hospital talking with detectives, not a doctor. Left in the dark as much as they were. He's in a bad way, he's unconscious was all any of us knew at this point.

Gerald Shaw was an ex professional boxer, complete with flattened nose, his dark brown eyes sunken back in his skull. He looked like he had been hit once too often. He was an old school copper. Happy to go with the obvious choice and the easiest route to conviction.

Kirsty Jackson by sharp contrast was not. She stood average height and build, plain looking other than hair so blonde, her eyebrows and eye lashes would have appeared almost invisible if not for mascara and tinting. Jackson was exceptionally bright. She had worked her way up the hard way, from beat officer at just 18 years old having left college. Not some privileged, fast-tracked graduate but an officer which grafted harder than any of her peers and had made it to detective after eight years loyal service to the force.

Having reached the rank of detective, Jackson was promoted faster than any detective in the history of the force. Just 18 months to detective sergeant. With the promotion came relocation away from her beloved Met Police and East London roots and upheaval to Brighton. Not even 28 years old and just one more promotion, she'd be leading all detectives in homicide and violent assault cases across the entire county of Sussex. Not bad for the daughter of a betting shop manager and café waitress.

I recognised the tomboy characteristics in her from myself right away. The easy, somewhat manly stance, feet wider apart than many women would stand. The confident, streetwise attitude. Here was a detective that would have been fist bumping her colleagues well before Covid-19 became the reason for a new, alternative handshake.

Detective Sergeant Jackson indicated for me to take my jacket off and take the seat beside her colleague. I did so as she found a seat opposite from me to start the mild interrogation.

"Who do you know who has it in for your friend, for Gareth?" Shaw asked.

"No-one at all detective," I replied, shrugging my shoulders.

"You sure about that? Think upon it for a moment longer… perhaps you do know someone or some people."

I twisted my body around, so I was facing him.

"I just said very clearly detective that I did not know. IF I knew anything, do you think I would withhold such information?"

Jackson leant forward, her elbows resting on her knees and looked up, staring into my eyes.

"No one is suggesting that Ms. Santoro. Don't get defensive at this stage. We have a lot of questions to ask and the sooner we understand the background surrounding Gareth, the more likely we can progress this case, which is what we all want. Right?"

Her removing her jacket earlier and now sitting open palmed allowed me to see the tattoo on the inside of her right forearm.

Never give up.

"That a promise to me Detective Sergeant Jackson?"

Jackson glanced down at the tattoo, then looked into my eyes as her raspy, East London accent took hold. "It's not specifically to you, Ms. Santoro. It's to any victim of violent crime which ends up in my lap."

"Regardless, I'm going to hold you to that!" I said, turning my head toward the ITU ward.

I ran my hands through my hair, looking blankly at Shaw then Jackson. "I just can't believe this is happening. Gareth is so lovely, so funny and kind. It makes no sense."

Shaw responded, "Sadly, that doesn't prevent extreme violence from occurring. It's seldom we see this level of violence whereby the victim does not know their attacker, but it does happen."

"If not a robbery, it's possibly a hate crime."

"Expand for me on that Detective Sergeant."

"Is Gareth a practicing Muslim, Jewish or perhaps belongs to a group who believe certain things which is strongly opposed by others?"

"Why would that matter?"

Shaw interjects, "Hate crimes sometimes have religious connections. We have seen a recent spike in attacks on people of the Jewish and Muslim faiths."

"That's awful but no, Gareth is agnostic," I said before adding, "But Gareth is gay."

Jackson gave Shaw a passing glance. Jackpot.

"You think this could be a homophobic motivated attack?"

"Too early to say Ms. Santoro but we won't rule it out."

"In Brighton? Like the gay capital of Europe!?"

"So what?" Shaw suggested.

"Are you seriously telling us that everyone living in Brighton is pro-gay relationships? That everyone is tolerant and happy to live and let live?"

"Well, I've lived here all my life and gay bashing is a rare occurrence from what I know."

Jackson looked upwards to the ceiling and cracked her neck left then right.

"Yeah, you may be right Ms. Santoro but as my colleague suggests that doesn't mean everyone is on board with their way of life. Hatred builds in people, sometimes silently over many years then it comes to the surface and the bile of hatred pours out like a volcano erupting. They smile and talk pleasantly, whilst angry emotions simmer underneath."

"If people have attacked my Gareth solely because of his sexuality, I'll fucking kill them."

Jackson sat back and stared at me. "I'll pretend Detective Shaw and I did not hear that Ms. Santoro."

Silence followed.

If they were waiting for an apology for my aggressive outburst, they'd be waiting a very long time.

"You mentioned if people have hurt Gareth? Why are you so

sure it wasn't a single attacker?"

I laughed as I stood up.

"I'm going to get a coffee. Why don't you google me and work out between yourselves why that did not happen."

CHAPTER THREE

So, now what?

"Gareth? It's ok, I'm here now. The Doctor said you won't hear me, that you cannot respond but just in case you can, I'm going to talk to you and be here ok. You just rest there. It's all going to be perfect boy. It's all going to be good. You're going to be fine."

Did my best to sound convincing. I was talking to comfort myself as much as I was Gareth. Holding his hand in mine, I'd pause now and then to kiss his hand, to rub his hand against my cheek.

It's not an easy thing to look upon your best friend, laying helplessly in a hospital ICU bed. What makes it harder is not being able to recognise him. He had taken such a beating; I wouldn't have known he was my Gareth without being told. His face was so swollen, the tissue damage forced both eyes shut, surrounded by deep set purple and black bruising. I'd seen the aftermath of bare-knuckle boxing and Gareth looked far worse. One side of his face lopsided where his cheekbone had been shattered. Half his face collapsed inwards due to someone stamping on his face when most likely lying unconscious.

"That's enough for this evening Ms. Santoro. I'm sorry, I must insist."

"But I'm just sitting here Doctor Harman, I'm not hurting him. Perhaps Gareth can hear me, he'll find such comfort hearing my voice."

Doctor Harman was a tall, heavily built man with a deep baritone voice.

"I'm sorry, but no. Please. You must leave," he repeated, whilst putting his hand on my arm and squeezing just enough to let me know no further conversation was to be that night.

Whilst I had been by Gareth's bedside, The ICU nurse was always present. There to monitor his condition, ever watchful in case he took a turn for the worse. The detectives meanwhile had spent time with Doctor Harman outside in the waiting area.

Harman had wished us all a safe onward journey and was gone from sight with just a few long strides.

I was fighting back the tears when Jackson spoke.

"Ms. Santoro?"

"Yeah, I'm ok." I replied, breathing out slowly.

"We have a development. I think you'd best know it."

"OK. Just give it me straight. No airs and graces."

I realised before I even finished my sentence how ridiculous my words sounded out loud.

Detective Sergeant Jackson was a feisty, to the point kind of person. I doubt she could dance about any topic. Blunt and as hard hitting as a hammer I thought wouldn't be unkind to describe her manner.

"Whilst you've been at Gareth's side, we've gotten a full run down of his injuries and why they had to sedate him to enforce rest. Had the CT scan shown more aggressive swelling on the brain, they would have put him into a medically induced coma."

"I know, the ICU nurse responsible for Gareth gave me everything. He's got a ruptured spleen which they may have to remove tomorrow most likely if they do the surgery. He has extensive internal bleeding. Collapsed right lung, 4 broken ribs, a shattered cheekbone and fractured eye socket. It appears there is swelling on the brain but that thankfully appears to be reducing by itself."

"Yeah, that's in line with our understanding," Jackson replied, flicking through her notebook. "No easy way to say this Ms. Santoro, so I'm just going to be real here. Ok? This is no longer being treated as assault and battery. This is now an attempted murder case."

I looked into Jackson's eyes, then to Shaw who, feeling uncomfortable averted his to study the floor.

"They left him for dead, Ms. Santoro," Shaw stated, finally finding his voice.

"It's hard to know precisely how much longer Gareth

would have survived left outside in the cold, without medical attention but their guess is less than an hour. It's a clear-cut case of attempted murder."

I clenched my fists and took a step closer to where Jackson stood, hands in her pockets.

"You get these fucking arseholes. You and your team. Grind them up, spit them out and put them away for twenty years. You promise me this Detective Sergeant!"

"We will do everything in our power to apprehend them and get the fullest sentence passed."

"We're sorry this has happened Ms. Santoro. It's a horrible thing to see your friend in this state."

"Thank you, Detective," I said, nodding in Shaw's direction.

"I need to go home to look after our dog." Suddenly aware of my responsibility to Ralph.

"Of course. One last question for now."

"Make it quick please."

"We did google you."

"And?"

"Jujitsu European champion. Team GB. Impressive."

"And?"

"We concluded that the reason you asked us to understand who you are was for us to grasp that Gareth would not have been taken down by a single attacker. It must have been two or more. You trained Gareth to know self-defense, right?"

"I trained Gareth to be an attack dog."

I left the detectives looking wide eyed at one another as I made my way out of the hospital to Nelly and a hefty parking fine.

The fine was £180. Half if I paid within 14 days. I threw it onto the passenger seat and turned on the radio. BBC Sussex was playing U2, "With or Without You." I started crying, sobbing uncontrollably as the song was building. I took myself home, driving erratically, only ever seeing half the road ahead and didn't stop until I reached my flat.

Two years ago. If I stop what I'm doing right now and close my eyes, I'm back in ICU. Like I never left his side. My emotions remain as raw as they were back then. It's like part of me died that night and a dark force was born.

My joy, my salvation as ever when life was hard for me was found within Jujitsu. Kelly's natural gift had been nurtured by Sean and she had been progressing beyond all reasonable expectations.

Her father, Addae had been released from prison having served his sentence for fencing stolen goods. A leopard doesn't change its spots, right? Or can it? In the UK, 75% of ex-inmates reoffend within nine years of release and 39.3% within the first twelve months. Nearly 40% re-offend within twelve months of being released back into society. Not a stunningly positive set of figures! Woeful might be a more reasonable description of how prison really doesn't work.

I had met Addae a few times and when he showed me how

proud he was of Kelly, seeing her beam whenever he looked in her direction it made me want to help him. I'm no saint. Anything I did for him was really done for Kelly. My investment in her development and that of Sean's was always in my mind. If she was happy at home, she'd sleep better, perform better and that double positive means not only will Kelly be happy but she'll also be kicking arse at Team GB.

Don't get me wrong. Her tenacity, her focus was incredible to date because Addae was inside. Getting bullied at school, just channeling all that shit into becoming a winner. But he was out now and if her parents are fighting constantly and he's getting into trouble, I doubt that will help her.

I had introduced Addae to a parent whose daughter, Melissa, attended my youth development programme in Brixton. The family owned two successful florist shops in the area. I had heard their long-term delivery driver had plans to retire as now in his late sixties and was finding the aggression and bad driving in London a bit too much for him.

Addae had a clean license. In fact, was a qualified HGV driver when he was in Ghana. Melissa, whilst jealous of Kelly in the classes, envious of her natural athleticism, becoming a part of Team GB, knew that her life was a good one. She had been brought up well by loving, supportive parents and ultimately wanted Kelly to have a dad. A dad worth having at that. Not one in and out of prison constantly causing Kelly and her mother untold misery.

"Sensei!!" Addae had beamed at me; outstretched arm eager to shake my hand.

I took it and smiled easily back at him.

"Now there's a broad smile if ever I saw one!"

"Sensei. I cannot thank you enough for helping me get this job with Melissa's family. I am so happy to have been gifted another chance."

"Don't fuck this up, Addae." I advised.

"I won't. I am so proud of my wife and Kelly. What they have had to endure because of my lazy, selfish past. I am a changed man. I want them to be proud of me. Perhaps one day they will be."

"Found religion huh?"

"No! Ah, everyone asks the same thing. That a man cannot change without the hand of God guiding them."

"So, what then?"

"As I've said Sensei. I am grateful for another chance. I met many men in prison who just cannot cope with life outside in the real world. It terrifies them. Prison is structure. It is three square meals a day. It is hot water, a clean bed and companionship. It is less scary than the outside world for many. I do not want to become a fearful man. I want to live. To provide for my family as a father and husband should."

"I'm thrilled to hear these words, Addae. Don't be solid for your wife nor for Kelly. Do it for yourself and they will see the benefit."

"Would it terribly bad if I asked you for a hug?"

I smiled, stepped forward with my arms open and hugged

this man with warmth and love.

When I stepped back from our embrace, a tear fell from his eye, slowly sliding down his cheek.

"It's all going to be aces right!"

Addae smiled back at me, a brightness in his eyes, gracefully bowed to me and went to sit on the side-lines, watching his daughter do what she did best.

I turned my attention back to the mats, just in time to see Marie-Claire force a furious girl whom I did not recognise into tapping out of the strangle hold she had been held in.

They bowed to one another and Marie-Claire came skipping over and threw her arms around me.

"Sensei!!"

"Bonjour Marie-Claire." I replied laughing.

"Bonjour. Ca va?"

"Oui, Je vais tres bien merci."

"You seem very happy today."

"I'm in Team GB for real. We are taking on Germany next month. I'm in the team!"

Bearing in mind she was the reining under sixteen French national champion, one might have expected this but it's no guarantee, of course. It was good to see her so humble. It is always pride before a fall in competitive sports.

It wasn't so long-ago Marie-Claire shyly approached me, shaking my hand nervously and bowing to me all beside herself at meeting her childhood hero. Now she confidently hugs me as does Kelly, as do most of the girls if they so wish.

I'm used to a certain level of affection. The physical connections with Gareth, with Sean, were not there at this time, so I needed these hugs perhaps more than I was letting on.

Kelly had finished her contest and casually walked over to join us.

"I guess you're in the team too Kelly?"

"Yes, Sensei. I am alongside Marie-Claire in the juniors," she stated, giving her friend a dig in the ribs.

"Wow, it's like they'll pretty much take on anyone these days!"

Kelly faked a how dare you pose then gave me a high five.

I met her hand and nodded to Steve Smith, Director of Team GB who began to read out all the names of the fighters which would take on Germany the following month. By the time he had finished, I had moved myself away from everyone to the side of the room and pulled the release cord on a huge net set above the center of the mats. The balloons cascaded like a beautiful waterfall as Nena's epic 80s pop song, "99 Red Balloons" began.

One of the most joyous moments of the past two years, without a doubt, was watching the team dance and jump about throwing balloons at one another, popping them excitedly in time with the music.

"That's a very nice touch Angelique."

"Thanks Sensei," I replied to Sean who remained a few feet

away. It had been a fucking awkward period ever since he told me that he loved me and had done so secretly for the past decade.

Not hugging him felt so alien but at the same time the right thing to do. I didn't want to give Sean any hint of false hope. He was my mentor, my sensei, my dear friend. In my eyes Sean was the big brother I never had. Like Gareth. I could never see him as a lover.

Don't get me wrong, I did entertain the idea. He's a highly attractive, incredible man and for sure I was flattered that he wanted me. What woman doesn't wish to be desired by a man of such caliber?

All that said, it's Sean and well, you know what I mcan. Some guys are never going to become your lover or husband, are they? It's like the universe has other plans for you. It felt like there was no choice in my decision but to respectfully reject his advances.

"What's new?"

"Well, I've quit academia."

"Yeah?"

"Steve Smith offered me a full-time role here as Director of Development, which I have accepted."

"And what? I'm only hearing about this now? There was a time, I'd be the first person to know anything good or bad in your life."

"It was only made official last week, Angelique. I thought this news could wait until I saw you face to face."

"Yeah, of course. No more idealistic students and stuffy old coffin doggers telling you how best to teach the students. You must be devastated."

"I'm still adjusting to not hating my day job," Sean admitted with a wry smile.

"How is Gareth?"

"Step by step he's improving. I mean he's stable. We're not going to lose him. Well, not physically."

"Meaning what?"

"He's changed Sean."

"Impossible for such an event to not change somebody."

"Yeah."

"Are the police making much progress?"

"There's a Pitbull leading the investigation. She's a young, detective sergeant highflyer type."

"So, basically you if you were ever a cop."

"Yup. Pretty much. I like her."

"Oh yeah?"

"Get your mind from the gutter Sean!"

"Sorry. Too many years around university students."

We both laughed. Fuck, it felt so good to laugh around Sean again. I need him in my life.

I said a warm goodbye to everyone and walked out of the UK Jujitsu centre of excellence and got into Nelly. I checked my phone, no messages. I asked Alexa to play The Cult, "She Sells Sanctuary" and put my foot down, feeling an overwhelming pull to be with my Gareth.

CHAPTER FOUR

Part 1

Humiliation

My daily visits to Gareth in ICU were painful. His progress was slow. It felt like his body was determined to take the smallest, baby steps possible. His spleen had been removed. There was no choice as there was too much damage to save it. A splenectomy is rarely done, and it really is a last resort procedure unless all hope had been lost. When the surgeon advised me, it is less than ten percent of people with damaged spleens who lose it, it made me beyond furious. People involved in catastrophic head on collisions, their cars wrapped around them like pigs in a blanket at Christmas fared better. People shot, stabbed even, seldom had this procedure. This sums up the level of violence, the pure hatred these people had for my Gareth.

"How you feeling today, boy?"

"Same shit, different day, girl."

"Ralph sends his love. He misses you. I hope you don't mind too much but we've both taken to sleeping in your bed." Somehow the smell of him remained, however faintly and brought us both comfort.

"Of course."

"They said you might be able to come home next week."

"So they say."

You know what hurt the most during my visits? It wasn't seeing him lying helpless, weak and thin in a hospital bed. It wasn't his physical state which upset me the most as the human body given half a chance is robust and uncanny in repairing itself where possible. It was that the essence of Gareth was missing.

Gareth was a beacon of light in my world and always had been. From bullying at school. Saving one another in various ways, from failed relationships to the purest joy dancing together whether in a club or in our living room with Ralph jumping around, sharing the moment. Always Gareth. Always.

My Mother could have passed, and I would mourn her, feel the loss. If Gareth had died that night? A part of me would have died right alongside him, never to return. It's not a topic open for debate, it is fact. Dreadful to say out loud, to think such thoughts? Perhaps. But it is the truth.

"I've bought you the best supplements to boost your immune system."

"Ok."

"I'm going to get you strong again, boy."

“Ok.”

“I’m headed to the police station after this visit to see detectives, Jackson and Shaw.”

“Ok.”

“Would you prefer it if I didn’t visit you daily, boy?”

“Sorry. I just don’t have much to say. I’m exhausted all the time.”

“What can I do?”

“Nothing Angelique. Nothing girl.”

“I’d sooner not sit with the police ignorant again of the events. Is there nothing you can tell me boy?”

“Two guys jumped me around the back of the hotel. It was late. It was dark. I was hit on the head, hard from behind.”

“I know. But why?”

“Fuck’s sake girl. I’ve told you; I don’t know.”

“You said last time they were calling you a disgusting faggot, a fucking queer.”

“And?”

“What else did you tell the police?”

“Nothing.”

“There must be more than this Gareth!”

“Why must there!?”

“People get hurt. People get attacked by homophobic arseholes. All over this cruel fucking world.”

"I think you got targeted because of the press, all the media attention on the local lad, openly gay, getting the big job. It's got to be connected. Why you otherwise? No one knew you before this announcement."

"Yeah. I was totally invisible, unlike you, huh."

"The fuck is that supposed to mean?"

"Team GB superstar. If it was you lying here, there would be a line out the door to visit you."

"I doubt it," I reply, shaking my head. "You've had visitors. Family and friends. You've told the nurses, the staff, you've not wanted visitors. I'm only here cause I either sneak in or refuse to be pushed away by you."

"I'm tired."

"Ok. I'll see you tomorrow."

"Sure."

I usually left the hospital sad, wiped out and ultimately feeling more alone than at any point in my life. I got it, he was suffering. But being pushed away by the person that matters most in the world to you, feels more painful than learning about him getting attacked in the first place. Does that make any sense to you?

I had driven to Brighton Police station tearful, whilst listening to Heart FM which was playing Paloma Faith, "Only Love Can Hurt Like This." Of course, there had been nowhere to fucking park. Brighton is a nightmare to drive around and even worse to try and find a parking space. The traffic wardens are on commission even though employed by the city council and like buzzards in the sky circling a dead animal, ever watchful, ever present to hand out fines.

I ended up back home and walked with Ralph to Police HQ. I went into reception, typically grey and depressing like most public buildings and asked for Detective Sergeant, Kirsty Jackson.

Jackson had appeared wearing black Doc Martins, black skinny jeans, blue t-shirt tucked in and a faded grey bomber jacket. Her beautiful, natural blonde hair tied back in a ponytail. She looked more like a street wise drug dealer than a decorated police detective. You can take the girl from East London; you can't take East London from the girl," I thought to myself as I took her outstretched hand and shook it firmly.

"Dogs not allowed unless police or guide dogs in the building Ms. Santoro. Let's take a walk."

"Fine by me. It's looking set to be dry. Seafront not too far for you?"

"That's fine," Jackson replied, looking skyward.

"You alright?"

"Been better."

"Tough being the victim's friend at times such as these," Jackson offered.

"Yeah, that's putting it mildly."

"You and Gareth are really close, aren't you?"

"Yeah, we are. We were."

"Were?"

"Like a total fucking stranger to me at the moment."

"Don't worry. That's normal. It hurts a lot, but it is normal in these early stages."

"This you trying to be empathetic, Jackson?"

"Is it working?"

"Not really," I said, looking through her.

Jackson coughed.

"Just left the lab this morning, Ms. Santoro."

"Fuck's sake, just call me Angelique, will you?"

Jackson gave me a look which suggested this was fine but didn't much appreciate my tone.

"Left the lab this morning, Angelique....Got DNA."

"Excellent development."

"Takes a while to run all the tests but yeah it's a good start."

"DNA from Gareth's clothing, I assume?"

"Correct."

"So...?" I remarked, shrugging my shoulders, looking at the waves crashing before us.

Jackson drew a large breath and released it slowly before speaking.

"It's a mixture of urine and saliva."

"What?"

"They spat and urinated on him. Perhaps whilst he was lying unconscious, perhaps not."

"They pissed on him?"

"Hard to understand how else his clothing would be soaked in urine."

"And it's definitely not his? Like if he had pissed himself whilst unconscious?"

"Wouldn't matter if he had. It's not his DNA Angelique."

"Fucking cunts! Those fucking arseholes!!" I shouted, making poor Ralph jump and hide behind Jackson.

"What are you looking at!? Keep fucking walking why don't you?!" I yelled out to passers-by, who had decided to stop and listen in on our conversation.

"Calm yourself. This is our business not for the public."

"Yeah. Alright. I'm sorry."

"Look this is a lot to take in. Come see about me tomorrow?"

"You think the DNA will have been run?"

"I can't promise but hopefully the test results will have been cross referenced to information held on the national DNA database."

"If the scum has offended before you'll have them?"

"Yup."

"I mean, this kind of offence can't be their first?"

"It's unlikely but it could be. If it is, we know it's not a violent existing criminal, so we won't waste our time looking at the usual suspects."

"You had people in mind for this?"

"Well, we know nasty people. It's our job."

"Huh. OK. Alright then. Until tomorrow."

Ralph and I made our way back to our now lonely, empty flat wishing more than ever that we weren't. I picked up my phone and called the only person whose voice I wanted to hear.

CHAPTER FOUR

Part 2

Excitement

"Hi Joshua."

"Hello Angelique. Hang on one minute please." Joshua sounded stressed. I could hear him telling his team of roofers off in the background.

"Sorry about that."

"Everything ok?"

"It will be. I swear one of the guys is a moron of the highest order. That scaffolding rig wasn't secure. At any moment it could have collapsed."

"Shit. That's hectic."

"Final warning in writing when I get back to the office, I'm afraid."

"Ah, repeat offender huh?"

"Repeat Muppet more like!"

"Don't bring Kermit into this. What's he ever done to you!?"

Joshua laughed. "Cute Angelique."

"Thanks. I would say I try but well, you know it's just me huh."

"As ever, a welcome distraction."

"Thank you."

"Any purpose behind the call today?"

"Yes. Absolutely. I need a distraction and after long, careful consideration, I have decided this will take the form of a good looking, sexy surfer bum look alike."

"Ride out?"

"Yes, please. Scare me, thrill me, JoshUA."

"Understood. When?"

"Now."

"Drive over to my place. I'll see you in an hour."

"OK," I agreed, ending the call with a cheeky smile wrapped around my face.

I hopped into Nelly, feeling horny, alive, mischievous, and well, finally me!! I put the radio on, finding Gaydio and drove way too fast out of Brighton listening to Fedde Le Grand, "Put Your Hands Up for Detroit."

I had decided during my drive through the country lanes to

Joshua's home in the Sussex hills to say nothing about Gareth. I also promised myself nothing deep, nothing other than fun and laughter. You deserve this, Angelique. Just be free. Live life to the fullest. Own the now, girl."

The gate was open and I parked Nelly to the side of his house away from the garage since it wouldn't be long before we were out riding his Ducati.

I could hear Fatboy Slim, "Right Here, Right Now," booming from Joshua's house. "Fuck yes," I muttered under my breath. If ever there was a dance track to mirror my soul in that moment, it was this track.

The front door opened before I got the chance to ring the bell. Joshua stood there, dressed head to toe in full Dainese, Italian leathers, wearing that easy going smile of his. A look which made me know instantly that calling him over any other man, was the right decision.

"Look at you all leathered up!"

"You approve?"

"We riding bikes or going to an S&M club?"

"Not sure we'd look very elegant on the dancefloor with all this body armor."

"I can rock elegant in green wellington boots, walking the dog in the rain, JoshUA."

"Yeah, I don't doubt that's true Angelique. Come on in, let me get you a glass of water. It gets hot and sweaty riding in full biking gear," Joshua said, walking back towards the kitchen.

"Hmmmm," is all I could offer up, my eyes glued to watching that muscular, perky bottom moving gently in those leather trousers.

Having had some refreshment, we moved to the garage.

"Here. Try the jacket on."

I took the jacket from Joshua, deciding not to make a big deal out of the fact the last woman to wear this was now working some high-flying job in America. True, the relationship was never going to last. Joshua had made that clear the night we met but the head-hunter had created an earlier than likely exit for her, which she grabbed with both hands by the sounds of it.

I put the jacket on, zipping it right up to the neckline. Like me, she was a size ten with boobs, I was guessing. It was a great fit. Not loose. Not too tight.

I took my time studying Joshua. Seeing someone new wearing this sexy, black and red leather jacket wasn't bothering him from his facial expressions. Or was it and he was just masking his feelings? I'm not ashamed to admit, it was turning me on wearing his ex-girlfriends kit. Had they fucked with her wearing it? Did I look hotter than her? I smiled to myself, looked up into his eyes and slowly turned around, casually putting my weight on one leg then the other knowing he would be staring at my arse in these tight jeans.

I looked over my shoulder. "So?"

"Perfect."

"Me or the jacket?"

"Both," Joshua smirked, moving closer to me. He placed his hands on my hips, leaning into me. I could feel his warm breath upon me. Pushing my hair up and over, away from his mouth I stretched giving his soft lips full access to my neck. Sighing deeply, I closed my eyes, feeling the tip of his tongue between his lips then those full kisses, warm and lasting, unrushed, sensual, heaven.

I pushed my hips back against his, running my hands through those gorgeous blonde locks. Joshua kept one hand on my hip, the other was in between my thighs, moving swiftly up to cup my pussy. Rubbing his fingers, circling his hand through my jeans, I could feel the heat burning up inside me already. Tearing my jeans open so aggressively, I heard a button fly off, hitting a metal oil can away to our right. Squatting down to undo the laces on these stupidly well-made Caterpillar boots cursing why I hadn't just worn trainers, then recalling Joshua had said, "No boots, no riding."

Flinging the boots left and right, I managed to get one leg free from my jeans before Joshua was upon me, grabbing my arse with one hand, the other clutching a handful of my hair, yanking me towards his Ducati. Having reached the bike, Joshua lifted my leg up so that I ended up with my foot resting on the rear pillion seat. He ripped my knickers to one side, put two fingers in my sex and went deep, stayed deep, vibrating, rubbing inside me. I gasped as he yanked my hair harder.

"You want this?" Joshua whispered in my ear.

"Yeah, fucking get it. Get it." I snarled back at him, twisting my head around to lock eyes with him.

Joshua quickened his fingering, pressing right up against my upper vaginal wall, hitting my g-spot time and again making me cum so hard, I lost strength in my leg supporting my body nearly knocking the bike off its side stand!

"You broke it, you bought it," Joshua joked, grinning cheekily at me.

"Shut up and fuck me."

"Bend over."

I did as I was told. Placing both my hands across the tank of his motorcycle, spreading my legs wide, arching my back so my sex was open for him.

That moment of anticipation, right girls? That glorious moment when you know a man you desire so badly is about to get inside you and fuck you to within a moment of your life. I moaned, as I reached between my legs, rubbing my clit, circling my bud.

I could hear Joshua spit on his hand followed by silence as that saliva was being worked all over the tip of his swollen shaft. Each passing second felt like an hour. I was about to turn around and tell him to hurry the fuck up! when I felt that thick cock of his stretch me wide open.

Nothing loving or gentle about Joshua that day. No easing in, inch by inch. Just stuck that hard cock in me with one aggressive thrust. My mouth was wide open yet not a sound created. Silence. Like as he entered me, he stole my voice, my vocal cords torn from within me. I closed my eyes. When I opened them, I saw stars, bright flickering light across where my vision should have been.

The only sound in the garage was Joshua's base grunting like deer rutting during mating season. That man just pounded away at me, grabbing at my hips, pulling me onto his rock-hard cock. My palms, clammy with sweat, making it impossible to grab at the tank anymore. I was just being moved forward and backwards, my hands slipping, gliding, like a speed skater at the Olympics.

Eventually, I managed to twist my body around just enough to enable me to push at Joshua's throat although was aiming for his chest. He stopped, slipped out of me, taken aback by my actions.

"I need to kiss you," I said, breathlessly.

Joshua smiled, then passionately embraced me as I jumped up to wrap my thighs around his hips. I gasped as he re-entered me then returned to kissing this gorgeous man, running my hands through his blonde locks. I found myself pinned up against the rough wall of the garage adjacent to a large, framed picture of the album cover from Pearl Jam's Ten.

I dug my fingernails into Joshua's back, enjoying him wincing before getting used to the sensation of pain and pleasure as one. I kept one hand, claw like, dragging down his back as the other wrapped around his neck, kissing him, like this was my last minute on planet earth before being hit by a giant asteroid. Whilst kissing. Whilst being impaled on his perfect cock, stretching my insides my friends?

I was smiling. This perfect, expensive, Italian leather jacket, unmarked, used but mint condition, within twenty minutes of Angelique Santoro wearing it, is getting ruined. Hoisted, dragged up and down the wall, scuffing that Italian flag! Imagining his ex-girlfriend stood in the doorway, watching us, touching herself. Enjoying our pure lust unfold, made me even wetter.

I wrapped myself even tighter around Joshua's hips, grabbing at his neck, his back for support as he fucked me harder. Feeling the back of my head scraping against the sandpaper rough wall as yet another orgasm tore through my body. Joshua didn't pause for a moment even, he just kept on at me. Relentless. Insatiable. Weeks of pent-up desire for one other, exploding in a lustful connection.

Before I knew what was happening, Joshua stopped abruptly and released me. My feet finally touching terra firma. He removed his jacket, reached for a dirty, oil streaked cloth and wiped the sweat from his forehead. Throwing his jacket, inside out, on the floor by his Ducati, he commanded me, "Get on all fours."

"Yes, Sir!" I replied, turning around. Slowly getting on my hands and knees, like a big cat stalking its prey. I took my sweet fucking time reaching his jacket. Arse up, chest down girls. Always.

"Start slow yeah?" I said, looking over my shoulder.

Joshua was panting so hard. Blushed red to his face. I didn't need to be calling an ambulance to his house!

Joshua laughed, "Slowly, it is then."

I stuck my arse up high, wiggling it like a bitch on heat. Joshua gently eased into me. Slow, deep, deliberate trusts. Deep.

You know that feeling when a guy cares about your pleasure as a woman right? His breathing becomes one with yours. Exhale, thrusting in. Inhale, as he draws away from you, teasing you. Keeping that swollen tip inside you but only just right? Fuck. Having been taken to within an inch of my life the past twenty minutes, the sharp contrast from hard, crazed fucking to passionate love making is bliss. Heaven on earth.

"Get it Josh. I'm ready," I yelled out to him.

Joshua had caught his breath. Sounded less like a man needing urgent medical attention.

He grabbed my hips and began fucking me harder. My hands were slipping inside his jacket so I reached out at the rear wheel of his motorcycle for support, some stability, as Joshua got more aggressive with me.

That feeling. I'll recall it vividly until my dying day. The smell, the texture of that tyre rubber, combined with the oil off the chain, made me feel like I was being fucked in a factory. Harder, faster, harder, faster. Joshua reached forwards, grabbed my hair in both his hands, yanking my head backwards.

"You like this? You want it like this?!!"

"YES!! Fuck me hard, come on, fuck me!!" I yelled back at him. My neck hurt. Sweat pouring down my forehead, stinging, as it found my eyes.

"I'm going to cum!" Joshua shouted out. I felt another hard yank at my hair followed by a low lustful moan and four jerking pumps as he lost himself deep inside me.

I had driven back home to Brighton, a big smile upon my face singing along to Katrina and the Waves, "Walking on Sunshine."

CHAPTER FIVE
Swimming Pools

"Spent more time with Detective Sergeant Jackson."

"Thrilling," Gareth mumbled.

If you've never had a conversation with someone following surgery for a broken jaw or in Gareth's case, facial reconstruction, it is not unlike watching a ventriloquist on stage.

Gareth was home. You'd think I'd have said that with joy in my heart, wouldn't you? You'd think, logically that would have been the case, would you not?

OK, OK. One might expect a man following double surgery to be poor company. Splenectomy had been a success. The facial reconstruction for his shattered cheekbone completed. Sipping protein shakes in a lot of pain, watching shite on the TV, doesn't make for a happy camper. I'm not a total idiot. I just want my

Gareth back. MY Gareth.

Teeth clenched, like an angry rodent cornered by a vicious cat. You can understand them well but it's rather off-putting as even when not speaking aggressively at you, every sentence makes you feel as if they are at boiling point.

"I know.... Everything."

"Meaning what?"

I took Gareth's hands in mine, bit my bottom lip hard enough to draw blood and said, "I know they urinated on you. Spat on you boy."

Gareth took his hands from mine, covered his face and started weeping. I repositioned myself towards the back of the sofa so I was spooning him, whilst calling out to Ralph who left his dog bed by the kitchen and automatically curled himself under Gareth's arms. We lay like this for over an hour. Not a word spoken. Holding my boy to me. Kissing his head, stroking his hair.

My drive to see Aveline later that day wasn't helped by a traffic jam and Heart FM playing Fergie, "Big Girls Don't Cry." They fucking do Fergie. Tearful. Silently listening to that song tearing away another piece of me.

I took a few slow breaths before getting out of Nelly, telling myself, "Woman the fuck up Angelique," and walked up the steps to the villa. I felt like the star of a movie. A sci-fi movie, having managed to escape from something dreadful which had been sucking my lifeforce dry. Like Han Solo in Star Wars, Return of the Jedi, when he was in that contraption and required help just to walk, once freed.

The door opened without me having to ring the doorbell.

"Angelique!" a bright eyed, healthy looking Aveline cried out.

"Hey lil' sis," I replied, opening my arms wide to embrace her.

"Come in, come in! Cup of tea?"

"That would be lovely, thanks," I hesitated, wishing I was being offered a large vodka soda.

We passed through the spacious hallway and through the living room to the kitchen.

"Must be good having Gareth back home, finally."

"It's amazing. Like, such a blessing. First, you get well and now Gareth is on the mend. It's been a hard time for us all but brighter times ahead for sure."

"I am better yes but…" Aveline trailed off.

"But?"

"Well, it's not easy for me to admit this, to say this out loud to anyone," Aveline began, looking anxiously up at me.

"Go on. It's ok."

"I am better but I'm an addict, Angelique. I'm an addict and I will always be an addict."

"I'm so fucking proud of you," I stated, leaning across the kitchen table to ruffle her hair.

"Well. That is an odd response!!"

"Not to me it isn't. You had a problem and you acted. Takes guts sis."

"I collapsed in the VIP area of a club, doing lines of coke with a client. I was then rushed to hospital for an OD."

"Hey! I never said it was classy," I said, winking at my younger sister.

"You're such a dick," Aveline giggled back at me.

"Been called far worse and I'm sure you're right! Pretty sure Detective Sergeant Jackson thinks I'm a first-class dick."

"What makes you say that?"

"I'm always emotional, so angry."

"Yeah, that's like, so not you. Wow, Angelique Santoro is human after all."

"Cute" I said, flicking her the bird.

"Surely most best friends or family members would be precisely as you have been? Being physically present, to bear witness to the aftermath of such a dreadful assault."

"Dunno. I've felt useless, lost, angry and hurt constantly. Been all over the place."

"That explains everything. I've been doing so well!! It's finally happened! You've become me and I, you!"

"You're on fire today lil' sis."

"Sorry. On a serious note? You had all my shit to deal with before as well as Mummy and Dad splitting up. That is a lot,

Angelique."

I never told Aveline about my sexual assault at the hands of Robert Jones nor about Sean, that very next day telling me he'd been secretly in love with me for the past decade. She was in no fit state to have me dump upon her and whilst seemingly looking brighter now, she remains an addict in very recent recovery. I simply smiled and stated, "Yeah. That's true. Shit really does come in threes!"

"I really appreciate you. I hope, all joking aside, you feel this and know it's real?" Aveline shared, looking at her hands, then into my eyes.

I took a deep breath and released it.

"Yeah. I know. It's good to have you in my back pocket though."

"Meaning what?"

"Anytime you really piss me off, that's it. One short phone call into Mother dearest and you lose your favourite daughter crown. Just like that," I claim, snapping my fingers.

"You're such a dick!" Aveline laughed and I joined her around the other side of the kitchen table for a sisterly hug.

As I held her, I whispered, "I got you."

Aveline took my hands, held me at arm's length and said, "No. I've got you."

"Shall we go and visit mummy?"

"Unannounced? Sure, why not. That usually works out so well."

"Mummy loves my unscheduled visits!"

"Sure. Your spontaneous visits have a different affect than mine Aveline."

"Well, you're with me so perhaps it'll be different today? I need to be kept as busy as possible. Supporting others, being less selfish and self-centered is key to my recovery."

"Fair enough. Heaven forbid I get in the way of that!"

We took Nelly, dropping the hood as we exited her driveway. Radio 2 was playing Shakira, "She-Wolf." There was something magical about holding Aveline's hand whilst we sang that song together. The sun warm on our faces, wind blowing back our hair. We pulled up outside the old family home, barely finding any room to park as there was a huge truck there. Various builder types chatting much to my mother's annoyance who had them hushed and scurrying back into the garden at double time!

"Well, hello girls!" Mother cried out.

I checked Aveline, thinking what fresh hell is this? Before joining her in a polite welcome back greeting. Followed by our well-rehearsed, standard awkward hug in sharp contrast to the easy flowing, loving sincere embrace offered by my sister.

"What's all this Mummy?" Aveline squeaked excitedly.

"I'm having a 25-meter swimming pool put in the garden along with some fresh landscaping."

Ah ha – The divorce. Of course. Dad mentioned something

about letting it all go her way at lightning speed, doing nothing to roadblock proceedings. He'd admitted all wrongdoing. Admitted adultery in the form of an on-going affair lasting some two years. I knew he was giving mother dearest the family home. I mean, it's only worth £3Million. Just give it away Dad! In addition to this, there was obviously an additional cash settlement, hence the swimming pool.

Still, I'd be no different. Just give it up. Get it done and move on. Better than giving up yearly fees from the import / export business. If business booms that'll cost far more in the future. Plus, this way, it's a clean cut. Done and dusted right?

What was the one thing Giovani, my dad had always said a big fat no to? Yup, a swimming pool. A showy offy, suburbia trinket, is how he felt about them. As was usually the case, I was with my dad on this. Totally ostentatious.

But ah! The timing was glorious for my mother. I'll give her that. To all the poisonous, insincere neighbours who had offered their false love and support for what she was going through? Ahhh, mother dearest. Not subtle. But a rather fun and glorious fuck off to them. Fuck it and fuck you all. Make 'em jealous mother. Why not give them something new to gossip about!?

"How fabulous Mummy!" Aveline expressed, whilst casting an easy eye over three hunky guys lifting some roman statue into place.

I casually enjoyed the eye candy on display. If they could build a swimming pool as well as they looked, it should be amazing. Ha!!

"Looks like they know what they're doing mother."

"At what they're charging, they ought to."

"It's very noisy mummy. Can we have a coffee back inside the house?"

We walked back and into the house, settling ourselves in the kitchen, as always.

"How is Gareth? Any progress on his case?" Mother turned around to face me, whilst fixing the coffee.

"We have DNA."

"Well, that's great news, Angelique!"

"It is in some ways. If the criminals have prior convictions, then it'll be a simple matching of DNA and even without witnesses coming forwards, it'll be hard to convince a jury it wasn't you and your cunty friends pissing and spitting on Gareth."

"Oh my God! Angelique! I didn't know they did that to Gareth. That's disgusting!" Aveline said, wide eyed.

I waited patiently for my mother to say something. She was bringing the coffee over, shaking her head, lost for words it appeared. It is a lot to get your head around. For me personally? It's worse than the punches and kicks given. It's de-humanising someone for being gay.

Black and white right? I mean, do you honestly think a bi-sexual person such as I or a gay man like Gareth have a choice in the matter? It's beyond fucking moronic of you, if you do!

Do you recall your life as a teenager? Tell me, truly look back and answer me this one question....Did you wish to stand out and be different OR did you want to blend in, fit in and be like everyone else? To be Normal? A gay person would NEVER choose to be gay. It makes teenage life confusing, isolating and even dangerous.

No. One does not choose one's sexuality any more than ones' skin colour. It is not a religion whereby you wake up one day and think bollox to Catholicism, I'm going Buddhist or whatever. That, my friends, is a fucking choice you make as an adult. Being gay, being trans, being bi-sexual are not choices.

CHAPTER SIX
Deceit

"The DNA is not a match to anyone on the database."

"So, whoever these arseholes are, they are not known to your lot?"

"Correct," Jackson confirmed, bringing her lips inward.

"Fuck!!"

"I know Angelique. It's a big blow. It is hard to believe people comfortable achieving that level of violence have not offended in the past."

"Oh, but they have offended. Multiple times, I would wager Jackson. The problem is they've never been caught!"

Jackson dug her hands deeper into her bomber jacket, kicked a pebble away from the footpath, back onto the beach.

"What we got now then?"

"Nothing."

"Nothing!?"

"CCTV doesn't cover where the attack took place. Door to door interviews have not given us much if anything worth knowing and it appears there were no eyewitnesses."

I looked at Jackson, shook my head and closed my eyes, feeling the biting wind skipping off the sea.

"So, the investigation is stalling. You've got no clues, no suspects, no answers."

"I didn't say that."

"Sounds like that's what you're saying."

"I've got our tech analytics team all over social media."

"To what end?"

"They're exploring all news feeds. All the comments posted shortly after the attack to present day."

"Go on," I said, suggesting we quicken our pace.

"Basically, these guys are the best at finding out who is out there spreading hatred, which is now officially an arrestable offence. It is a hate crime to encourage violence and intolerance in others."

"So, the game plan is sniff and poke about social media. Find some nasty trolls and see who they are, what they are up to?"

"It's a lot of deep diving. Kinda' stuff you as a civilian

wouldn't be able to do, so yeah we've got the technology and the people to explore, examine and ultimately give us names."

"So, you're hoping whoever these people are, they have likely bragged about it or certainly supported the violence in their posts."

"Exactly."

"Then arrest these people under hate crime offences and hope they have DNA which will match those we now have on the database."

"Pretty much."

"Don't mean to sound negative here Jackson but sounds like an awful lot of hoping."

"Detective work isn't glamorous Angelique. It's a lot of following up leads which often end up dead ends. It's leg work, sweat and tenacity. I want to get these fuckers just as badly as you do."

First time I'd ever heard Kirsty Jackson swear. It reassured me somehow. Her dropping that always polished, detective persona to meet me at my level.

She could sense the energy shift between us and smiled at me.

"Have faith in me yeah?"

"I'm trying Jackson. I'm trying," I replied and walked back towards my flat listening to Sam Fender, "Seventeen, Going Under."

The day after meeting Jackson, I found myself utterly bored

at work so took Ralph for a short drive to see my dad at his import / export business at the Shoreham business park. I found him, coffee mug in hand, sitting on a flimsy stool, enjoying the afternoon sunshine.

"Hey!"

My father turned his head around, stood up and gave me his best, warm Italian embrace.

"Hello, Angelique. You look tired."

"Feel like shit. I'm exhausted."

"Still not much progress in seeking out Gareth's attackers?"

"Police got nothing."

"I'm so sorry you and Gareth are going through this."

"I know, thanks. How's everything between you and Jane?"

"Amazing. She's a wonderful woman. I feel very lucky to have her."

"That's great. I'm happy for you."

"Seen much of your mother?" Dad asked, whilst looking at his feet.

"It's OK Dad. You don't need to keep feeling bad. What's done is done. Having Aveline back from the states obviously helps her a lot. She's her best friend."

"That's a relief. I thought she was only to be gone a week or two. Was almost a month in the end wasn't it?"

"Yeah, close to that," I confirmed, now my turn to study the ground. Fuck! I hate lying to my dad. Aveline was in the recovery, addiction centre for two weeks longer than was originally planned. Her cravings were brutal and the doctor in charge, Dr Rahman, was not comfortable with letting her out. He wasn't comfortable. I'm still not comfortable. Just a shit show. It's about time I got used to playing the lead actress, yet here I was, my stomach tied up in knots.

Dad and I chatted about this and that before an urgent shipping issue meant our time together had to be cut short.

Whilst driving home my head was full of various thoughts, many of them surrounding Gareth's case. It was like my thoughts were so clear, so precise, I could not ignore them. Catatonia, "Road Rage" was playing, so I turned the volume up and let my mind spark freely.

"Sup, boy?"

"Hey, girl. You alright?"

"Yeah, I'm ok. Just been with Giovani. He sends all his love and best wishes to you."

"Love your old man."

"I think most people do."

"Well, other than your mother, who I'm pretty sure hates his guts."

"Yup. That's fair," I said laughing.

I stopped myself from fussing over Gareth a few days before. Making a conscious decision not to bang on about the case, which he seemingly cared so little about. I stopped asking how he was feeling. I was not his mother, yet remain his best friend and this best friend knows when to wind her fucking neck in.

I was sick and tired of the short-tempered responses. Nothing I said was right or what he needed so there was far more silence than usual not aided by Gareth being more stoned, more often, than I had ever seen. You know when someone is smoking too much weed? The dog prefers sitting in their dog bed in the kitchen away from your cuddles and warmth!

Feeling utterly conflicted. Allow me to explain my friends. I had been Gareth's best friend for twenty-two years. A long time eh. In all this time, it had never occurred to me to snoop, pry, to disrespect his privacy in any way. But during that car ride home, all I could think of was why are you lying to me, boy? What are you hiding? What's going on?" Followed by other sharply focused points such as, why are you not frothing at the mouth like a rabid dog? Why are you not as livid as me? What do you know? What are you withholding from me, from the police?"

Can you guys cast your minds back to a point in your life when you had taken a good hard look in the mirror and been brutally honest with yourself about a failing relationship? A lover, a friend? How did that make you feel? Sad? Angry? Frustrated? Disappointed? Disillusioned? All these things and more perhaps? But at the same time, you could no longer go on living within yourself. Stuck in your own mind, having taken those deadly few steps towards honesty, you are now done in! There is no going back! You cannot shrug those feelings off. Oh, as much as you want to be a coward and just hide away from yourself, you can't, can you? You have to say or do something.

I communicate well. I'm an agent. A Headhunter. Being able

to communicate effectively, is a key skill essential to my job. That said, all my best efforts to communicate with Gareth had failed. There are times when words are not enough and that time had come. Frustrated and angry by the lack of developments in this case. Exhausted emotionally, I was seemingly willing and ready to overstep any previously existing boundaries.

Three days later, I saw an opportunity and grabbed it. Gareth wanted to clear his head, get some fresh air. He and Ralph left the flat. He wasn't in great shape so I guessed I had around 20 minutes to myself. I checked the bay window and waited until they were off the steps and into the street below. Picking up Gareth's phone, I was relieved his pin had remained unchanged despite upgrading to a new phone a few months ago. My date of birth. 110386. In we go.

Inbox was busy but nothing of interest. Well-wishers. Some I knew, a few I did not but nothing useful to be found here. Sent items, the same. Shit. Ten minutes had passed and I had learned nothing.

Deleted items. Hang on! Who the fuck is Paul Hardcastle?

His text had read. "We need to stop. I can't do this any longer. I'm the new head of this church. I should never have allowed myself to do this. Forgive me."

Gareth had responded, "Don't do this to me, to us, Paul. I love you and I know you feel the same way about me."

My mind was racing. I said Paul Hardcastle out loud four times as I put his phone back where I found it. Is this what's been missing? Who is this Paul Hardcastle, where is he from?

Which church group is he the head of? How did he and Gareth ever meet? How could Gareth keep a new relationship from me? I thought we were like twins. We shared everything, didn't we?

It was a strange place to be, having all these questions firing about in my mind, coupled with a sadness that he lied and deceived me.

Moments later, I'm feeling wretched and guilty that I have gone and invaded his private space. Ah, snooping through someone else's phone, Angelique!? Let's talk about deceitful, sneaky behaviour shall we, you fucking hypocrite!?

Realising in that moment, I would look guilty as sin if he walked back in, I hurried myself into the kitchen and started chopping vegetables. Coq Au Vin was one of Gareth's favourite meals. He would smile seeing me prepare this for him and I would smile sweetly back, kiss his cheek as would a wife poisoning her husband's food.

I'm ashamed to admit this but I felt exhilarated. I had a rush of energy which I had to play down so as not to alert Gareth. Is sneaking around usually so invigorating? Is this how people feel cheating on their partner? Stealing money from your company and getting away with it?

All I can share with you is I had a burning desire to research the web, find out everything possible about Paul Hardcastle, his church and anything in-between. Angelique Santoro. Private Investigator had a nice ring to it.

CHAPTER SEVEN

Part 1

Sherlock Holmes and I

A bomb could have gone off down the street from where I was sat and I'd have not flinched a muscle, nor looked up from my research. Listening to Stevie Wonder, "Superstition" transfixed by what I was reading. The internet café called ABC Tech, served decent coffee and was located just off Sandpiper Lane. Whilst I was not an ex-police detective or experienced private investigator, I was someone that had watched a thousand hours of Bosch, CSI, Silent Witness, NCIS, Criminal Minds and read enough crime thriller books, to fill a huge bookshelf.

I knew I did not want to leave any trace of my sleuthing visible. Nothing could be found online on my phone or laptop linked to me. Why I was being so cautious at that time I cannot tell you. I wasn't being investigated or looked at in reference to Gareth's attack. Angelique Santoro was the hurt best friend, right? Maybe it was just too many hours reading and watching crime related stuff, it just felt like I should be cautious and seek to protect myself.

I sat back down with my second coffee, gave Ralph a bit of fuss and a dog treat from my coat pocket and powered on. Paul Hardcastle. Your church. Something felt wrong. Very wrong.

You know when someone is bullshitting you, taking you for a fool? For example, a young girl comes up to you in the high street and says, “I’m sorry to bother you but I’ve lost my purse, my mum was expecting me home an hour ago, I just need £2 to get a bus home. Can you help me?” Translation? Truth? I’m an addict and I need £10 for a fix of crack or heroin and you’re going to get me closer to my target. All been there, right? Oh, a few times I was a sucker! Only after it happens to you too many times do you suddenly realise what a fool you were and how good at looking lost, sad and helpless these people are. Not an Oscar winning performance but worthy of a nomination!!

Hardcastle was a highly educated man. Left Harvard with a law degree, practiced law for a few years with various large, global corporates specialising in merger and acquisitions before feeling the calling of the Lord. At the age of 32, he decided to give all his energy and focus to the church, to helping others. Admirable indeed!

So, what was wrong with this? Surely a person should be congratulated for turning their back on corporate money and lofty social status to presumably earn far less and serve the everyday man? I’m still working out what I believe with regards to faith, spirituality, and such topics. Agnostic or unsure is where I stand.

I believe in being kind and decent to people and to support and encourage them. To some, these are good Christian qualities.

I think you can be a good person, do good things without having a specific religion in your life.

Paul Hardcastle's church, "Eternity Saints" seemed a bizarre combination of Scientology and Latter-Day Saints. It was its own identity, taking various bits from other churches and faiths and making out they somehow were the only church that really understood how God operates and how one can truly be saved, find lasting salvation. The wording made me scrunch up my face and for sure this outfit was controversial. Various articles from around the world suggesting like Scientology they were not a church, a religion, which took kindly to any form of criticism and often responded by attacking the attackers, as it were. "You speak or write poorly about us and we'll dig up dirt on you and discredit you, your family." Whilst it stopped short at, "You'll be sorry." The articles I read, had suggested that aggressive, threatening behaviour had been experienced by some members of the public.

This group had money. I remember reading somewhere, "If you really want to get rich, start a religion." Plenty of people give ten percent or more of their annual income to the Catholic church. I had no idea how this group worked but they offered various spiritual courses and counsel which all came with a hefty price tag.

One of the things which they did appear to line up with and it read like the Old Testament was that this church was anti same sex marriage and believed homosexuality was a sin. You will go to hell for being gay.

I sat back, drained my coffee, logged off and left the internet café in a daze. My mind was hectic. How the fuck did my Gareth get involved with this person? Everything Gareth and I believe in. Who our friends are. Sure, not all my friends are gay, bi, or trans perhaps one in three are. We live in Brighton; the gay capital of Europe and this church is growing. Its UK operations are based here.

Suddenly, I bumped into a heavily built man carrying his daughter in his arms, apologised and kept walking.

Locating a bench in Preston Park, I sat myself down encouraging Ralph to jump up and join me so I could stroke him whilst assessing my thoughts. I recalled my first meeting with detective Shaw. "You think everyone in Brighton is happy about people living a gay existence, Angelique? Or perhaps some people are seething, angry but just keep it all quiet?"

Is this true? Is this really where we were at in 2022? Is this how some people were feeling in large numbers in this bizarre, fucked up, post Covid world we are now living in? We have less tolerance, more anger. Did all the self-isolation breed less love and kindness for our fellow man or woman and increase intolerance? Or was this always there and it was just good timing for this outfit to invade our minds?

There was a growth in right wing politics and beliefs. In Italy, a political party were openly anti homosexuality. In the UK, we read in horror that in America there was a bill being passed to make abortions illegal. That a woman would not be permitted to terminate her pregnancy even if the victim of rape and abuse. A woman's body was not her own, to do with as she saw fit.

Strange times. Most of the time, I look at the world in awe and wonder thinking how amazing it is, how incredible and beautiful people can be. I'm an optimist. Good things don't happen to negative people is one of my favourite sayings. Obviously, that is not a dig at people who suffer from anxiety, depression or other mental health complications.

I became a hero at Team GB. The first British woman to win the European championships in my sport. I did that by being ridiculously positive and putting myself in a bubble of calm, good energy. At that moment? My legs were heavy, my soul drowning in a depressed state of sadness and confusion. I just didn't get it. Why would I?

The only lead we have is this guy and his church group. I had to make sense of this. Find answers to the questions.

Paul Hardcastle did not do this. I was certain of this but what if people who worked for him did? What if members of his congregation somehow found out about Gareth and Paul's secret affair? Had attacked him to prevent news getting out their leader was a homosexual? It was possible. It would have sent a firm, clear message to their leader, "It'll be you next time." I nodded my head. I'm on to something with this train of thought. Cold shiver down my neck, arms, all the way down my spine only ever occurred when something was happening in my life which was very wrong, yet I was seeing it crystal clear.

The following fortnight had me thinking a lot about Kirsty

Jackson. "Detective work is leg work; dead end leads and tenacity." She wasn't wrong. I had located the church HQ. A modern, newish built property, off Lewis Road, about a mile north of the seafront. I'd revisited ABC Tech internet café a couple more times, doing some "deep dive" research on the church, its' founders and trying to establish who was senior in the UK and who had the most to lose if numbers suddenly fell.

It was a warm, sunny morning and I was parked up 50 metres or so from the church entrance watching the comings and goings through a small pair of military spec binoculars, I'd purchased recently from an army and navy surplus store in Southampton.

Simon Smitherman, head of membership care, which I think was like a parliamentary whip, came out of the church and went towards a new BMW which was on double yellow lines, just a few doors down from the church. For those of you not from the UK? Double yellow lines mean, "You cannot park here ever."

A traffic warden, a slightly built man in his 50s, was in the process of writing up a ticket when Smitherman came up to him and started yelling at him. Right up in his personal space, throwing his arms around, pointing his finger in the poor man's face. The warden took a step back, put the electronic device away and started to walk away from this arsehole who yelled more abuse, before getting into the BMW and driving away at pace.

I waited until the warden was a few feet away from Nelly, got out and gently said, "Excuse me, Sir?"

He glanced up at me, clearly anxious. Distressed.

"Yes?"

"I saw what just happened over there. Are you ok?"

"Not really. Not my first encounter with him. I should have stood my ground and called the police."

"From what I could see, if you had, I think he might have hit you."

"Yeah, perhaps. He's a nasty piece of work that one."

"What makes you say that?"

"He's from that whacky bunch of freaks. Some new age church thingy. All odd balls, you mark my words but he's different," the warden claimed, pointing back towards the church.

"Different how?"

"Well, you saw him. How aggressive he was. Not normal, is it? I mean, I get sworn at, it's part of being a traffic warden in Brighton. But the way he is? Unhinged is the word. That man is unhinged."

I put my hand on his arm and said, "I'm so sorry that you've had this experience today, Sir."

He smiled at me and suggested, "You're alright you, ain't ya? One of the good uns'," nodded his head and walked away.

Jackson didn't pick up when I called. I left her a voicemail asking her to call me ASAP then got on with my drive to London. This evening was Team GB Vs Germany and for the first time in a while I had good reason to smile to myself.

CHAPTER SEVEN
Part 2
Fight Night

Singing poorly but enthusiastically to AC/DC, "Back in Black" I entered Crystal Palace. Such warm, fond memories of the Crystal Palace National Sports Centre. It was the venue which played host to the Jujitsu British championships, when I won the title, becoming the "youngest ever national champion." Remarkably, I still am, after all these years. The place was heaving. Back in my day, we might have a couple thousand people present and over half would be supportive friends and family with zero interest in Jujitsu.

The internet has played it's part in making Jujitsu more cool, more visible and when you have the likes of the famous actor, Tom Hardy on Instagram competing in the sport, of course it positively affects popularity. There were TV crews parked up. Eurosport and BT Sport were covering the contest with major

German television stations. I pulled my baseball cap lower and picked up my pace carrying my smart tailored trouser suit and blouse in a suit bag over my shoulder.

"Isn't that Angelique Santoro?" A teenage girl asked her girlfriend, as I walked past them.

"OMG, it like so is her!" her friend yelled out.

I stopped, turned around and said, "Hi girls!"

They ran over and before I knew it, I was surrounded by teenage girls and boys, signing autographs. I love giving energy to people and to see so many now into a sport I've always loved but had often found myself explaining what Jujitsu even was is really something.

How strange at 36 to now be semi-famous. Whilst competing, I was totally unknown to the British public. Part of the reason is Marie-Claire and Kelly, of course. They have a crazy number of followers on TikTok and Instagram as always posting funny videos and just generally being total bad asses and I'm in some of these videos.

Security came and ushered me off towards where the media hub was, so I could get changed and sign in.

It was something of a relief the championships were being held in the UK and that I had been invited to commentate on the event. Santoro Recruitment Services aka SRS was not doing well. Interest rates were sky high, nurses and paramedics out on strike. The NHS which provided me with around eighty percent of my income, were making cuts, not getting new hires and SRS was struggling.

I am not blaming my business doing poorly just on things outside of my control, to do so would be both inaccurate and dishonest. My mind had been elsewhere ever since the attack on Gareth. I wasn't doing half the things I should have been, so being offered ridiculous money to commentate on the contest wasn't something I was going to pass up. The Hilton group had placed a temporary general manager in place until Gareth could return but he wasn't on full pay, he'd only just started working for them, so money was tight. This gig had perfect timing and meant my detective sleuthing was being funded!

The event schedule was explained to me. I was given strict instructions about where to be and to be aware when filming was being halted and adverts being run. I paid close attention, nodded, and smiled easily.

"Oh God, the camera loves you, Angelique. You're a doll!" Melanie, the lead producer for the channel, called out. Melanie was late 40s, impeccably dressed and just like Jennifer Saunders's character from "Absolutely Fabulous." Everything was "Oh, darling this" and "Glorious that" and "Oh, would you, that's marvelous!"

She was lovely however, loved her job and fun to be around. Now that I knew my schedule and what was expected from me, I removed my posh, high heeled shoes, slipped on a pair of Converse all-stars, blue, of course, to match my suit and went off in search of Kelly and Marie-Claire.

I found the pair larking around in the changing rooms.

"Hello you two!"

"Sensei! Oh, don't you look all posh n' proper!" Kelly cried out, jogging over to embrace me.

"You look very chic Sensei." Marie-Claire suggested as she casually walked over to join her best friend in the group hug.

"Who's going to kick arse and take names today?"

"We are. We are!!"

"Correct answer. You girls feeling it today huh."

"I'm so nervous Sensei but I'm happy you are here with me. Marie-Claire has been helping me."

I smiled at Marie-Claire who gave me a look which suggested, "Kelly is my best friend. Of course, I'm helping her."

"Do you need anything from me?" I asked, holding each girl by the hand.

"Nothing in particular, it's just great you are here to support us," Marie-Claire said, answering for them both.

"Look, I've got a busy day working for the television and media company but I'm going to be as close to the mats as I possibly can. I promise, I'll be watching every contest. Every second of every fight. Just because you can't see me, doesn't mean I'm not right there with you. Ok?"

We high-fived one another and I wished them all the luck in the world and reminded them how special their gifts are. That I believed in them as much as I did myself, when I was fighting.

I asked the woman doing my hair and makeup to go easy and not make me look like a circus clown. She laughed and said, "You need some makeup, as the bright lights and the way TV cameras work they flatten and dull your features. Don't worry, I'll do the minimum, I've been advised how you like things done, Ms. Santoro."

I was taken aback. She'd been advised how I like things done? I'm not Madonna or Taylor Swift! I smiled to myself and thought it was great the PR rep for these people had listened to me but I wasn't really expecting it to have been keenly observed and acted upon. You know me. Bit of lip gloss and mascara, I'm good to go. Full face make-up? Nah!! But, I have to say by the time she finished, I did look good!

The afternoon was progressing well for Team GB. Of course, some of the athletes for both countries found themselves not progressing to the evening quarter finals. A few surprises with athletes expected to be in the semi-finals not making the cut. Never bet on sports is my advice. The form guide, studying who should do what in any sport, come the day itself, well, it often goes differently. It's why the people owning the betting shops have the yacht in St. Tropez and not the punters frequenting their premises.

Kelly and Marie-Claire both delivered truly gutsy, focused performances reading their opponents beautifully, counter attacking with grace and poise. I don't think I did a very good job at the end of the afternoon session at being all cool and media professional! I was clapping my hands and shuffling about in my seat, punching the air and well just being me. Pretty sure if I had an agent, he or she would be rolling their eyes and thinking, for fuck's sake Angelique be cool, be measured, be professional and refined! I'm not very good at hiding myself. I wear my heart on my sleeve and like my dad, I'm passionate, excitable, and real, always. I wasn't a cool kid in school, was I?!

There was time for a quick meal before the evening finals and again I was taken aback by how these media darling types got looked after. It was more like a five-star hotel. I even got the catering manager's business card for my own personal reasons, like if in the future, I might throw my dad a surprise birthday party or something.

One of the screens was zoning in on Kelly and she was looking so anxious. I felt like a mummy bear seeing her cub in distress.

"How long do I have?"

"What?"

"When am I joining you on air, Melanie?"

"Less than ten minutes!"

"OK. I'll be back!" I said, as I put my suit jacket on and ran out of the studio to cries of, "There's no time, where are you going? Come back Angelique!!"

I ran to the mats, dodging people as if in a computer game then slowed up, looking calm and graceful, in control, as I found the Team GB camp. Kelly saw me and I mouthed "Stay there." As I reached her, I pulled out two earbuds and with one hand put a bud in my ear and gently placed the other in Kelly's ear.

Moments later, we were kneeling, facing each other as "Welcome to the Jungle" by Guns N' Roses commenced. I turned the volume up high, placed my hands on her shoulders, encouraging her to do likewise, as we got into the music. Staring into Kelly's eyes, smiling at her, not a word spoken. She just needed to see how much I loved her and believed in her. That's all and to remind her this is fun! We're here to have fun. Enjoy this moment. Live it, own the now! Love it!

After a couple minutes, I left her mouthing, "You got this." She beamed back at me. That smile of hers, could light up the darkest night sky. Once I was confident the cameras were not on me, I sprinted back to the studio and got back just in time as the evening show got going.

Commercial break, a couple minutes to breathe and better compose myself.

"Sorry about that, Melanie. You must think I'm a terrible guest commentator."

"You're different, Angelique."

"Is that bad then?"

"No. Different is always good. You're the Lady Ga-Ga of sports commentary." She laughed and said, "The camera loves you; the people love you."

I recall being so relieved. I needed the money and not being invited back in the future would have been a bitter pill to swallow.

It was just as well me being me was going down well with the media folk. I was even more excitable in the evening show! When both Kelly and Marie-Claire got through to the semi-finals, I got off my stool and ran around the commentary room shouting, "Yes, Yes. C'mon England. COME ON!!!!"

The guest from Team Germany, had sat quietly and without emotion throughout the day, clearly thought I was a total mentalist and I just didn't care. I'd sooner cut my hand off with a meat cleaver like in those bloody "Saw" films than be like her, all stoical and lifeless. She had competed in my era but we'd never fought one another. I could read what was behind her eyes. How did this excitable child beat everyone in Europe time and again?

Passion is why, you dullard! My eyes said back to her.

The next two hours were the highest and lowest for me. It's far worse watching people you care about, you love, performing in sports than being the athlete. I now understood how my dad must have felt all those years supporting me. It's horrible! My stomach was in knots, my palms sweaty. It's so passive. You can't do anything to help. Just sitting or standing, every second feeling like an agonizing minute.

Kelly was being schooled by a crazy talented German fighter. It all ended in tears, when Kelly landed awkwardly, two fingers forced back the wrong way, breaking instantly. These people knew their job. The cameras were on her, on me, back to her soaking up the agony, the tears. I had my hand covering my mouth, my eyes wet. Kelly was crying openly, holding her hand up, supporting her best he could, was Sean.

Felt like someone was squeezing my heart. My chest was tight and I just didn't want to be in this commentary box a moment longer. I needed to be with Kelly but couldn't. I'd taken the piss enough today and reminded myself this is what they wanted. My joy, my sadness. Angelique Santoro unable to hide herself away was television gold. Kelly hurting herself was television gold. It's high drama. All good for viewing figures. All and any drama are, right?

Marie-Claire had progressed her semi-final as if a walk in the park. Sean was talking with her. She looked pissed. Looking past Sean, staring across the mats to the girl she would be fighting in the final. The girl who had just hurt Kelly.

Marie-Claire was a cool cat. Old way beyond her years but she had me worried now. High emotions can be a gift to the opposition. It needs to be calm, controlled aggression, not wild, angry, I'm coming for you!

Fuck! I so wanted to be there on the mats with Marie-Claire, but she was with Sean. My mentor. My Sensei. I knew Sean understood clear as day what was going on with her. The cameras had zoomed right in on them, and I could see he was doing exactly what I would. Holding her hands, talking calmly to her. Reminding her that she was going to win this contest but only if she remained calm and collected.

It was a tightly contested final. Both athletes showing why they were perhaps the best juniors in the world right now. Steinberg, like Marie-Claire was a tall, rangy fighter. Last year's junior national French champion taking on the best junior fighter Germany had produced in many years. You could have cut the air with a knife. Silence in the commentary booth at times. Gasps and me biting my lower lip being recorded for more than verbal commentary. With just forty-five seconds left on the clock, Marie-Claire threw Steinburg over her hip, pouncing catlike upon her, putting her in a strangle hold.

I jumped up, knocking my stool over and shouted, "That's it Marie-Claire. Hold her tight, keep her down!"

Twenty-five agonising seconds passed, and Steinburg's face was starting to turn blue and red. She tapped out.

I squeaked, punched the air, as Marie-Claire stood up, utterly exhausted, her arms held high, head back as the crowd went crazy. Air horns, usually associated with Ice Hockey, blaring around the stadium. The crowd on their feet chanting, "Engerland – Engerland – Engerland!!!"

CHAPTER EIGHT

You again?

"Hey Jackson."

"Morning Angelique. Sorry, I missed your call yesterday, what's so urgent?"

"I have a name; I want you to get your analysts to explore, please."

"You have a person of interest to the case? How?"

"Doesn't matter how. Will you run the name?"

Jackson breathed out, sounding a bit cheesed off at my unwillingness to be open.

"Obviously."

"Simon Smitherman, head of membership at Eternity Saints, a church group based on Lewis Road."

"You have reason to think he could be involved or may know Gareth's attacker?"

"I think he's someone your team should explore with an open mind."

"Fine. I'll get on it."

"Thank you," I said and having wished her a productive day, hung up.

Team GB had beaten Germany on total fights won, as well as overall points scored. The next day, I thoroughly enjoyed myself reading about the performance. The British media is typically over the top in praise for a national sporting team or brutal in its criticism. The Lionesses had won the European Football Championship 2022, lifting the profile of women's football and making these amazing women household names. The media loved them, the people loved them and it was fabulous. Other teams, in other sports would get slammed. Not sure how it is in other countries but the Brits love to either celebrate a team or slam it! There is little in between, it seems.

Lots of great pictures focusing on Steve Smith, Sean, other coaches with the team and a disproportionately high number of me with Kelly and Marie-Claire.

Fast forward five days.

The coverage, the video of Kelly and I crouching down together listening to "Welcome to the Jungle" had gone viral. Over a million hits on YouTube and even more across Instagram and TikTok. Kelly had been interviewed at length and of course people wanted to know how her hand was but more than anything,

"What song were you and Angelique Santoro listening to before that fight?!" It's true, the energy between us was beautiful. Our broad smiles, glorious togetherness, captured perfectly by the camera crew.

"Welcome to the Jungle" was being played on the radio and there were rumors it was going to be re-released. I guess, it was like a smaller scale buzz but similar to Kate Bush, "Running up that Hill" all because the hit TV show, Stranger Things used it.

Must be an odd feeling being the recording artist getting that phone call, suggesting, "We might have a number one hit with that song you wrote over thirty years ago!" Life is odd, funny and weird at times for sure, but if it brings people together and creates a good buzzing energy for all the right reasons, then fucking aces, right?!

Gareth had taken to changing his ringtone from "Murder on the Dancefloor" to this Guns and Roses track, so whenever I called him, he could feel super proud of me. Wow. Signs of my Gareth returning. Meant more than words can ever say.

Jackson had called and we arranged to meet up for a coffee in town.

"So, this Simon Smitherman character…" Jackson began.

"What did you find out?"

"American born, as a lot in this group are. Well, the more senior, leaderships guys certainly. He's been vocal about Gareth's attack, but he's smart enough to know when to stop, doesn't incite violence and thus skips under the radar."

"You're fucking joking," I replied, shaking my head.

"Nope. He knows the line and he's not crossed it. For sure, he's displaying no empathy and is all about how God works through men and that gay people will burn in hell but that is not hate speech."

"Sorry, all gay people will burn in hell is not provocative and hateful?"

"I didn't say that Angelique. I said, it stops short. If he wrote, this is an encouraging start, do God's work on earth, seek out these sinners and do likewise to them? Then he's fucked. Then we could arrest him."

We discussed other possible scum bags and Jackson said they were doing their best and analysing other unpleasant characters but reminded me to be patient and these cases take time.

Three days passed, no further communication from the police. I'd had just about enough of watching this building, snooping online and decided action must be taken. Directly, by me.

It took me two days of walking around Brighton, before I found him.

I bumped into him, coming out of a betting shop, tearing up a ticket and looking mightily cheesed off.

"Oh, hello, fancy seeing you again. How are you?"

"Oh, it's you. Erm, I'm ok I guess and you?"

"I'm well, thank you. I'm Clare Rustling, by the way." I said, removing my hand from my pocket and shaking his.

"Richard Lees," he smiled. "Nice to see you again."

"Are you busy?"

"Day off. Why?"

"May I buy you a drink, Richard? It's 5pm somewhere in the world, right?"

"Sure, why not?" He replied and we walked on together chatting casually about this and that before entering the King and Queen public house.

I paid for two pints of beer, and we found a table around the side of the bar.

"How much did you lose today?"

"How do you know I didn't win?"

I laughed and suggested I'd seen him ripping up the losing ticket.

"Oh, right, yeah," he mumbled. "Fucking Arsenal."

"You bet on just football or other sports?"

"Mainly football, sometimes the horses."

"Look Richard, I'm going to be straight with you, alright? I work for Harrington, Lexington and Pulsner. We're a criminal law firm." I stated, watching his facial expressions closely before handing him a business card, supporting my claim.

"Alright. So, what's this all about? What do you want from me? I ain't done nothing."

"No one is suggesting you have, Richard. The name, Simon Smitherman mean anything to you?"

"Who?"

I repeated the name, sitting back. Casual, yet in control.

"Look luv, I don't know what your game is here, asking a man my age out for a drink then ambushing me with questions. It ain't right. I thought you was a good 'un!" He finished with a snort, defensively crossing his arms.

"I am one of the good ones."

"Yeah? Prove it. I didn't come down with the last shower, luv."

"I'd prefer it if you called me by my name Richard. I'm Clare, not luv."

He shuffled uncomfortably in his chair and muttered something that sounded like, "Sorry. Yeah, ok."

"We have a client and we are pressing charges against Smitherman on her behalf. Smitherman is the man who verbally assaulted you a few weeks ago. When we met."

"Ruddy arsehole!"

"He is and far worse, we believe."

"Go on then."

"Look, I'm not at liberty to go into details, suffice to say she's been sexually assaulted, and she's scared. So scared, she won't leave her house."

"That's terrible. What's this got to do with me though?"

"We want you to go to the Police. Report him for assaulting you verbally in the street that day, make a formal statement."

"Look. I dunno about that. He's a big, scary bloke and what you just told me don't exactly make me wanna' stick my fucking oar into this mess."

"You have a daughter?"

"Nice try, Clare. No, I don't."

"But your sister has? You've got family which are young girls, don't you?" I asked, smiling at him whilst thinking, fuck Angelique! He better have. That was a serious wild card you just threw out.

"Yeah, younger sister has 3 kids. A boy and two girls.

"So…How do you feel that someone like Smitherman is going to walk free? Someone like him, gets to terrify, rape, or sexually assault another girl, another woman in the future? We have DNA Richard. But it doesn't match any known criminals on the National DNA database."

"He's not on the database then?"

"Precisely. We believe it's him. You report him for assault which quite frankly you should because what I saw was assault. Police will arrest him, take a swab. He scared a civil servant, just doing their job. That's the truth, isn't it? We're not asking you to lie."

I could see his mind rushing. His eyes flickering, ignoring the pint he was enjoying not long ago. Time to close this deal, Angelique..

"£1,000 cash now. Another £1,000 when you show me the crime reference number."

"You what?"

"Not messing about Richard. You go and do the right thing. You can treat your nieces and sister, still have a nice tidy sum to make a few winning bets."

I know, not very nice to poke a gambler, Angelique. Still, I also suggested he spend some of that money on his nieces, didn't I? So, take off your judgmental hat.

I placed the money on the table. "Fifty, £20 notes there, Richard. Fifty more, as crisp as they come, in a couple hours from now."

He looked up at me then picked up the money.

"Alright then. Piece of shit deserves to have his DNA on the system. I hope it is a match for you, for this girl. Poor thing."

"Appreciate you, Sir. Goes without saying you never met a Clare Rustling."

"Who?"

I smiled at him. "Three hours from now at the Wagon and Horses pub, you'll get the rest of your money."

"OK, see you then, little red riding hood." He gave me a pervy look and was gone.

Man likes a redhead. Ah, they all do, I thought to myself, as I left the pub with a spring in my step.

CHAPTER NINE

Be sure thy sin will find thee out.

The letter holding the crime reference number, was burning a hole in my jacket pocket. I walked home, grinning like a fool, listening to Jason Derulo, "Want to Want Me." Richard had appeared at the Wagon and Horses, exactly three hours after we had parted company, looking rather pleased with himself.

"I enjoyed that," he admitted, sitting himself down opposite from where I sat.

"Feels good standing up for yourself and doing the right thing, eh?"

"Yeah, it does. I've always avoided conflict. Ever since school. When you're small, you kinda' do that."

"Well, you can walk like you're ten foot tall today. Keep it quiet. Don't go bragging how you got two grand for this and that. It's not safe for any of us."

"Don't worry. I keep myself to myself. Telling people you've had a right touch gets you nowhere other than pissing 'em off. It ain't like they're going to be happy for you, is it?"

"Absolutely correct," I agreed, giving him an easy smile, grateful he was a low-key kind of person.

He coughed and handed over the police reference letter.

"You got something for me?"

"Give me your jacket."

He did as instructed. I put an envelope with £1,000 cash inside his jacket, zipped it up, set it down beside me, before requesting he wait a few minutes for me to be on my way before he left the pub.

"Understood," he replied brightly. "See you around then."

"No, you won't." I said and was gone in the blink of an eye.

Walked for a few minutes to an area I knew wasn't covered by CCTV cameras, before removing my red wig and thick horn-rimmed glasses. I ran my hand through my hair, enjoying the fresh air. Those wigs are so fucking hot and uncomfortable to wear. It was always a delight to take it off!

Opened the front door and called out to Gareth. No response. He must be out and about. Good for you boy, I thought, whilst making a fuss of Ralph before going into my bedroom. Located one of the four burner phones, bought in Southampton the same weekend I purchased the military spec binoculars.

"10043/22 Smitherman. Detain. Cross ref DNA. Hold in

cells."

Sent the text to Jackson before taking a hammer to the burner phone and destroying it.

I had just finished picking up all the shattered pieces of the phone, placing them in a food freezer bag and binning it, as Gareth walked in.

"Hey, girl."

"Hey, boy."

Gareth walked over and gave me a loving embrace. I held him for as long as I could. Then held on a little longer.

He laughed. "You trying to put me back in hospital? I did break a few ribs not so long-ago pet!"

"And look at you now. Walking about, being a dick. Somethings never change, eh?"

"Ooohhh, sharp as a guillotine, you today!"

"I'm in a rather fantastic mood, it's true," I replied, winking at him.

"What's happened now. Hit two million likes on your video!?"

"Possibly, no idea boy. Just happy to see you, being more you. It's been hard on me."

"I know pet, I know. But hey, the worst is past. Got a date to go back to work, so just been chatting with my boss, sorting that out."

"Amazing. Now, that is great news. Let's celebrate. I'll make us a gorgeous, fresh pasta dish and we can just hang out, watch a movie or two."

"Spot on. I'll come with you to the delicatessen, then pick up some good wine from that off license you like."

I smiled broadly at Gareth and off we went. Arm in arm, down the steep steps from our flat to the street below.

Was I still hurting that Gareth had lied to me? Yes. Was I upset but didn't show it? Absolutely. To what end? He was still my Gareth. A tainted version in some ways but when he was like this, it was enough, especially how life had been without his essence. All that mattered to me was getting justice for him.

OK, my turn to lie. For sure, "Justice for Gareth" could be a flag waving banner outside the courthouse, but it had better also say "Justice for Angelique" because hell hath no fury, like a woman scorned. You arseholes should have thought about me, before nearly killing my best friend.

The following day, Smitherman was arrested and brought to the Police station. Verbal assault or physical assault in today's world? There is little difference in terms of being arrested. The difference comes from it being highly unlikely you'll go to court or suffer even a fine or community service, especially if your first offence. That all said? You will most likely have both your fingerprints taken and a swab for DNA. The text message I sent to Jackson, letting her know to expect Smitherman, would mean he would definitely be getting a swab done.

"Appreciate the text Angelique. We're holding Smitherman in the cells whilst awaiting the results of his DNA. See if there is a match to Gareth's assault."

"What text? I haven't done anything. You've arrested him? I thought you didn't have enough evidence to do this?"

"Really, Angelique? Are we going to start playing games with one another, after all this time?"

"I don't know what you're on about. Truly."

"OK, I'll play along with you. A Traffic Warden reported him for threatening behaviour. 'Bout two weeks ago, the incident happened. Same time as you made me aware of Smitherman."

"Coincidences are funny, eh?" I said, trying not to smile.

"Not so long ago, we'd not have been able to take his DNA but things have changed. New laws passed surrounding cyber stalking and online bullying. It's all under hate crime. It's changed how we view and act towards verbal abuse."

"About time you guys got lucky."

"Anyways. Thought I would call to let you know. It'll be a tense six to eighteen hours for the DNA to be processed. Depends on how backed up the lab is, but it's marked high priority."

"How did he react to his DNA being taken?"

"He kicked off. Took three strong officers to hold him down and after two failed attempts at taking a cheek swab, they gave up. One officer grabbed at his hair a bit."

"Right. DNA from hair follicles, right?"

"Yes, correct. Look, I've got a meeting now. I'll see you tomorrow."

"Good work detective sergeant," I said, hanging up the call.

I rubbed my head and went to the kitchen to get another glass of water. Gareth and I did eat all the gorgeous food I made but washed it down with two bottles of red wine. My head was banging. Whether or not Smitherman was our guy, we didn't know but he'd certainly been a bad boy. Such a fuss over a little cheek swab? Why? Because you know somewhere your DNA is waiting to be discovered, matched to a crime reference number.

If he was guilty of the attack on Gareth, he knew leaving his mark at the crime scene mattered not. He knew there was nothing on him, certainly not in the UK. In America? Who knows, perhaps. I read about a guy getting picked up for not having road tax or insurance, driving his car at one am, from Dorset to Kent with twenty-two kilos of cocaine in the boot. The traffic police pulled him over for these two motoring offences. They didn't have a Scooby-doo about the drugs! Why would they? Traffic cops don't know this information. I mean, how moronic do you have to be, to choose that time of day when nothing on the roads and not have your car in road legal condition?

IF Smitherman is guilty of attempted murder? Well, he got caught because he was a total arsehole to a Civil Servant. Being an aggressive twat was nothing compared to the real crime he committed, which to date, had gone unpunished. Be sure thy sin will find you out. Nice. I smiled to myself whilst taking a couple of paracetamol.

I had time to kill and sure as heck wasn't in any mood for work. I'd not seen much of Caitlin and Olivia since everything kicked off, so I checked on Gareth, who was still passed out, snoring peacefully and indicated to Ralph it was time for his morning walk.

Gaydio was playing house anthems, so I turned the volume up and sang as best I could to Ralph, Mike Posner's, clubbing re-mix, "I Took a Pill in Ibiza." What a gorgeous track to drive fast to. We were in Stanmer Park in just under twenty minutes, passing through those stunning black, wrought iron gates and parked outside Caitlin's home.

Before I had a chance to knock on Caitlin's door, she opened it and threw her arms around me.

"Angelique! What a lovely surprise. I heard Nelly from a mile away!"

"Yeah, I was giving it some beans just now," I said, giggling back at her.

"Come on in for coffee. Been far too long you know.

"I know. I'm sorry. Been a shit friend."

"Ah, calm your mouth. You've had a lot on your plate, for sure." Caitlin replied, smiling at me from over the kitchen table. "You're here now and that's all that matters."

"Thanks, Caitlin. How you been lately?"

"Well, sit down whilst I make the coffee."

I did as I was asked and waited patiently for Caitlin.

"Right then," she said, handing me a double expresso, whilst sitting herself down with a cappuccino.

"I'll tell you what it is."

"All ears, Caitlin."

"So, there's this guy right!"

"Oh, is there now?"

"Oh, there is a guy! Make no mistake about that."

"I got a feeling we're going to have a conversation better suited to wine than coffee?"

"That's most likely true but it's 11am and you're driving."

"The suspense is killing me. Go on, spill it, Caitlin, now!"

"So, I've been seeing this man called Jason. Well-built, stocky man, bit like your Joshua. Mixed race. Think his mother is Syrian and his father Japanese."

"Love mixed race people."

"I know right? Got these gorgeous green eyes against olive skin. Like something from the Vampire Diaries. You know, Hollywood hot."

"You deserve all that and more, Caitlin," I remarked, as I reached over the table to squeeze her hand.

"Thanks Angelique. Look, I'll tell you what it is. He's like a man for sure but sometimes more feminine you know, like girly?"

"You referring to him going down on you in a way most men couldn't possibly do?"

"You fucking know I am!!" Caitlin laughed.

"Oh, sweet heavens above. There is a God," I said, giggling with her.

"It's like in a former life he was a lesbian. A very unselfish lesbian at that."

"You won the lottery girl."

"Feels that way. You know what, Angelique? In the past whenever I've had a man good in bed, he's been a total shit out of the bedroom. Either a loser, can't hold a job down or got drink and drug issues or gambling. If they are nice and lovely, I'm as dry as the dessert with them, bored and sex becomes a tedious chore. Probably rather be cleaning the house."

When I'd finished pissing myself and found some sense of composure, I replied to her, "Well, that's aces, Caitlin. I'm thrilled for you. I've never seen you excited about a man; in all the time we've been friends."

"Never had it all, Angelique. I'm terrified he's going to bolt on me, or I find out he's got a wife and five kids, and I'm being played for a fool."

"You trust him?"

"Yeah, I mean for how long we've been together, sure, I think so."

"Well, you've got Olivia. Just saying."

"Ah, I know but I'd feel a total shit for doing that."

"She could just deep dive the web for you. Just find out if he's still married or whatever. Just basics to put your mind at ease."

"Isn't that a shitty thing to do? I mean, you've not done that to Joshua or have you?"

"Totally different. I'm not ready for another full-on relationship just yet, you are."

"OK, put it this way. IF he had a lodger and that person was a crazy tech geek superstar, like Olivia, wouldn't he do the same? It's not like you're going out of your way and paying someone. It's just using the gifts of a friend at your disposal?"

"Angelique, you have an inner darkness in you girl." Caitlin laughed. I didn't.

I knew she was right.

CHAPTER TEN

What do you say Kirsty Jackson?

I had lingered as long as possible at Caitlin's home but eventually she had to crack on with a work assignment, so Ralph and I left and headed back to Brighton. Heart FM was playing, "Balance" by Lucy Spraggan. Such poignant lyrics, about self-harm, addiction and struggling within herself for better mental health. I changed direction, doing an illegal U-turn and drove straight to Aveline's villa, off Dyke Road.

I missed drinking wine with my sister. Alcohol was the precursor to cocaine use, as it is with many addicts. Aveline never had alcohol dependency, but you can't drink any alcohol, do any substances whatsoever as a recovering cocaine addict. Clean means squeaky clean.

Aveline's appearance had changed dramatically. Her hair was luscious, shiny. Her skin tanned from a lot of walking and outdoor PT sessions she did twice weekly with a neighbour. The skinny size six legs were now a muscular size ten and she filled out her jeans more like I did, her bum visible from both the side and back for the first time.

"You look so well, lil sis!"

"Thank you, I'm trying hard. Obviously, you look amazing, Angelique, as always!"

"Oh my God, that video of you and Kelly is everywhere. It's been so great having Martin and well, everyone talking about you. It's taken the pressure off me. It's not all, how are you feeling today and are you ok if I pop out for a few hours," Aveline said, as she faked a huge yawn.

"I'd not thought of that."

"Yeah, I mean don't get me wrong, I'm so grateful for the love and support but I'm strong now. I'm eating, I'm exercising. Looking at studying perhaps getting into something new."

"That's amazing. I'm so proud of you. How are the cravings now?"

"People talk about good days and bad days? It's not really like that for me. I have good hours or bad hours."

"Of course. You must be different, even in your recovery!"

"You're such a dick! Why on earth do I tolerate you at all?" Aveline jested, pinching my upper arm fat.

"Ouch!" I cried out, moving around the coffee table, taking her little finger in my hand, twisting it back so she cried out too, her torso automatically lowering towards the floor.

"Are you going to play nicely Aveline?"

"Yes! Yes, I'm sorry. Let me go!!"

I released her. As soon as Aveline was free, she pinched my arm again, twice as hard as before and ran out of the living room, heading for the garden.

I sprinted after her but shit she was fast. She darted in between the fir trees, heading for the neighbour's driveway. Stopped, turned around, flicked me the finger and ran off.

All I could think of was how lucky I was to have this relationship with Aveline now as grown-ups. We never had this growing up. It was beyond special to me, especially in the aftermath of Gareth's attack.

It was dark when Jackson finally called me. Dark and cold. I'd done everything to kill time including a gym session and a long dog walk. Had tried to work but I just couldn't get any kind of useful focus. Unsurprisingly, this meant I was to be found in my local dive bar, drinking alone, a large gin and tonic in hand.

"Angelique. We got him. We got the nasty fucker!!" Jackson shouted down the line.

"Yes! Fucking yes!" I cried out, too high to care whose evening chilled out vibe I was interrupting. "So, now what?"

"Now he stays in that cell, is what."

"You told him we've got his DNA matched to the crime scene and he's going down for attempted murder?"

"No. Wanted to call you first. I'm going to do that right now."

"Shit! Wish I could be standing beside you when he gets to hear of this development."

"Of course."

"You'll be off duty once this is done and the case notes logged?"

"Yeah, that's right."

"Join me for a drink?"

"Sure. Think I owe you that much. I'm buying. Which bar do you want to meet at?"

I knew I didn't want Jackson this close to my home address, this close to Gareth.

"Where do you live? In Brighton?"

"Yeah. Well, on the Brighton side of Hove – Fourth Avenue."

"How long you going to keep me waiting?"

"I need time to progress my report plus getting there so let's be safe and call it an hour and a half from now."

"Perfect. I'll try not to get too pissed," I said and hung up.

Finished my drink in two un-lady like gulps, reaching the bar in four strides. "Same again, please."

"Well, well, well, Ms. Santoro," I muttered to myself, returning to my table by the window.

"If you ever want to leave recruitment, you've got this whole private eye shit down to a T girl." I hopped onto Instagram to nose about Kelly and Marie-Claire's profiles.

Kelly had a few pictures with her fingers strapped together looking happy and grinning with a caption saying, "Tough sport. Tough girl." Marie-Claire had liked it and commented, "Medal winner next time out!!" I joined the comments with, "Lioness on the hunt. You won't be denied your prey next time Kelly. Go Team GB!!"

I thought my mind would be rushing with the news that Smitherman had been charged. That he wouldn't be leaving that cell anytime soon. Well, he would. He'd be transferred from the Brighton police station holding cells and transferred to a proper secure prison. I thought, I'd feel more.

Truth? I didn't feel much at all. Happy he wasn't going anywhere? Yes but I just think deep down I knew it was him. From witnessing the way, he behaved outside the church that day. It was so over the top, so unnecessary. If anyone in that church group had hurt Gareth, it was him. Every cell, every drop of blood in my body knew it. My mind had progressed. This information gave me a rush of energy for ten perhaps twenty minutes, mixing beautifully with the gin.

"Who joined you? Which piece of shit from your church also put the boot in? Which scumbag pissed on my Gareth? Which arsehole hates gay people as much as you do Smitherman? Which member of the church sought to protect Paul Hardcastle?"

I was getting angry. Wow. Twenty minutes of happiness and then my stupid mind drags me back to darkness, yet again.

Perhaps an evening away from myself would be in order? I finished my drink and left the pub hoping that Kirsty Jackson would provide me with what I desperately needed.

Listening to Prince on my way to Hove, enjoying "Sign of the Times" as I reached the Blind Busker pub. From where I was in Seven Dials to Fourth Avenue it was about two miles, so a brisk half-hour walk.

Sat myself down with a long island iced tea and texted Jackson which bar I was in. Killed that half an hour waiting for her by reading the BBC news feed on my phone. The news was dominated by the UK Government having another Prime Minister. Boris Johnson had been removed from power for being a lying, deceitful, untrustworthy bastard. He was replaced for sixty days by the stunningly incompetent Liz Truss. Now, she was out on her ear. Three Prime Ministers in six months! "Jeez, Louise" I mumbled to myself. "No wonder the French, the Germans and probably the rest of the world are ripping the piss out of British politics. What a total cluster fuck of incompetence." I shook my head and put my phone away just as Kirsty Jackson reached my table, pint of lager in her hand.

"You want another whatever that is?"

"Not just now. You're playing catch up as it is."

She smiled, took her brown leather jacket off and sat down opposite me.

"Congratulations," I said, smiling easily at her.

"And to you," Jackson replied, staring into my eyes.

Stare all you want, I thought. I'm giving nothing away now, nor in the future.

We clinked glasses, said cheers, took a long sip of our drinks and then eased ourselves back into the compact, yet deep leather armchairs.

"How did the arsehole take the news, that he was being charged with attempted murder?"

"Calmly."

"You sound disappointed."

"I am. I was looking forward to him being a difficult and obnoxious prick just as he was when trying to prevent us taking his DNA in the first place."

"Accepting his guilt?"

"Doubt it. The church has mega bucks and he lawyered up immediately."

"How the hell does he plan to contest hard physical evidence such as this?"

"How the hell does a person become such a nasty cunt in the first place?"

"Arrogance and a ridiculous sense of entitlement?"

"Sure and being a sociopath. Half the CEOs' and global leaders are."

"Not a psychopath?"

"Nah. I don't think so. He shows a lot of the characteristics of sociopathy."

"Which are what?"

"Lack of empathy for others. Impulsive behaviour.

Attempting to control others with threats or aggression. Using intelligence and charm to manipulate others. Tendency towards physical violence."

"Sounds about right."

"People often use the term psycho incorrectly. Far less common. Many super successful people, both men and women are borderline sociopaths."

We fell into silence for a moment taking a little time to enjoy our drinks. I casually studied Jackson. Her blonde hair had almost a platinum tinge to it under the spotlights of this pub. Her eyes a pale blue showing anyone paying attention her brilliance. You know when you meet someone super smart? Yes, of course their language, how they speak, the concise intelligence of how they might construct a sentence is clear but for me, it's always in their eyes. Truly brilliant people have an alertness, a bright sparkle in their eyes.

She knew I was studying her.

"Saw you with Team GB on the TV. Highlights showed the contest on BT Sport."

"You follow Jujitsu?"

"No. Boxing. That's why I have the BT Sport app."

"You box?"

"Not as often as I'd like."

"How did you get into it?"

"My brother boxed. Was a professional as well as a police officer."

"You followed in his footsteps."

"Yeah, pretty much. We were always close."

"Do you have any other siblings?"

"Have a Sister. Younger than me. I was the middle child."

"I'm sensing lot less love for her than your older big brother."

"Isn't that normal, Angelique?"

"Probably. Can't answer from personal experience as I have just one sibling."

"You close to her?"

"I am now. Not growing up. Couldn't stand one another."

"Standard!!" Jackson laughed, as she finished her pint.

"My round," I said, standing up. "Same again?"

"What you having?"

"Long island iced tea."

"Why?"

"Tastes good plus has five different spirits in it!"

"Oh, we're having a proper evening out, are we?"

"I think we should. We deserve it don't we?"

"No argument from me there, Angelique. Sure. Fine then. I'll join you."

I smiled at her, letting my hand glide over her shoulder and headed to the bar.

We spent the next couple hours chatting, drinking, then

drinking some more before ending up in Gareth's boutique hotel. Well, the hotel where Gareth used to work before he secured the Hilton gig.

"What were you like growing up at school?"

"Bit of a loner. I wasn't interested in what the other kids liked."

"What were you into?"

"Boxing. Drawing. Comic books. Tattoo art."

"Not one of the cool kids then, eh."

Jackson laughed. "Oh, no. Not like you. You were probably the most popular girl in your year. Beautiful Angelique with her French Italian looks and all that money."

"I wasn't with the cool kids Kirsty!" Felt strange, so odd. That was the first time I had ever used her first name.

She clocked it right away, despite being half cut.

"Kirsty now, is it?"

"If you like?"

She blushed. Impossible to hide, when your skin is as pale as a vampire in need of a feed.

"How do you know I come from money?"

"Doh! Google? Basic police 101. Know who your victims are, their family and friends?"

"Oh right, sure, I guess."

"I'm guessing based on the google street picture of your

family home that you come from money, went to posh school n' stuff like that?"

"You already know I went to Hogwarts."

"Yeah, I do."

"That bothers you somehow? You think, I think I'm better than you because I come from privilege?"

"Fuck you get so defensive at times," Jackson replied, shaking her head.

"Just because I come from the streets of Bethnal Green, you think I feel inferior to you or something?"

"I don't want you to feel that way and I don't mean it that way."

"So, what do you mean, Angelique?"

I stood up, took her hand and walked with her to the corridor leading to the restroom.

Abruptly, I stopped. Pushed her up against the wall and kissed her.

CHAPTER ELEVEN

Justify My Love

We fell through the front door to Kirsty's flat, locked in a passionate kiss. My hands cupping her face, as she ran her hands through my hair. The taxi ride to her home had gone by so fast, it barely felt like we'd gone more than 200 metres but it was closer to three miles. We were all over each other. Kissing, giggling, grabbing, lip biting, hair pulling, all in that ten-minute journey.

I'm usually hyper aware of my surroundings but that night? If my life depended on it, I could not have told you what age the driver was, nor indeed what he looked like. If I did see him, my mind refused to recall an image.

I tore open Kirsty's blouse, the poppers sounding like firecrackers on Chinese New Year. She stood still, like a statue. Breathing hard, her pupils enlarged. Silent.

"You're sub, aren't you?" I asked.

"Yeah. For you? Always."

I stepped forward and whispered in her ear, "Let's see how much you can take."

Kissing her forehead, I directed. "On your knees, but first take your jeans off. Slowly. Let me see you."

Kirsty silently did as she was instructed.

"Get in front of me. Lead the way to your bedroom. On your hands and knees like a dog. Crawl. Keep your chin dragging on the carpet, arse up."

Once in the bedroom, I grabbed her ponytail, dragging her onto the bed.

Jackson cried out.

"Shut up, slut."

"Yes Mistress. Sorry Mistress."

"Lie perfectly still as if your very life depended upon it."

Letting my eyes linger on her firm breasts, her twisted body. Enjoying the power and control, Kirsty was allowing me. I moved around the bedroom, stopping now and then to pick up and study a picture frame, or some make up or beauty products, returning them, silently. Knowing every step I took, every pause I deliberately made, her eyes never left my body, not even for a second.

I went to the living room, picked up her brown leather jacket from the floor and returned to the bedroom. Holding the jacket aloft with one hand, the other reached into the pockets. I pulled out her purse, opened it and one by one examined the bank cards, gym membership, receipts from various shops and scattered them like leaves to the floor. Found a fifty-pound note, two twenty-pound notes and threw them onto the bed beside her. Mobile phone dropped flippantly, whilst I locked eyes with Kirsty. Unzipped the inner pocket and took out her police warrant card.

"Kirsty Jackson. Detective Sergeant. Sussex Police," I said dismissively, before discarding it.

"Now, this is more interesting, Detective Sergeant." The silver, steel handcuffs rocking to and fro in between my fingers, like the pendulum of a clock.

"Are these police issue?"

"Yes Mistress."

"Where's the key?"

"Inside my jeans pocket."

Locating the little key, I placed it on the bedside table. I took hold of both her wrists, telling her to lie back and reach, so I could cuff her to the iron bedframe. Arms stretched above her head, looking utterly helpless. Felt a growing warmth in between my legs as my eyes took a walk all over her taut body. Picked up another pillow and positioned it under the one she was lying on, propping her up.

"I want you watching me."

"OK," Jackson said, breathlessly.

I yanked her bra up and over her firm, perky breasts and started licking, sucking her erect nipples. One at a time before pulling at them, pinching them together. Returning to kiss Kirsty's lips. Reaching to plant loving kisses all over her neck.

"Don't stop."

"Be quiet, slut," I sneered, repositioning my body so my hand was over her mouth.

"I won't ask you a third time. Show me you understand. Blink twice."

Jackson did as instructed and got rewarded with a passionate kiss.

Followed by a sharp slap across her face.

Jackson remained tight lipped. "Good girl. You stay quiet." I said, planting dozens of gentle, playful kisses where my hand had just stung her cheek.

"You got Amazon music in this bedroom?"

Kirsty nodded her head.

"Alexa. Play Justify My Love, Madonna."

Arguably, one of the hottest songs ever written. I smiled at Kirsty as the song started, letting my fingers glide softly up her thighs, up her inner thighs, rubbing her pussy just for a few seconds before stopping. Just standing there, delighting in her sexual anticipation. Watching her as she lifted her hips off the bed, arching her back. Her eyes pleading with me to return to her.

"No. Not just yet. You must wait. You may speak."

"Thank you, Mistress. I know, I'm not worthy of your

touch."

"I like your ink," I expressed, whilst admiring her toned legs.

Jackson had both legs heavily tattooed with black ink, in sharp contrast to her skin which was pure snow white.

"Thank you."

"Did it hurt? This black Cobra crossing, twisting itself across both your legs?"

"Yes, it hurt a lot."

"What do you need more detective? Pain or pleasure?"

"I need both."

"Hmmmmmm, OK," I muttered back.

I kissed her mouth. Letting my tongue explore hers in a playful dance. Sucking her tongue, gazing into her eyes. One hand playing with her nipples, circling them gently, then without warning, pinching, pulling at them. Enjoying her gasp out loud as her pupils widened.

Kirsty closed her eyes, moving her hips up and forward to meet my hand now exploring her damp sex through her knickers.

"Open your eyes."

"Yes, Mistress."

"Keep them open. I need to read your body. I want to own you."

Holding her gaze, I slipped my hand down the front of her knickers. More boy shorts, you know the type. Tight, hugging, coy and cute all at once. Girls just look so hot wearing them, plus it suited her character. Boxer. Boyish. Street tough detective. Mean and complete yet with me in the bedroom, totally submissive. What gorgeous contrast. Nothing hotter to me than being pleasantly shocked or surprised.

Teasing her again. Letting my fingers open her labia, wet. So wet for me. Dipping just the tip of my finger into her pussy then out. Slowly running my fingers to her clit and lingering there. Gliding, running, circling my agile fingers over and around her engorged bud.

"Mistress. You're killing me!" Kirsty moaned.

"You've been bad. You must wait. Only good girls get to cum when they want."

I smiled at her as I removed her boy pants.

Such a cheeky, lustful grin replaced my easy-going smile, when I saw her little tuff of blonde pubes over her mound. No hair whatsoever around her labia, her pussy, just this perfect blonde haircut!

I put myself in between those toned thighs, breathed in deeply her scent and tasted her sex for the first time. Kirsty groaned, as she squeezed my head between her thighs. I love going down. Giving oral perhaps even more than receiving it. Love the power, the control over another woman. Every gasp, every moan, every twitch of every muscle fibre, directly linked to my agile, willing tongue. I pushed her legs back, licked her arsehole, flitting my tongue over and around that cute hole before ever so slowly, dragging my tongue through her labia, circling her clit, licking, and sucking her swollen bud. Swiftly darting down again, probing inside her pussy. Tongue fucking her sex. I brought Kirsty close to orgasm then abruptly stopped, with just seconds to spare!

Kirsty's eyes were wide open. The lust. The passion, burning from her eyes into mine. She was twisting and pulling on her shackles, the bed shaking to join the clanking vibrations. Her torment. My delight.

I sat back, put my head to one side, a wry smile wrapped around my face.

"You look frustrated Detective Sergeant Jackson."

"Mistress Angelique. Please, Mistress. I'm begging you. Let me cum. Please, just make me cum!"

I said nothing in reply. I just sat there, staring into her eyes. Loving every second of control over this woman.

I licked two fingers, soaking them in my saliva and thrust them into her wet sex. Her back arched; her legs started convulsing as if I'd struck her with a cattle prod. As if electricity was being sent at 10,000 volts though her body. I laughed, as I went deeper into her pussy. Knuckle deep and started to work my magic upon her. Vibrating, pulsating those fingers, whilst rubbing her clit aggressively with my other hand. East to West rubbing of her clit whilst circling my fingers up against her vaginal wall. That was it. She was done in. Twenty seconds, if that, before that first, glorious orgasm tore through her body. Kirsty cried out in ecstasy as the shackles made an eerie, metallic, scraping sound against the iron bars of the headrest.

Once you get a woman to this point? Never stop. Not until

they are so sensitive, they are begging you to stop. I carried on, easing a finger into her arsehole. Two fingers in her soaking wet pussy, one going deep into her bum hole. There is nothing better. If you don't believe me? Try it!

Thrusting into Kirsty, until I was breathing hard, my wrist killing me. Savouring my reward, as orgasm followed orgasm. I stopped counting after her seventh.

"Mistress. Enough. Please, enough!" Kirsty sounding as desperate as she looked.

I stopped abruptly. Left the bedroom and returned with two large glasses of cold water. Helping her drink, supporting her head, before placing the glass beside mine on the side dresser. I lingered briefly over her to lick the sweat off her forehead and brush back her beautiful blonde hair from her face. Blowing cool air over her.

"You have crazy skills, Mistress Angelique."

"So, they say," I replied, grinning at her whilst massaging my wrist.

I took a finger, slowly waving it in front of her.

"Oh, God. Please, Mistress. I'm begging you. Give me time to recover before going at me again!"

Remaining silent, I took that finger and eased it back into her pussy before gently removing it.

"Taste yourself." I said, as I placed my finger into her warm mouth.

Kirsty held my stare as she sucked on my finger.

I slowly peeled off my jeggings and black, lacy thong. Eased two fingers into my wet pussy, then placed them into Kirsty's open mouth, feeling her tongue move in between my fingers, sucking them clean.

"Do I taste good, slut?"

"Like honey," Kirsty whispered, her eyes full of sparkle and light.

"If I release you from your shackles, do you promise to be a good little sub? I don't need to restrain you, for you to behave yourself, or do I?"

"No. I'll behave, I promise. I want to use my hands on you, to touch you, please, Mistress."

I removed the cuffs from her wrists and gently massaged them. Found some body lotion and gently rubbed it around her wrists and hands where the skin was grazed and red.

Removing all my clothes, standing naked before Kirsty, I enjoyed watching her reaction.

"You're so fit. So hot!" She exclaimed.

"Knew I fancied you when I saw you on the TV that time. You are beautiful."

"You want to touch me?"

"May I?"

"You may, my little sub slut. Pleasure me."

"I'll do my best Mistress."

"No. Do better."

Kirsty stood up and kissed me, making me feel light-headed. I felt like I was back at school with Alessia. As you know, I'm no stranger to enjoying women but this was different. I sensed a strong, super powerful connection between us. This spontaneous role playing, nothing discussed, just like a river flowing to the sea. Natural. Nothing forced, nothing awkward. It's like I'd known her ten years not a couple of months.

Kirsty moved to my ear and whispered, "If it's ok with you Mistress, I'm going to lie on my back and have you straddle my face. Will you honor me?"

I pushed her back on to the bed and told her to make herself comfortable before climbing on top of her, dragging my wet pussy up her torso, over her chin to rest on her mouth, already open, her tongue eager to explore me.

I grabbed the headrest of this iron bed, aware of the cold metal in my hands, as I gazed down upon Kirsty. Her eyes full of cheekiness. Pure mischief. Her tongue went straight into my hot, wet sex, whilst her hands grabbed at my big Latino arse. Always loved horse riding. Riding a hot girl's face is precisely the same as a rising trot. Lift your hips forward and back, up and down, just gliding over the leather saddle. Substitute a saddle for Kirsty's face and you get the picture beautifully.

Skimming her lips, feeling that wet, warm tongue skipping, dancing playfully over my clit, her fingers, her nails digging into my arse.

"Don't stop. Keep on at me."

I quickened my pace, feeling my first orgasm build within

me. Like a wave rising before it crashes onto a rocky beach. I cried out as I came, Kirsty pulling on my hips preventing me from going anywhere. Her eyes had the determined look of a fighter not letting up on their opponent. Moments later I came again, harder, longer than my first, feeling my juices on her face, sliding down to my inner thighs.

I removed myself and crouched down beside her, licked my sweet cum from her face and kissed her passionately.

"Where's your paddle at?"

"Bedside table, first drawer."

"And your toys?"

"Same drawer Mistress."

"Lube?"

"I don't need any."

"Get on all fours. Let me see your holes."

Kirsty did as instructed. Arching her back, knees forwards, making her bum as big and wide a target as possible for me.

Without warning, I drew my arm back and whacked her with the paddle. The satisfying noise of leather on skin barely audible over Jackson crying out. Again, my arm withdrew, my eyes took aim and I unleashed another violent whack to her bum.

"Fuck!" She cried out.

"Hard enough for you, slut?"

"Yes. Hit me again!!"

Not sure I was meant to be taking instruction from my sub

but I was having too much fun seeing how much delight she was taking from experiencing pain and did as I was asked.

After the fifth assault on her rear, her right bum cheek was glaring red at me. Before going at her again, focusing my efforts on the other bum cheek, I dropped the paddle, picked up a large, pink dildo I had found in her bedside drawer, spat on the tip and entered her sex. Kirsty moaned as pleasure started to balance out the sting and pain which would linger a good while yet, due to the force in which I had struck her.

I fucked her slow and deep with that pink toy. Pushing all eight inches into her sex, then easing back, inch by inch before thrusting in again, taking her voice away completely. Slow became normal, became fast, became frantic. Kirsty screaming in pleasure as wave after wave of orgasms tore through her body. I abruptly stopped.

"For such a small slut, you make a lot of noise."

Kirsty said nothing, panting hard, trying to regain some kind of composure. I was having none of it. I picked up the paddle, raised my arm to shoulder height and unleashed a whack to her virgin skin on the other buttock.

"Owww!" Kirsty yelled out.

Again, I ignored her and continued at pace. I hit her a second, third and fourth time in rapid succession, before I dropped that paddle and reached for the pink dildo. I massaged her arsehole, spat on my thumb, massaged it some more before entering her hole at the exact same moment, I eased that pink toy into her pussy.

Working that toy and my thumb together in perfect harmony. Sliding in and out of both holes with the grace and precision of a dancer. Kirsty never stopped moaning, gasping for air, twitching uncontrollably, as I worked her. Yes, I worked her. This is the image you need to see, to feel, to understand. I had this little slut under my control. Whatever I wanted her to experience, whatever reaction I desired? I created it. She was helpless. Powerless to prevent my will being executed.

Kirsty collapsed onto the bed, her eyes rolling, pulling me to her.

"Hold me," she panted.

I located the duvet and covered us, as I held Kirsty to my breast, stroking her hair.

"You're amazing," she mumbled. These were the last words she spoke that night, as within minutes of being held in my arms she was lulled into a deep, peaceful sleep.

I waited a few minutes longer before leaving the bed and getting dressed. Smiling to myself from the kitchen, I could hear her gently snoring as I fixed myself a double vodka. Drank it down like an alcoholic with terrible cravings and left her flat as quietly as I could, listening to "Electric Dreams" by Phil Oakley, as I walked home.

CHAPTER TWELVE

Love is complicated.

"Yes, I understand. I'll be there shortly."

"Everything alright, boy?"

"Yes. That was Detective Jackson. They have arrested and officially charged some bloke. His DNA is a match to my clothing."

I walked over to Gareth and hugged him. His body felt limp. Passive.

"Why are you not excited, boy?"

"Oh, I am. Just shocked, I think. Been so long with nothing and now they have someone in custody being refused bail, so they must be confident he's their man."

"One of them," I added.

"Oh, yes, of course. One of them." Gareth trailed off, looking shell shocked.

"So, you're off to the police station now?"

"Yeah. I'll finish my coffee, take a quick shower and get myself down there."

"Great. I'll come with you."

Sometimes Gareth was my Gareth. At other times, he was a stranger to me. I've been patient. Fuck my life, how patient I have been!

Love is complicated. It always is. He was in love or still is in love with Paul Hardcastle. Who am I to judge his life, how he feels? For Gareth to have fallen so hard, he must have been head over heels in love with Hardcastle. Gareth seldom felt anything for any man. He was always, "Yeah, they're ok, I guess." Men fell in love with him constantly. He did not feel the same way towards them.

We had walked to the police station holding hands, taking the piss out of one another.

"What time did you get in this morning? You still smell a bit boozy girl!"

"About three am, I think."

"Someone got a bit jiggy jiggy with it last night!" Gareth said, whilst nudging me in the ribs.

"I might have done."

"Oh, for sure you did. Miss, I go to bed at ten pm, up at 6 am to work out with Caitlin or go punch and kick the shit out of people, in that new mixed martial arts gym in Portslade, you love so much."

"A lady never kisses and tells, boy."

"Well, you aren't a lady, so spill it!"

I released my hand from his and punched him hard on his arm.

"Fucking ouch!" Gareth cried out.

"Well, behave yourself. If I wished to tell you about last night, I would have done so. I do not, so button it, boy."

"You're becoming more and more like me with each passing day. It's reassuring. Like you're growing or something."

We stared at one another before falling about the place in a fit of giggling.

"I don't know how you just said that and kept a straight face, boy."

"I know, right!!"

I reached up and kissed him on his cheek.

"You know I love you, right?"

"Yes, I do. I know, I've been impossible these past few months. Appreciate you never wavering in your love for me."

Squeezing his hand, I smiled back at him. We walked the last half mile to the police station in silence.

"Detective Sergeant Jackson and Detective Shaw please," I asked at reception, explaining who we were and that they were expecting us. Well, they were expecting Gareth, not necessarily yours truly.

"Hello Gareth. Appreciate you coming so swiftly, thank you," Shaw said, before smiling at me and saying it was good to see me too, under brighter circumstances.

I smiled agreeably back to him before locking eyes with Jackson.

"Good to see you both," Jackson offered, as her eyes flitted between Gareth and I, before a very quick look back into my eyes.

They were still bright and sparking with the passion from the previous night spent adoring each other.

Gareth and Shaw walked ahead of us, chatting casually, this and that. Kirsty and I walked side by side and having checked there was no-one behind us, I stole the opportunity to cup her perky bum cheek in my hand.

Kirsty pushed my hand away, giving me a cold stare but I knew she loved it. Last night wasn't going to be a one off. She didn't want that any more than I did. The chemistry between us was electrifying. I could feel my heart in my throat and knew without a doubt Kirsty was struggling to maintain her professional, polished appearance around me that day. Call me immature if you so wish but I felt so alive in that moment, just like being back at school with my first love, Alessia.

You know that feeling, right? Can you cast your minds back to school or college when someone made your heart skip, butterflies flying around your stomach? You felt lightheaded, drunk even, almost physically sick? Are you here with me right now? It didn't matter if they even felt the same way about you, did it? Those overpowering, adolescent feelings. The ones which as mature, experienced adults, we are not meant to give in to. We are grown-ups now! Put away silly teenage thoughts and feelings, perhaps all too aware it leads to nothing but heartache and despair. And as adults, we must surely have far more important things to be thinking about or doing?

I did not. On the one hand, I was developing feelings for Joshua. I was now seemingly developing feelings for Kirsty. The one thing which has always terrified me more than anything, was being alone. I was enjoying being single. It was a huge step for me, after being in relationships, time and again purely for safety and security. To find myself buzzing with thoughts of both my lovers, was not concerning for me. I felt alive, my friends! To me, feeling alive is more important than anything else. Being stuck in a relationship, without feels, is a fate worse than death.

We settled ourselves in interview room 3a. Was there an interview room, called 3b? If so, why not just call it interview room 4? Why does my mind always come up with pointless shit, that has no significance or bearing on anything?

The room was painted grey. Like an aircraft carrier. You know that dull, naval battleship grey? The lighting was still strip lights, not less harsh spotlights. Again, perhaps the point. It's not meant to be a pleasant place to find yourself in. Perhaps, other interview rooms had more aggressive lighting, designed purposefully to make one feel even more unsettled?

"Oh, do shut up, Angelique," I told myself.

Jackson ignored me, focusing her energy solely upon Gareth, who was doing his best to not fidget about.

“What does the name Simon Smitherman mean to you, Gareth?”

“Nothing at all.”

Jackson pretended to flick through some notes, then sharply looked up and stared at Gareth.

“Let me re-phrase that question. Perhaps, that’ll make it easier on your memory. Who is Simon Smitherman?”

“I don’t know that name,” Gareth replied, slightly more edgy, aggressive even.

“What does the church group, The Eternity Saints mean to you?”

“Never heard of them,” Gareth claimed, lying through his teeth.

I could sense his body tightening up. OK, I am like the twin sister he never had. I sense things others cannot, but I clocked it in both Shaw and Jackson. They gave one another a look which may as well have said, you fucking liar!

Shaw continued the interrogation, “Smitherman, is Head of Membership for that church. His DNA was all over your clothing, along with one other, we have yet to identify. What do you make of that?”

Gareth looked directly back at Shaw and responded, “What do I make of that? What do I make of the news, that some religious prick sought to send me to hell faster than his God intended? Is that what you are asking of me?"

"Are you religious, Gareth?"

"No. Not in the least."

"So, you've never been to this church. It's on Lewis Road."

"No."

"Never spoken with or met anyone associated with this church group?"

Gareth sighed, closing his eyes for a moment before answering. "Pretty sure I just said that Detective Shaw."

"He unleashed an extreme level of violence upon you Gareth. It's seldom we come across such anger from a total stranger towards their victim," Jackson stated, leaning back in her chair.

"To quote you Detective Jackson? It seldom occurs. Not impossible and not unheard of then, is it?"

"You've seen the aftermath response to my near-death experience on the web?"

"I've seen an outpouring of love and support for you and sadly a certain level of praise and encouragement from certain religious groups or individuals, which felt it was God working through chosen men, to carry out his will," Jackson finished, shrugging her shoulders.

"Well, then?" Gareth said. His turn to sit back in his chair nonchalantly.

"How do you think he knew who you were then?" Shaw asked, finding his voice.

“I’ve always thought it was linked to all the positive media coverage about Gareth landing the big job at the Hilton Group. You know, openly gay, local lad comes good?”

“Appreciate that, but we’d like to hear from Gareth just now please Angelique.”

I smiled easily at Jackson, whilst my eyes said, “Don’t be a dick Kirsty!”

She stared back at me, her face expressing, “This is my universe. You are a guest in it. Don’t you dare act like I’m your little sub, bitch. I’m warning you.”

All that did was excite me further but I didn’t show it.

“So, to summarise,” Shaw began, stretching his ape like arms over his head. “You don’t know who this guy is. Never spoken to him and your best guess is that you share Angelique’s train of thought that he simply disliked all the positive media attention you got for landing a dream job, whilst being openly gay?”

“I think it’s plausible, Detective Shaw. It’s a rather significant coincidence otherwise, I would suggest.”

Jackson placed a picture of Smitherman in front of Gareth.

“Nothing at all, then?”

“Nope. Never seen him before.”

“Right, I think that just about does it for today.” Jackson said, standing up, reaching across the table to shake both our hands.

“Thank you both for catching him. I’m sorry, I’ve been little help, but I am grateful to you both.”

“Appreciate that. Thank you, Gareth,” Shaw replied, as he put on his jacket and left the room.

Told Gareth I had a few things to take care of in town and I’d see him back at the flat before his evening shift started at the hotel. He gave me a loving embrace, kissed my forehead and went on his way.

Jackson and I waited until Gareth was out of sight before she suggested, “Want to get coffee somewhere along the seafront?”

“Yeah, that would be good Kirsty.” I smiled at her.

“I know he’s your best friend and all that jazz but he’s lying through his teeth.”

“Yup. I know.”

“You think he’s met Smitherman?”

“Not necessarily but he knows The Eternity Saints church and he knows precisely where their church is situated.”

“You thinking the second attacker is from the same church?”

“I’m thinking, he’s either a work colleague or a member of the congregation.”

“Agreed. So now what?”

“We wait patiently and see who says what, who writes what on social media. Smitherman’s arrest will create anger and resentment in certain people. Most will just be arseholes, having a rant. One, on the other hand will mean everything they write and may well have used extreme physical force in their past. We will be deep diving these people.”

"What failed first time around may yet bear fruit this time around?"

"Yes. Like, I've told you before Angelique. Police work is hard work and keeping on, no matter what. It's not glamorous but it's tenacity which always wins out. You must want to catch these people more than anything else in your life."

"Is that why you're single?"

Kirsty stopped walking. Dug both hands deep into her bomber jacket and looked out to sea.

"Probably. Plus, I'm new to Brighton. What's your excuse?"

"Who said I was single?"

Kirsty laughed. "You usually play with girls like you did me last night with a boyfriend or girlfriend then?"

"There is a guy, Joshua that I'm seeing."

"But he's not officially your partner or anything?"

"Are you fishing Jackson?"

"Just want to know if last night was a one off for you."

I smiled at Kirsty.

"It's fine if it was. I just want to know is all."

"Would I have grabbed your arse in the police station if it was a one-night stand?"

Jackson looked directly into my eyes and said, "That was very uncool. Don't ever disrespect me like that again. I would never do that to you, representing Team GB, in public."

“Oh, is that where this is going? You’re going to be at my side when Team GB take on America in a couple of months’ time?”

“Everything’s a joke to you isn’t it, Angelique?”

I cupped her face and kissed her passionately.

Having released her, I smiled. “No, not everything is a joke with me.”

CHAPTER THIRTEEN
Big in Japan

It had been an uneventful fortnight since Gareth and I visited the police station. I was struggling with SRS. The UK had slipped into a recession and as a result the recruitment services I offered, were in slight demand. Nurses and Doctors were out on strike as were the paramedics and ambulance drivers. Teachers were next joining the picket lines, whilst train services ground to a holt over drivers' pay. Inflation was at its highest since the mid-1970s and the UK felt depressed and depressing. This was not aided by the Tory party being involved in scandal after scandal, demonstrating their total lack of integrity. The public became ever wiser to the facts, that there were rules and laws governing us, which the people in power clearly thought did not apply to them.

It was around this time, having finished my second cup of

coffee at Caitlin's home, following a highly enjoyable training session, involving lots of sprints and pad work that my phone rang.

"Hi, it's Angelique," I said, warily unsure which international area number was showing on my phone and why.

"Angelique Santoro?" A bright, youngish, female asked.

"Yes, speaking."

"I am Akira Suzuki from Sony corporation, Tokyo."

"You're calling me from Japan? How did you get this mobile number?"

"From Steve Smith. Team GB, Director. He did not think it would be a problem to call you directly. I am sorry if this is not the case."

"No. It's fine. I'm just a little surprised is all. What does Sony want with me?"

"It's not just you we want potentially but, Kelly, your student."

"You want Kelly and me? To do what exactly?"

"We are going to be running a new advertising campaign, for our JPSO5 Headphones. State of the art. Best in the world, we believe. We want or are thinking perhaps we want you and Kelly in the advertisement."

I put my phone down on the kitchen table, enabled the speaker function, and put my finger to my lips, as I looked over at Caitlin.

"Tell me more."

"If you are both interested in this opportunity, we will fly you first class, of course to Japan and you'll spend a couple of weeks here until we are satisfied the filming is perfect and then you can go home."

Caitlin was nodding her head, giving me two thumbs up. She knew my business was on its arse and the way the UK was, particularly the NHS well, it was potentially something significant, you know. Keep me afloat until better times and organisations start recruiting again.

"Perhaps it is best, I discuss the specifics, such as money, compensation for your time with your agent. What is their name please?"

I pulled a funny face at Caitlin before answering. "I do not have a sports agent."

Akira couldn't help a small snigger escaping.

"Angelique Santoro does not have representation! This is so strange. Everyone in Japan knows who you are!"

"I very much doubt that."

"Your video with Kelly was received here differently than to other parts of the world. Here, it reflects our values. Master to pupil. Elder to child. Love, respect and honor between Sensei and student. For us, it is a thing of great beauty."

"Thank you. I feel the same way."

At the same time, Caitlin put a hand over her heart and mouthed the words, "Oh My God!!"

I gave Akira my work email address and we agreed she would send me a suggested contract offer of employment and would advise what steps need to be taken to secure a short-term working visa in Japan. She ended the call reminding me they were Sony and if they wanted us, it would happen.

"Holy fucking shit, Angelique. This is huge!"

I stood up, moved around to her side of the kitchen table and hugged her.

"Looks like I've got a fast drive to London then."

"You're not going to call Kelly first?"

"Heck no. I want to see her face light up."

"I need to see Sean and Steve first. I have no idea how this works. Like, what is the Team GB cut on something like this?"

"Why would they get a cut? You don't work for Team GB officially, Angelique. You are not a paid member of the staff."

"Yeah, but without them, without Britain Vs Germany, the TV crews and stuff, this whole thing would never have happened, so I don't know what their stance is. If happy for me, then fine, I'll just donate twenty percent of my fee back to them."

"You've a big, generous heart my friend."

"Team GB is part of me Caitlin. I'd be lost without it."

I had Alphaville, "Big in Japan" playing way up loud, as I left Brighton heading to Team GB, HQ in Wandsworth.

I'd barely stepped foot inside the building, not even checked in with security and administration before I spotted Steve Smith and Sean walking down the corridor which led to the board room.

"Morning Gentlemen!" I called out.

They both turned around, smiling at me.

"Oh no, look who it is!" Sean said, rolling his eyes.

"Hello, Sensei" Steve replied, ever the professional.

I jogged over and presented myself with a girly curtsy.

"Cute," Sean said.

At the same time, Steve remarked, "Forever the joker in the pack, Angelique. Always a joy to see you."

"Always nice to be welcomed to my home, from home Gentlemen."

"We're just heading to the monthly board meeting. Is there something you need?"

"If you could kindly spare me a couple of minutes, please?"

I explained my phone call earlier that morning from Sony, in Tokyo. Steve and Sean listened attentively before looking at one another and shrugging their shoulders.

"Sounds like congratulations are in order. This is all you. This is the essence of Angelique Santoro. You make us proud. This is a reward for you caring, for being who you are."

"Steve's correct Angelique. It's your money. Typical you to ask if we expect a cut or to even think we do. Nothing to do with us. If you want to donate something to the youth development programme here or to your beloved Brixton youth club, we are not about to say no!"

I smiled, wished them both a productive meeting and headed back to Nelly, beyond excited to see Kelly.

I don't have children. Been a long time, some twenty years since I was at school. What time is lunchbreak? It was still morning, just gone 11:30am, so I called the school and asked the grumpy woman who answered the phone when lunch break began.

Half an hour to drive the 4 miles sounded doable. I texted Kelly. "Kelly. I've got some exciting news for you, for us. Meet me at the main school gates, shortly after noon ok. Sensei X"

I asked Alexa to play, "Left my heart in Tokyo." Mini Viva. Sang loudly, without a doubt badly out of tune and smiled at a hot black guy, whose car stopped adjacent from mine on a red light. He smiled back and revved his engine. I pulled a "You're not being serious mate!?" face, to which he nodded back at me.

Lights went green and I floored Nelly. Within a few seconds, I hit 80mph and his dated, older BMW was in my rear-view mirror! Silly boy. An Alpha Romero 4C, is a missile. Had he had a new BMW, M3, it would have been close, but he didn't.

Kelly met me about ten past twelve with a string of friends. No idea who any of them were.

"Sensei!!" Kelly called out, before flinging her arms around my neck.

"Hey, Kelly!" I replied, hugging her warmly.

Part of me was aware Kelly was being like this, a little over the top, to show off and impress her peer group. Fine by me. I was the seriously unpopular kid at school and my fighting talents just alienated me further, not helped by getting suspended for kicking Robert McCormack's arse in front of fifty kids! "Psycho Dyke." Such a charming nickname for a fifteen-year-old girl to have, for well over a school year!

It wasn't so long ago, Kelly was being called "Scum" at this very school, a reference to her father being in prison. No doubt, some of these kids are not real friends, rather just hangers on but if two are, plus Marie-Claire and me, then she's doing ok!

Kelly introduced me to everyone and I smiled and waved to them all, making sure not to miss anyone out. I know how badly being left out or feeling you are, hurts and affects teenagers. One of the boys was clearly a future petrol head and asked me if he could sit in the driver's seat. I opened the door for him and smiled at him as he passed me to get in.

"Totally sick, Miss!! She in neutral? Can I start her up, please?"

"She is. Be quick about it. I don't want the headmaster coming."

The boy pushed the big red starter button and Nelly roared to life. Cheeky monkey then gave a couple of hefty goes at the throttle pedal, grinning ear to ear as Nelly barked and spluttered, the engine growling, the exhaust system back firing like a machine gun.

I reached in and removed the key as the boy climbed out and said, "Ah, she's wicked, Miss!!"

The noise had gotten the kids so excitable and my heart leapt with joy to see Kelly finally happy at school. I wasn't jealous of her. Sure, it would have been nice for me to grow up, look back on such fond memories as these being created but ultimately, I was content one of us would look back upon our school days happily.

"You got ten minutes to talk with me?"

"Of course, Sensei," Kelly replied, telling her friends she'd see them later.

"Oh, and James? You wouldn't mind keeping an eye on Nelly for me, would you?"

"I'd love to, Miss."

I handed him a twenty-pound note and waved goodbye to Kelly's friends.

He beamed and stood soldier like by the hood of my car. The school was in a shitty area and whilst unlikely anything would happen whilst away with Kelly, I thought it best to engage the big lump but moreover, I thought it would be a fun story he could share with his friends.

Kelly and I walked around the school grounds, keeping to the tree line away from everyone.

"So, what's this exciting news?"

"It's not official yet but it's quite likely you and I are going to Japan to work on a commercial for Sony!"

"What!?" Kelly exclaimed, grabbing my arm.

"It's true. I got a call this morning from Sony corporation in

Tokyo. Our little viral video is big in Japan. Like really big. They totally love the vibe, the energy we shared on the mats that day and want to use us to promote their latest headphones. It'll be a global advertising campaign."

Kelly put her hand to her mouth, tears flowing freely.

"Hey, you," I said gently. "This is good news, why the tears?"

Kelly wiped her nose and eyes with the sleeve of her school sweater.

"It's mum and dad. I've heard them talking about wanting to move away from the council estate where we live. To buy somewhere."

"Well, that's potentially a positive move. Why are you upset, Kelly?"

"I overheard them talking last week in the kitchen. They can't save enough for a deposit and even if they could because dad's been to prison, no mortgage broker will touch them. I heard him crying the other day. He's doing so well Sensei. Working overtime, saving and being so good to us but it's like game over for him. His past is always going to stick to him."

"I get that. I'm sorry, Kelly," I sighed, putting my arm around her shoulders.

"Will this be like real money, Sensei? Would I get enough to help them get a mortgage? I mean, if they could go somewhere with a real deposit perhaps someone will see past his criminal record."

"Well, they both work full time jobs and could get good

references from their employers, so who knows. Money talks, Kelly. It always talks."

"What could we make?"

"I don't know. I just wanted to make sure you were up for it. Just you and me on a little adventure!"

"That would be so cool. I can't wait to tell Marie-Claire! Does Team GB know?"

"Yes. I spoke with them earlier today. We have their full support to go enjoy ourselves."

I gave Kelly a hug and suggested she get herself ready for afternoon lessons.

Watching Kelly run back to class or well, doing anything with joy in her heart just lifted my spirits. It always did. Whatever she gets out of our relationship, I get just as much back, if not more.

Driving back to Brighton, listening to Lady Ga-Ga's, "Poker Face." All I could think of was how much can we earn out of this job and would it help Kelly's family if a certain Angelique Santoro would be willing to put her name down on the mortgage application? To act as a guarantor for them. If I could find a mortgage broker which loves martial arts, then perhaps it would be possible!

CHAPTER FOURTEEN
Troll

"You're kidding me."

"Nope. We arrested the little shit yesterday."

"Smitherman has a cousin working alongside him at Eternity Saints? It's him, you think joined the assault on Gareth?"

"Can't say 100% Angelique. DNA is on its way to the lab, highest priority request made."

"Tell me everything."

"Look, it's like I suggested it would be. You arrest someone for attempted murder and some people will jump to their defence. Slate the system, start talking up conspiracy theory, start making out the police are corrupt, that it's planted evidence. Very angry people. Look at Andrew Tate. The man is a total scumbag but look at the global outpouring of support since the Romanian police arrested him."

"OK Kirsty. So, what has this guy been saying?"

"Definition of a toxic troll. Combine that with extreme Old Testament bullshit. Smitherman is innocent. The police are the devil's servants. Immoral. We must take to the streets, demand his release. He is a servant of God."

"Sounds like a douche but that isn't enough for you guys to arrest him. You told me before it must clearly fall into hate crime."

"I'm getting to that. He went on to say that all gay people are an abomination and that wiping them off the face of the earth would be a service to humanity. And that we must stop listening to politicians and weak, cowardly people that think it's fine to have such impure sinners living amongst us. How disgusting it is to share the same air as them, whilst taking a train, sharing a carriage with them."

I laughed. "Oh, he's properly fucked himself!"

"I knew someone would. Smitherman's arrest. The negative publicity towards his beloved church group in the media the past two weeks. It's like when we first studied the Eternity Saints, Scientology or Latter-Day Saints. Incapable of accepting criticism from the media. For once, the media really helped us out here. They poked the bear, we got to reap the rewards."

Oliver Scott. twenty-eight years old, slight build with badly potted skin, having suffered acne growing up. His strawberry blonde hair was already thinning, nails bitten to the quick. He had that nervous, intense energy about him. The kind of metabolism caused by an overactive thyroid. He could probably eat 4,000 calories a day, take no exercise and remain a lean as a greyhound.

Originally from Utah, he had moved around various states in America with his family. His father was a preacher. Well, he called himself a man of God, whilst believing such nonsense as we are all God's children and had a gentle, passive attitude towards homosexuality and perversions of the flesh.

Since joining Eternity Saints, he had severed all ties with his family, including his mother whom he loved dearly but could not get passed how she could tolerate to live with someone who preaches the word of God, so inaccurately. The New Testament is for worshipers which cannot face God's wrath to sinners. Weak people. His father was a weak man.

Smitherman had encouraged such behaviours in Scott. Pressing upon him, that to be a true soldier of Christ, meant not compromising on what you know to be right. To stand up against abhorrent sinners, who have the devil breathing air into their lungs and to promote the cleansing of society, one sinner at a time.

"I want to see you."

"When?"

"Tonight."

"Can't tonight, got plans."

"How about tomorrow evening."

"Nope. No good for me. Joshua is taking me out to that new

Thai restaurant in Hove."

"Nice. I've heard it's good."

"We're so lucky living in Brighton & Hove. I know London is fantastic for food, different cuisines but here we have over twenty world cuisines, all walking distance from the seafront."

"That's true. Eating out here is wonderful. So much variety."

Silence fell upon us.

"Kirsty?"

"Yeah?"

"You, ok?"

"Yes. Of course. Why do you ask?"

"It's just whenever I mention Joshua, you shut down, go inwards."

"Not sure what to say to that, Angelique."

"I've been honest with you from the start."

"Not saying you haven't. You're seeing someone. I'm free to see people. All very Brighton."

"But you would prefer it, if I wasn't seeing someone else?"

"Would I prefer it, if I knew when I'm not making you cum, some hot guy isn't?"

"We've not really talked about it."

"I rock your world, you rock mine. He's the lead rocker in orgasms! Whatever, Angelique."

Silence fell upon us once again.

"Look, I've got a lot on today. Just text me when you think you're free."

"OK. Sure. Well done for the arrest. Great work, detective sergeant!"

"Sure. Catch you later," Kirsty muttered, abruptly hanging up on me.

I put my phone down on the bedside drawer and asked Alexa to play, "Mood" by 24K Goldn, featuring Iann Dior.

I was trying to be cute. Playful, in how I ended the phone call with Kirsty but the way she shut me down, made me feel sad. For sure, I understand. Most people see one person at a time, right? But then a lot of people out of a long-term relationship, like post-divorce, date more than one person at a time, "play the field," have fun, right?

So why do I feel like a total shit? Is it because I never have dated two people at once? Angelique, you now "have" Joshua and Kirsty. Yay!!

Well, it is, and it isn't. I like men. I like women. It's complicated. It does not matter how sensitive and metrosexual Joshua is, he's still a hunk of testosterone fueled man and thank the Gods for that! Kirsty isn't like anyone I've ever met. This feisty, fuck you, street cool detective is something I can handle. Well, I think I can. However, when we get it on, it's insane. Her submissive ways in the bedroom, bring out my dominant sexual prowess, which is addictive. No one has ever made me enjoy my dom side so much. Always been comfortable being a tomboy. Being highly masculine as well as feminine, but it's different with her. Sorry. I'm not doing a very good job of explaining myself. Perhaps, I like her because like me, she's a contradiction in many ways.

The PDF in my inbox from Akira Suzuki left me dumbfounded. Sat in a daze, stroking Ralph absentmindedly, I read and re-read the letter of engagement. Sony corporation was offering me £10,000 a day to go and work in Tokyo and £5,000 a day for Kelly.

"Holy shit, Batman," I muttered to myself.

"What do you make of that Ralph?" I asked, whilst massaging behind his ears.

I put on a silly Scooby-Doo voice and replied to myself, "That's a lot more than you're worth Shaggy!!"

"You're quite right of course, Ralph. This is bonkers."

Spent the next two hours reading through the contract terms and conditions, the dates proposed, travel arrangements and visa requirements. The hotel they were going to put us up in was something else. Mesm hotel, Tokyo was listed online at being around £400 per room, per night. In the end, the flights being offered were standard business class not first class as Akira had said they would be over the phone that day but since Kelly and I are both under average height, leg room and such things are not the highest priority. I was confident it would be a significant upgrade over economy. Never flown anything but economy. Could never justify the additional expense. To me, that was eating out and cocktail money for a holiday saved right there!!

"Jesus wept Angelique, that's a lot of money."

"I know, Caitlin. I'm beginning to understand how Olivia feels. All that money she earns being an internet gaming queen."

"Well, I guess for so many, it is luck and timing but, in your case, you truly deserve it. Look, I'll tell you what it is. If you think of the thousands of hours you dedicated yourself to becoming a European Champion. All the hours from just seven years old to thirty, all the sacrifices you made. Now, add in all the days since you retired six years ago coaching, supporting others?"

"It's a lot of work for zero money Caitlin, that's true," I said, nodding my head.

"Still, all feels a little unreal. All from that video going viral."

"It went viral because it meant something to a lot of people. To some, perhaps mothers and daughters, it was just a beautiful moment captured unknowingly by you guys. To others, like Sony and big business, it represents something far greater. It's like Simon Cowell's face on X-Factor when someone nails their audition. He always turns around slowly, sees the audience on their feet, giving a standing ovation, right!? There's that gentle, wry smile of his.

"Ka-ching, Ka-ching!!" That's all he's thinking.

"Yeah. You're right, as always, Caitlin."

"I'll see you for training tomorrow. We can go over that contract, make sure you're good to go."

"Aces. Thanks Caitlin. See you then," I said and hung up.

It was dark by the time I arrived at Kelly's family home. A two-bedroom flat in a large concrete tower block built in the

1950s. That people would choose to live in a concrete tower block might strike some as bizarre. And yet at their inception they were hailed as an escape from the slum housing of post-war Britain. Like so many things, intentions were honorable and well positioned at the time. The reality? Not so great. Fast forward seventy years and these structures have not fared well. Lifts were seldom operational and Kelly's family would have to carry their heavy shopping bags up eight flights of stairs.

Unemployment was far higher in these areas. Two out of three youths on her estate were not working which enabled gang culture to thrive. I knew the drill. Stand beside Nelly and wait for the young men to appear. Like hyenas, looking for an easy meal. It's important, I explain to you that I bear these young men no ill feelings. They often form part of my club in Brixton. Children from the estates have a poor, sometimes physically rough start in life. Who am I to judge their teenage behaviour coming from privilege?

"Yo! That's a nice car innit," a voice called out, belonging to a tall, skinny white man with a neck tattoo of something in black, I couldn't make it out under the poor lighting from the streetlight above.

"Thanks. She's alright," I said, looking directly at him.

"Something you need, Lady?" he asked, taking two steps closer to me, whilst three other youths appeared from the darkness of the underpass.

"I do. How much for an eighth?"

"You talking coke or weed?" he said, looking me up and

down with a pervy grin.

"Weed."

"£60 luv."

"Don't take the piss. It's never more than £40 and that's when it's something worth smoking."

He laughed and turned to his gang, "You hear that boys? Lady here knows her gear."

"So, £40 then?"

"Not for Mexican Sativa honey."

"That what you got?"

"For the right price it is. Classy Lady like you, don't wanna be smoking the cheaper shit."

"More for my flat mate. He's a connoisseur of the herb."

"Can do for you £50," he offered, digging a hand into his hoodie pocket.

"Not now. I'll give you £100 in half an hour if when I return, the car looks as pretty as she does now."

"Done," he replied, turning around to the younger of his crew to come forwards and stand by Nelly. He and the other two teenagers walked silently back to the underpass.

"Fuck's sake!" I said, breathing hard, finally getting to the eighth floor. I knocked twice on Kelly's door.

It opened and Kelly's mum, Sofia smiled and embraced me before inviting me in.

"Angelique is here!" she announced cheerily, shutting the door behind me and asking if I would prefer tea or coffee.

"Cup of builder's tea. Strong, just a dash of milk, no sugar would be lovely," I said, smiling warmly at her, placing my hand upon her arm.

Addae and Kelly hugged me as I entered the living room.

"Wow, now that is the kind of welcome I like!"

"It is the only welcome acceptable to you visiting us!" Addae exclaimed.

"I need to talk with you all together. You know about Sony?"

"Yes! Kelly told us all about it the other day. We can't quite believe it."

"Well, believe it. I've checked the contracts out. Everything is in order. Kelly and I are to spend a fortnight in Japan working for Sony corporation on their global advertising project, to promote their latest high-tech headphones."

"This is really something," Addae said, putting his arm around Kelly who leant into him, blushing a little.

"£5,000 a day."

A stunned silence followed my words as the family sat mouths ajar, staring at one another. Finally, Addae spoke.

"£5,000 a day!? For Kelly to work with you in Japan. No, it is not possible, Angelique."

"It is and it's happening, Addae."

Silence turned to cheering and clapping as Kelly's parents

embraced her and kissed her head and cheeks.

When everyone had calmed down which did take a while, Kelly found her voice.

"It's for you, Mum. For you, Dad. Get that mortgage deposit together. Let's move away from this shitty estate, have our own home."

"It is your money, not ours."

"No, Mum. This is for us. I want us to all benefit."

Addae looked at his wife, shaking his head. "You raised the most perfect daughter my Sofia!"

She smiled back at him, appreciating that he recognised it was her efforts not his that contributed most to the way Kelly had turned out.

I advised the family to keep quiet about this adventure, especially the money. No-one will be happy for you in this time of suffering with the cost-of-living crisis across the country.

"Oh, and by the way? If you struggle to secure a mortgage, despite placing down over £50,000 cash deposit, I will be your guarantor. You are buying your own home!"

I left them all looking delighted and stunned.

"What a rather lovely evening," I thought to myself as I skipped down the stairs and back to where I had left Nelly in the capable hands of the local gang.

I had the £100 in my left hand, dug deep into my jacket pocket. My right hand free to take the bag of weed.

"Got the money Lady?"

"Yup. Got my weed?"

"Right here," he said, moving up close to me, letting a hand slide over to grab my arse.

I took hold of his wrist, twisted my body violently away from his, bringing his hand up in the wrong direction.

"Get off me, get off me!" he screamed.

One of his friends took a step towards us.

"Don't even think about it," I said, glaring at him.

The youth stopped dead in his tracks.

"Give me the weed now."

"You‘re hurting me!"

"Give me the weed and I'll stop."

He reached into his pocket and slowly held up the bag.

I took it from him. "This the good shit, yeah? You're not trying to fuck me over are you?"

"Deal's a deal! Where's our oner?"

I took the £100 from my pocket and dropped it on the ground, releasing the youth at the same time. He knelt down, massaging his wrist as I casually got into Nelly and drove away.

CHAPTER FIFTEEN

Now, we wait.

I usually like to put my foot down as you know, get places swiftly. That evening was different. I left Brighton, driving well under the speed limit, my mind hectic. You know those times when it's impossible to focus on one thing? Ideas, thoughts, images, memories, all mixed up in a bundle you cannot untangle. I was excited about Japan, about the upcoming contest with the USA. I was anxious waiting on the DNA results for Smitherman's cousin. Concerned that SRS would go under and my love for recruitment would fade right alongside it. Strong, freshly developed feelings for both Joshua and Kirsty, invading the space in my heart, I had to date saved for Alessia and Gareth.

Some days, I am utterly carefree. Almost childlike. The previous evening being surrounded by four members of a street gang, having to put one firmly in his place, did not lose me even a minute of sleep. I returned home, cool as a refrigerated cucumber. Tossed the bag of weed to Gareth who was standing over his beloved decks playing, Spiller, Groovejet, "If This Ain't Love"

"Oh, nice one darling!" he beamed, opening the bag and inhaling deeply over it.

"Mexican Sativa.... Apparently."

"Smells divine! Buds are shiny, like tinsel on a Christmas tree."

I laughed at his passion for the herb. Gareth's love of house music and weed probably equals my love for him and Team GB. That's a whole lot of love!

"To what do I owe this unexpected gift?"

"Part of an arranged cost, for the secure parking of Nelly in a certain council estate, on the wrong side of London.

"Kelly?"

"Yup."

"Her family must be over the moon with the news about Japan. Serious amount of coin for a kid her age to be earning."

Obviously, I had told Gareth. Sean, Gareth, and Caitlin always know everything. Every detail of my life. Well, except for my detective sleuthing and seeing Kirsty. Those were my secrets.

Whilst Gareth skinned up a spliff, I helped myself to one of his cold, Czech Pilsner beers and eased myself down on the sofa, taking a moment to appreciate that tune. Gotta love Sophie Ellis-Beckster's voice.

"You coping ok, being back at work?"

"In the main, yes."

"Go on."

"Well, I'm there mentally. I feel sharp and excited to have secured this job. My team is amazing."

"But?"

"But it is a struggle physically, girl."

When you have a splenectomy, your liver steps up and takes on additional duties the spleen once did. That is all well and good however your immune system will never be as robust as it once was. You are frequently run down if not very careful with diet and specific supplements. I'm not entirely convinced smoking weed has been scientifically proven to enhance one's immune system, but Gareth has enjoyed the herb since we were kids at school so not likely to stop anytime soon!

"You been taking the supplements, I bought for you?"

"Yes, girl, I have indeed."

"Twice daily, boy?"

"Not always but definitely every day."

I smiled at Gareth, and he blew me a kiss. Working long shifts in a hotel is hard work, mentally and physically. Truth be told, emotionally too, as some guests are total wankers. "I'm a paying guest, therefore it's my right to be a total prick."

"It's unfortunate you have a tiny penis and such a huge wallet, that you feel entitled to be such an enormous cock!"

Gareth said, this is how he'd love to respond to some of the rich older men with their trophy wives upon their arms.

I arrived at Joshua's home feeling an overwhelming need to be held in his big, strong arms. It was early evening, the garage door was open and light coming from within. Hearing Nelly pull up Joshua came out, walking beside him was a stunningly attractive blonde woman. They were both fully kitted out in biker gear.

"Hi Angelique," Joshua said casually, as I got out of the car.

"Evening all!" I replied, making sure to smile warmly at Catwoman. You recall that Batman movie were Michelle Pfeiffer totally killed it? I swear to you, she was the real deal. High cheek bones, classically beautiful, with a heart shaped face, short, bobbed hairstyle. Dressed head to toe in expensive Italian, black leathers, she had a ridiculously confident manner about her. Smaller in the boobs perhaps than I, which she more than made up for with toned, shapely thighs.

"Angelique, do you have competition?" I thought to myself, as I hugged Joshua and introduced myself to this gorgeous creature.

"So, finally, I get to meet Angelique Santoro," she said, with an easy smile. "I'm Melanie."

"Hi, Melanie. Lovely to meet you too."

"Finally?" I asked.

Melanie took me by the hand and walked me inside the garage.

"There," she remarked, pointing to a corkboard on the wall. Pinned to it was a cut out from a newspaper showing Kelly and I holding one another on the mats. That now famous moment captured in so many forms of media.

"Oh, yes, right, yup, that's me. Guilty as charged."

"I must have seen that video clip with the Guns N' Roses song, like twenty times. It's just brilliant." Melanie beamed at me.

"Oh, you clever girl, you." I thought. What would turn Joshua off faster than you being a catty little bitch toward me?

"Bit creepy, you putting cut outs of me around the garage, Joshua. Are there others to be found about the house, life sized, cardboard ones perhaps?"

"One or two but I'm careful to put them away in the attic before you show up."

"Clever boy," I said, wearing a wry smile.

"I fancy a drink. Gin and tonics all round?"

"Lovely," Melanie and I replied together.

Joshua smiled as he left the garage. I was eager to see if Melanie would change her tactics, her nature or would she remain constant? Was she a genuinely nice woman or was she a clever bitch, wearing a brilliant disguise? There are some women who like magpies to silver foil get drawn to married men at a bar. They see a wedding ring and think, "game on." Is it because they are a challenge or perceived to be? Is it the whole forbidden fruit thing? Or it is they simply find a man attractive, which is not scared of commitment and perhaps they can steal them away from their wife? Perhaps, it is their desire to be a mistress or have a fun sexual relationship, without the man turning into some lost puppy and falling in love with them? Joshua wasn't married. Nor was he mine. Not that I believe people "own" others and I dislike it when people refer to their partner as a possession, whether they mean it or not.

"You're a proper biker then Melanie," I suggested, looking down, studying the knee sliders over her leather trousers. The plastic, rubber compound worn down significantly.

"It's easier than it looks, getting your knee down," she replied casually, as if she were referring to tending roses in her garden.

"You're too modest."

"I grew up around bikers. My older brothers did Moto X, so I ended up getting into bikes young."

"How old were you when you started riding?"

"I was six."

"That's really young."

"Same as you probably getting into martial arts?"

"Yeah, think I was seven but it's true what they say. Gotta start kids young if they are ever going to be any good."

"True, Angelique. Like skiing, bike racing can be dangerous. It's all about confidence. Pushing limits without fear. When your little you are close to the ground so when you come off, it's not that big a deal really."

"My mother would have had kittens. She hated my taking up Jujitsu. Motorbikes would have put her into an early grave!"

"I know for sure! My poor Mum!" Melanie exclaimed. "She had three sons really, well four if you count my dad."

Interesting. Melanie sees herself as a tomboy, despite being a highly beautiful woman. Who does that remind you of? Does Joshua have a type or is this just a coincidence? I don't believe in coincidences. "This is not good news Angelique. She's got it all and probably not dating another woman. If I were Joshua, I'd be weighing up my options. What's she like in the bedroom? Is she a good kisser? She's smart, engaging, confident, sassy as me, shares his love of motorbikes.

I don't do jealousy. It's a lame human emotion, which I refuse to let into my being. I'm simply assessing her attributes and seeing how Joshua might perceive her. Have I pushed Joshua away by being honest about Kirsty? Telling a man, "Oh I can't see you tonight, I'm hanging out with Kirsty." Translation in his mind my friends? "Angelique is getting off with a sexy detective ten years younger than me. How can I compete with that?" Is this what he feels now? He needs a back-up to Angelique because she's too recently single to commit to him? How would I feel being in his shoes? Is my openly bi-sexual nature no longer a turn on for him but rather a perceived threat? Do I need to ramp things up, bring another girl into our universe, make him the centre of everything? What man doesn't want two women at once? If only, for the odd night of pleasure, here and there. Gives Angelique a rather unique selling point does it not?

Joshua returned with our drinks and asked me if I was ok.

"I'm aces. Why?"

"You just looked a bit spaced out a moment ago."

"Oh yeah, right. Just a lot on my mind, with work crap, NHS not hiring, state of SRS."

"You're in recruitment, right?"

"That's right Melanie. How did you know that?"

"Oh, Joshua mentioned it when I asked if you were a full-time coach at Team GB, he told me you weren't. I'm in business leadership coaching, so like you, feeling this recession big time. Sucks."

"Self-employed?"

"Yup, you know it."

"Feast or famine. Chicken or feathers!"

We laughed together and she touched my arm fondly. No. She wasn't a bitch. In another world, we would become great friends. But this is planet earth, 2023 and we won't become this to one another. I already have you in my life and her name is Caitlin.

The question I was dying to ask was, how did you guys meet or how do you know one another? Want to give power to your competition ladies? Gentlemen? Well, go right ahead and ask that question, see where it gets you. It reeks of desperation. A fishing trip. Oil exploration. Drill that fucking hole. Go ahead, I dare you.

Nothing is less sexy, less alluring than neediness. Not easy, is it? All you crave is information. Knowledge is power right!? How does one get that without asking questions? How indeed.

Patience.

Play it cool. Be cool, Angelique.

CHAPTER SIXTEEN

There you are, Dumbo.

“Well, our Melanie is rather lovely.”

“Our Melanie?”

“Oh, I’m sorry. Would you prefer your Melanie?”

“Cute, Angelique.”

“Of course.”

“I appreciate you not making that awkward.”

“Well, I have turned up without invitation or prior arrangement. Sorry about that. I did call a couple of times but you weren’t picking up, as you were riding.”

“You got that right.”

“What I didn’t get right, however, was that you were riding solo,” I said, giving him a cheeky grin.

"You're finding this amusing, aren't you?"

"As opposed to what?"

"I think most women, most people, would be feeling uncomfortable."

"How do you know I'm not feeling like this?"

"Oh, I don't know. You lounging about my sofa, both feet up on the coffee table?"

"Would you like me to remove my feet?" I asked, casually sipping my second large, gin and tonic.

Joshua laughed. "You're something else, Angelique Santoro, you know this?"

"Sure. Perhaps."

Patience. Like I suggested, right? Let the boy come to you, girls. Always. They love the chase. It's in their DNA. It's also genetics that acting like you couldn't give two fucks makes you as a woman, far more attractive to them. I didn't need to poke about did I? Joshua's last remark said everything to me. I was safe. For now. The cut out helped my confidence, of course.

Melanie was a cool customer. I was suitably impressed with her. To lead me by the hand and point to the corkboard, behave as she did in front of Joshua and on her time? Impressive indeed.

Not sure what a normal response to the situation would be but as I'm not very normal, I accepted Joshua's assessment. All joking aside my friends? Message received. Incoming threat detected. Do I need to launch a missile offensive? No. Not yet but the system is now armed.

"Dearest Melanie. I like you. A great deal in fact. I wish you were not my enemy, but you are just this. How to deal with you? This is a question I must ponder upon. I'll not sabotage what you may be developing with Joshua. Not my style. Angelique will prevail should she so wish. Play your games. Be the best version of yourself. All you've done is make me realise how much I feel towards this man. For this wake-up call, I thank you."

Joshua had put on George Ezra's "Budapest."

"Love his voice, his vibe."

"He's great, no question."

"Do we address the elephant in the room or be wonderfully British and bury our heads in the sand?"

"My mother does a superb ostrich."

"It is something we Brits are rather good at Angelique. Avoiding awkwardness. Pretending it's not there or happening."

"On a par with queuing, according to Bill Bryan's book, Tales From a Small Island."

"He got that right. If there is a long queue for something perhaps not that important, the Brits will form an orderly line with military precision and stand in it, until sandwiches and tea are sent for by the head of the household."

We both laughed and for a moment I lost myself in those gorgeous blue eyes.

"The floor is yours, Sir Josh-UA of Sussex."

"Why, thanking you kindly, Lady Santoro of Paris, France and Amalfi, Italy."

I nodded gracefully to him, gently encouraging him with hands open to continue.

"You told me that you were seeing the detective. Kirsty, what's her name."

"Jackson. Kirsty Jackson."

"That's right. I am hereby announcing to you, Lady Santoro at 7pm on an otherwise uneventful Wednesday, I am seeing a woman called Melanie."

"I thank you for your honesty, Sir Joshua. Had I not pitched up unannounced today, when do you think you would have told me?"

"Next week probably."

"Probably?"

"Well, it's not an exact science telling the woman you've been dating that you are seeing someone new."

"Are you doing so to balance out me seeing Kirsty?"

"I don't think so, no."

"Do you think it's the same thing? You seeing another woman, like I am?"

"Not sure I follow."

"Well, if you were seeing a man perhaps that would be more the same? I'm bisexual Joshua. Not having a woman in my life affects me in a negative way. You're straight. But do you need two women in your life to balance you out in some way?"

"Oohhhh, I feel whatever I say, it is likely to be an incorrect answer!!"

I laughed. "No. For sure. Whatever, however, you feel, it is important to me, surfer boy."

Joshua shrugged his shoulders, his t-shirt riding up as he did so, showing me his gorgeous biceps.

"Angelique. We are both coming out from long term relationships. We have never said we are exclusive and bearing in mind how we met, I never assumed anything. I really love spending time with you and look forward to each visit or meal out, whatever."

"That's like super cool and reasonable. Good to know you're not angry or upset with me and fucking someone else to get some kind of leverage."

"Leverage? You thought I was playing mind games?"

"No. That's not what I was thinking at all. It's just reassuring that you are the man I thought you were and are in the same head space as me. I'm not seeing Kirsty to hurt you, playing games."

"I never thought this of you Angelique."

"Marvelous. Quick question?"

"Go on."

"Why are your leather trousers still on?"

"Because I've not been long off the bike!"

"Indeed. Well, that was then, and this is now. I'd like you to remove them. Now."

Joshua smirked at me, stood up and removed the biking

trousers.

“Now your boxers. I want you naked. Trust me. It’s in your best interests.”

I drove back to Brighton, having left Joshua breathless on the sofa. Can’t be entirely sure but I may have given him the best blowjob he’s ever had. Failing this, it was the best blowy I’d ever given him. Inspired by Melanie? More than likely, yes. But hey, inspiration presents itself in many different forms my friends. The secret is to somehow grab it, make it your own and take good advantage of it!

Back to my usual self, driving considerably over the speed limit enjoying the attitude of Wendy James, lead singer of Transvision Vamp in “Baby, I Don’t Care.”

I was just parking Nelly up outside our flat when the phone rang.

“Hello, Detective Sergeant Jackson,” I said mischievously.

“Good evening, Miss Santoro!”

“Oh, someone sounds brighter than in our last phone call!”

“We’ve just arrested and charged Oliver Scott for attempted murder.”

“Oh my God! That’s amazing. Well done, Kirsty. That’s so awesome!”

“My team is over the moon. Got them both, Angelique. Banged to rights.”

“Can we meet?”

"Still at work, got to write this up. Give me an hour, yeah?"

"Perfect. I'll grab a bite to eat and see you in Hove."

"Not a word to Gareth. I'll see him face to face in the police station tomorrow. Still got questions for your best friend!"

"Understood."

"Oh, and if you attend in person as you did a few weeks ago, don't go grabbing at my arse, yeah?"

"I'll make a very concerted effort not to," I replied giggling, before hanging up.

Got a taxi to a wine bar, called La Rouge, listening to "Sweet Dreams" by The Eurythmics. Wearing a green silk dress to my knees, looking elegant, classy, then in sharp contrast a pair of chunky, black Chelsea boots, to ensure I felt me at the same time. I love dresses but I'm not good in heels and always feel like I'm trying too hard. Do you know what I mean? Drinking and high heels do not go well together. I'm an athlete first and foremost, a party girl second! Not about to find myself on crutches, having torn ligaments in my ankle or foot from falling over, leaving a bar with wobbly legs.

Having located a secluded spot away from the crowd, I eased myself back into the leather armchair. The waitress appeared. Cute as a button, cropped boyish brunette hair with various piercings including silver studs, complete with polished rose-colored glass tips through both her nose and cheeks.

"Good evening, Miss. What can I get for you?"

"Evening to you too," I said flirtatiously, holding her gaze. She was into girls, if the subtle glance to my boobs was anything to go by. Well, this and her appearance was a telling combination perhaps.

"How long have you worked here?"

"Just less than six months."

"Ideal. Can I trust you to select a good bottle of champagne for me? You know, not the lower end of the scale but not a take the piss out of the customer one either!"

She smiled. "For sure. French? Veuve Clicquot yellow label, is in the same league as many far more expensive champagnes. Two glasses?"

"Perfect. Thank you so much."

I stole a glance at her curvy bum as she walked away, returning my gaze to my phone just as Kirsty entered the bar.

After the earlier tension between us, me checking out a young waitress, may not have gone down that well. Just got lucky, Angelique. Ha!! I thought to myself, as I got up to kiss Kirsty on each cheek.

"Fuck, you look hot."

"And you Miss. Jackson."

"Such a pretty liar. I look like shit and feel it. Been a frantic week getting this arsehole. Had stomach acid in my throat these past twenty-four hours worrying about the DNA from the lab."

"I love your passion and commitment."

"Love that you fancy me, despite being a total mess, Angelique."

"I find people who are intense attractive. You on this case, is like me getting ready for a contest. I see myself in you."

"So, you fancy yourself basically?"

"Tired but still lively, I see," I said, leaning forwards to tickle just under her ribs.

Kirsty squealed, those blue eyes waking up. As humans, we are funny creatures don't you think? A little surprise stimulation and we go from tired and withdrawn to wide awake and engaged.

The waitress arrived, with the bucket of ice, champagne already placed within, wished us both a pleasant evening and left us to our banter.

"Bit out of my price range."

"You're not paying for anything tonight."

"Well, in that case, shall I do the honors?"

"By all means."

Kirsty opened the bottle with the nervousness of someone expecting a bomb to go off. I get it. We've all opened a bottle and gasped as the cork sped off around the room nearly taking someone's eye out! In the end the bottle opened with a satisfying pop but was somewhat anticlimactic.

"Tell me everything, Kirsty."

"So, the lab results came back, as per Smitherman. Oliver Scott's DNA is in both urine and saliva."

"Dirty slag!"

"Birds of a feather, Angelique. I know he's under the control of Smitherman. He's beneath him in the Church but also as a person. Smitherman is the ringleader, I'm certain of it."

"I couldn't give a fuck about that. Guilty as the leader or by association or some kind of joint hand holding exercise. He played his part."

"Not saying he didn't. I'm just giving you my take on it, yeah?"

"Yes. Sorry. Continue."

"He's already lawyered up refusing to say anything but no comment."

"So, not even saying not guilty."

"Well, of course he said that repeatedly. Claiming this was a set up. The lefty Brighton green party and its wet nosed police force trying to get Eternity Saints shut down somehow."

"Unbelievable."

"Yeah, well what else is he going to say? Just like Smitherman, it was a well-rehearsed speech. Like listening to the shadow actor, ready to take over should that person suddenly fall ill the night before the big opening."

"What else you got on them?"

"The team have been working hard ever since we arrested Smitherman. He was smart leaving his mobile at home. We suspect Scott will be the same. The mobile company will likely show they were at home or rather the GPS signal will confirm they were."

"But?"

"But we've got Smitherman's new BMW parked half a mile from the Hilton at the time of the attack. New cars are fitted with tracking devices, especially the more expensive ones. Not something you can readily mess about with."

"Love that!"

"Additionally, we have both CCTV and doorstep camera footage showing two men walking in the direction of the hotel and what appears to be the same two men walking significantly faster back some twenty minutes later."

"Circumstantial?" I questioned, shrugging my shoulders, taking another sip of this delightful champagne.

"No. One image is a lovely close up of Smitherman looking right into the camera lens of a private household's door delivery set up."

"Thank you, Covid."

"Absolutely. These high-tech cameras are vastly superior to the often worn out, older CCTV cameras outside shops. Cutting edge technology, lights come on at night, with the slightest movement, the works. The inventor of these thought both about the safe delivery of packages and scaring off potential burglars. Clever bugger."

"Amazing. Well done, Jackson!"

"Thank you."

"When's the likely court date for the trial?"

"Yeah, well that's the kicker, Angelique. Due to Covid, the courts are backed up, just as the hospitals are for essential operations. We're looking at six months from now."

"Shit!"

"I know. It's brutal, having this on-going for so long. Must remain calm and strong. It is, what it is."

"Not sure Gareth will cope very well with such a lengthy delay to proceedings."

"He struggling?"

"Yes and no. Good days and bad days."

"Of course. It's always the victim who suffers. The guilty sleep peacefully even in remand or prison."

"Even when they win, victims still lose, right?"

"Not necessarily. Getting these wankers sent down will give us all massive satisfaction and Gareth will have this, plus you being his cheerleader, will ensure he keeps progressing."

I smiled at Kirsty, reached forward and kissed her hand.

"Thank you for everything."

"Of course, Mistress. Anything for you."

CHAPTER SEVENTEEN
Shield Maiden

I slept in Gareth's bed most nights since the night terrors began. Well, if he was on a night shift, I would stay over at Joshua's place or with Kirsty but if he was home on an evening, his bed became our bed. The terrors began suddenly and usually between 1am and 3am.

We had bypassed the typically useless GP and found an expert in PTSD which had advised us that nightmares and recurring anxiety entering our dream state was symptomatic of PTSD. It is the mind's delayed response to extreme stress, often associated with violence. Whether you committed an act of violence or were the victim of it seems to make little difference, he suggested. Paul Harrington was a decorated officer of the Army. Captain within The Royal Regiment of Fusiliers, Harrington had seen action in various parts of the world including Afghanistan and Syria. He served fourteen years, had an exemplary service record and left under a fanfare of warm congratulations and medal ceremony.

He had once proudly said the words, "Honi soit qui mal pense" quietly under his breath, whilst polishing his boots as part of his early morning routine. "Evil be to him who evil thinks." He lived and breathed army life. He never felt stressed. He won promotion swiftly and enjoyed the discipline, helping those beneath his rank and file to become better men. Hard working, honest and honorable men who could smile back at themselves looking in the mirror.

Within two years of leaving the army, Harrington was a shadow of his former self. Heavily bearded, homeless and lacking any self-love and respect he once so proudly instilled in his men. PTSD wasn't widely acknowledged back then and whilst plenty of men still don't open up and talk about their feelings perhaps as well or as often as they ought, compared to twenty years ago they certainly do. Paul was in a good place now and dedicated his life to helping others progress their condition.

The first night the terrors took hold of Gareth, I was in a deep sleep, dreaming about Kelly taking gold against the USA and us leaving for Japan on a glorious high. I leapt from my bed and sprinted into Gareth's bedroom. He was sat bolt upright, shaking, and crying. His t-shirt drenched in cold sweat, clinging to his skin. I tore the t-shirt off him, replacing it with my own, the one I had stolen from Joshua the previous year. Holding Gareth to my naked breast, stroking his wet hair until eventually, he passed out utterly exhausted.

Kirsty and Joshua both understood that with me, no-one ever came before Gareth. Not before all this shit had happened and now with this latest development, they accepted that for some time to come, they were not going to be my top priority. I had both Aveline and Gareth to be constantly mindful of. To their credit they handled it well. I was anything but a perfect girlfriend to either of them. Sometimes Gareth slept peacefully in my arms with Ralph snuffling quietly at the foot of the bed. More often than not, he would wake up scared, anxious and I would ease him back to sleep.

Trouble with this was that I was becoming increasingly sleep deprived so when with Kirsty or Joshua, I would be more prone to falling asleep on their lap watching TV after a good meal than making, mad passionate love to them. My sexy mannerisms and ways were my thing, always had been my unique selling feature. Without this, was I handing Joshua to Melanie on a polished, silver breakfast tray? Would Kirsty soon tire of me and find herself a more enjoyable playmate? With each passing week of poor sleep patterns, my mind started planting more unwelcomed thoughts and fears within me.

Three months had passed since that playful evening, drinking champagne at La Rouge. SRS was still struggling to secure business. The UK was slipping further into recession with corporate giants such as Tesco, Marks & Spencer, Google, Twitter, Microsoft and Amazon all laying off tens of thousands of staff, whilst scores of lesser known, smaller outfits did likewise.

I was drinking far less and exercising more in my own personal battle for increased inner calm and well-being. Joy was found and delivered upon by Kelly in GB Vs USA. Once again, I had found myself in the commentary box, this time letting the makeup artist do a little more than before to hide my tired eyes. I had consumed a double expresso on top of the double vodka soda from half hour previously. The result being an excitable, charming, and cheery Angelique. Before the event went live, I was told to be "exactly as you were last time but perhaps without the running off part!!"

I said, I'd do my best. Viewings were up over half million on the last Team GB contest against Germany. The interaction between Kelly and I, the reason for much of it so everyone believed. I said, "I doubt it was down to my expert commentary!"

Only to be hushed down with, "Oh, tosh and nonsense darling. Television isn't about perfection. That German woman was a perfectly accurate, experienced ex-athlete and a total bore! You're fun and don't mind being overcome by emotion. That's what the British public love. We're such a tied up, emotionally shut down people. You're all Italian and French yet British at the same time. You can't lose. Just be you!!"

With these kind words of encouragement banked in my mind, I forgot the TV crew altogether and allowed myself to get fully wrapped up in the event. As it was being aired live, the host did have to apologize to the viewers when I yelled out, "For fuck's sake Kelly!" after she lost her footing and nearly handed a contest to a lesser opponent. Opsy daisy, Angelique!!

I sat there like a naughty schoolgirl, biting my bottom lip, whilst looking at my host. In that moment, I was wondering how many people were watching at home laughing and enjoying my faux pas versus those offended by my language slip. Confident it would only likely increase my fan base, I did not offer up any sort of apology, sat up straight and removed my bottom teeth from my lip! "Who the fuck else can do for them what I do?" I thought.

Little controversy. A little *Oh, she's cheeky, that Angelique woman*, won't do me any harm.

Marie-Claire had pulled her groin days before the USA battle, which was a great shame on the one hand but on the other it provided a unique opportunity for Kelly to not only be the top junior Team GB athlete but ultimately the outright winner. Kelly progressed through the tournament with the controlled aggression and purpose of a Viking shield maiden attacking England's villages. Her hand fully recovered now; she was unstoppable. It's like the disappointment of hurting herself against Germany had enabled yet more personal growth.

Being recognised in the street, her newly uplifted status at school from being referred to as "scum" to *Oh, hey Kelly, is it ok if we hang with you?!* was doing her no harm. It was like Kelly grew a year for every three months of life she experienced. It's strange, yet true. She was the new me. Team GB had finally found the new Angelique Santoro. Well, to be more precise, I had identified and trained the new me but whatever! It was long overdue.

The final was a hotly contested fight with both girls giving it one hundred percent, which you may think is obvious Angelique, it is the final! Let me explain. Five fights must be won to reach the final. That is a very demanding day both physically and emotionally. The pressure to perform in the final to "bring it home" is huge. You are clearly good enough.

There you stand facing your opponent. A single win away from glory, yet your body feels heavy. You're now running on the last twenty percent of battery power before you stop moving altogether and the lights go out.

Kelly and I had spent a lot of time over the past two years doing short, intense meditation exercises. I was thrilled to see her, hands on hips, gently breathing, eyes closed as the TV cameras zoned in on both competitors. The American was edgy looking, wasting energy bouncing impatiently from one foot to the other. Kelly was the exact opposite. Using zero energy, she was refueling. In her mind, I knew precisely where she was at. We had worked on her meditation for different outcomes. Right now, she was visualising her body as a fuel cell, empty and tired. With each passing breath in, that fuel cell was being topped up. Five deep breaths and the fuel cell was at optimum.

When she opened her eyes, I knew she was going to win. Her opponent slipped. Kelly capitalised on the lost balance, helping the American find the floor with a glorious leg sweep. In the blink of an eye, Kelly had put the girl into a strangle hold that even I could not have removed myself from. She tapped out. Aretha Franklin, "Respect" blaring out of the speakers, as she ran off the mats into the arms of Sean.

The British fans erupted into raucous celebration, clapping and cheering, singing the RESPECT chorus as if their very lives depended upon it. I knew it was Kelly's favourite song and had requested it if she won, that this be played instead of the lame cheesy pop song they had planned on, which would have meant nothing to Kelly or her friends and family.

To my astonishment, the entire commentary box, other than the quiet American were dancing and singing about. The cameraman was grinning behind his apparatus, so who was I to not join in!?

The country was in free fall. The cost-of-living crisis being felt so intensely across our beautiful land. What lifts a country in times of sadness and worry? Victory my friends. It doesn't matter in which sport. Tennis and Wimbledon. The Lionesses in football. Whatever. It's having a reason to high five and hug your family, friends and neighbours. It is light. It is a lightning bolt of love, straight to the heart.

CHAPTER EIGHTEEN

Nihon, Kimashita.

"May I hold your hand, Sensei?"

I smiled at Kelly. "Of course. Anytime. Anywhere, you like."

Kelly took my hand and I squeezed hers just for a little bit for reassurance.

"Seats upright for take-off. Please ensure all electronic devices are either switched off or on silent flight mode." The stewardess said.

"Shit, it's happening."

"You know how you like it when I drop Nelly down a gear and boot her?"

"Yeah, I love it!"

"So, take off in a plane is similar. The engines roar and you feel the thrust as the pilot pushes the throttle fully open. It's the same thing."

"Except with Nelly we remain on the ground like we're meant to. We're people, not birds!"

"Well, today, you're a human, bird thingy!"

Kelly refused to take the window seat but as traveling business class it was just the two of us, not three or four seats in a row as per economy. Anytime she wanted to switch seats with me, she could.

The engine started to vibrate, then that slight pause before the pilot decided it was time and opened that throttle. Kelly squeezed my hand so hard I winced as the plane sped down the runway, reached its desired speed and eased off the ground into the air.

"Holy shit!" Kelly cried out, much to the gentle amusement of an elderly woman sitting across from us.

I pointed to the window to distract Kelly who fell silent as she lost herself watching the world she knew, fade into tiny, toy-like objects before vanishing from view altogether.

Kelly's parents had both flown previously. Once. Her mother coming from Denmark. Her father, from Africa. Neither had enjoyed the experience. Can't blame them. Flying economy is not fun or enjoyable and I'm five-foot, four inches tall. If significantly taller, it feels cramped and uncomfortable because newsflash! That is precisely what it is. I used to laugh when upon landing someone would say, "We hope you enjoyed your flight. Thank you for traveling with us and we look forward to welcoming you onboard again soon."

Business class? Now that my friends, is a whole other ballgame. Big, wide comfortable seats, fully reclinable. Luxury blankets and supportive pillows. Food, which I'd pay good money for in a restaurant and decent gin. "I could get used to this," I muttered under my breath as Kelly settled back into her seat, closed her eyes, and fell into a deep sleep, still holding my hand.

A month had passed since the glorious victory against the USA. That meant two things. First, Kelly was now famous. If she wasn't before, she was now with over a million Instagram followers and unlike so many celebrities, hers were active and engaging. It also meant I was, partly by association, partly because of the various media interviews I had done and TV commentary but mainly by association.

It seemed Sony had accurately predicted public opinion of the two of us and somewhat earlier than most. We would help shift their headphones. It wasn't even a gamble. Truth is their gear was probably the best on the market, so I didn't feel like a sell-out. This was essential to us both. Being real. Being the real deal not puffed up, flaky, sell out celebrity shit.

Secondly, the court date had been set and would happen exactly six weeks after our fortnight in Japan. I had mixed feelings about Japan. On the one hand, I was thrilled to visit the country, spend time with its people. A people passionate about history, food, old fashioned values and a true love and respect of martial arts. On the other, it meant two weeks away from Gareth, Joshua, and Kirsty.

Gareth was stable. He was spending time with Harrington which gave me both hope and some inner calm. Whilst I could love and care for Gareth better than anyone breathing, I was not the best qualified to progress his PTSD.

Gareth and I had sat down over a cold beer in the local pub and discussed my absence. He was thrilled I was having this experience but at the same time I could sense at this time two weeks without me was going to feel more like two months. We agreed two people would be around in the evenings if he would otherwise be alone. His good friend, Karl from his previous boutique hotel and Caitlin. Caitlin was ex-military and understood so many things us ordinary civilians couldn't possibly begin to grasp. I knew she had seen loss of human life. Had she also taken it? It was never a subject we discussed but something deep within me felt she had. With this trio looking after Gareth there was no need for me to feel guilty, yet I still found myself feeling a little edgy and apprehensive.

Whilst Kelly may have been a timid little rabbit on the plane once we landed, she was nothing but a bundle of teenage excitement and bubbly enthusiasm. I felt blessed. If I were here with another adult not a sixteen-year-old, I would have their shit to listen to. Their drama about husband or wife or elderly parents, this or that health issue. Such conversations would absolutely make me think more about my worries back home and my inability to hold Gareth or Aveline. Being grateful, I have learned is everything in this life. Grateful for whatever good finds its way to you. Love, friendship, opportunity, or the unexpected kindness of strangers. It matters not. Taking a moment to recognise and feel gratitude is a joyous and humbling feeling.

Akira Suzuki was waiting for us at arrivals, with her personal assistant, two security guards and a chauffeur all dressed up like in the movies. I glanced to Kelly and raised my eyebrows. "Shit is real, Sensei!" I laughed with her as we bowed respectfully to Akira. In Japanese culture, a nod of the head is for a casual greeting. A deeper, more considered bow from the waist is for a heightened, more formal level of respect. Kelly and I had decided unless instructed otherwise, we would do a full, slow bow to everyone we met, whether a full time Sony employee, or a sub-contractor. It was an easy decision to make despite being the honoured guests, the famous clients or whatever. In martial arts, one learns at an early age to bow and respect your Sensei and one cannot cause offence by demonstrating a higher level of respect for their culture, right?

"Welcome Angelique. Welcome Kelly." Akira greeted us, as she returned to a fully upright position.

"Thank you so much for this warm welcome and sending a car to get us. We could have got a taxi to the hotel."

"Oh, no. That would never happen Kelly! Please follow us. The limousine is parked in the underground car park. We can take the lift from just over there." Akari said, pointing away from arrivals to a sign saying car rentals and the subway.

Suddenly, there was a shrieking of young voices, as a group of teenagers ran towards us.

"Kelly! Angelique! Kelly!!" The youths excitable voices lifting to a higher pitch, as they closed in all around us.

The security guards were powerless to do anything but try to gently encourage some kind of order to their advances. Not sure if any of you have watched the Netflix documentary about Queen? There was footage from the early 70s when "Killer Queen" was a modest hit perhaps in Europe but when they arrived in Japan, it was not unlike Beatle mania. They had been warned but you could see in the faces of Freddie Mercury and Brian May, they were stunned. At that time, they could walk down Bond Street in London and do so without any bother from anyone.

I cannot fully express what a strange, overwhelming feeling it was. Never seen anything like it accept watching documentaries about Taylor Swift, Billie Eilish or Lady GaGa. It was insane! They were jumping up and down, shouting our names, thrusting pictures of us to autograph but there was really no space to write or do anything as we were being jostled about so much.

Airport security blew whistles and joined the Sony personnel. Eventually, there was a little breathing space and we did our best to sign various items including baseball hats and mouse mats. Kelly was stunned into total silence, whilst I did my best to say something but nothing very engaging or intelligent just, "Hello! How are you?" or "Thank you for coming to greet us!" I reached for Kelly's hand which she grasped onto as if her life depended on it. We followed the security team, which had now grown to eight large men, yet as swiftly as the teenagers had arrived, they left in a quiet, orderly fashion.

"That that was insane, Sensei!! I mean, what the actual fuck!?"

I shrugged my shoulders, looked blankly at Kelly, words

failing me in that moment.

"We are so sorry." Akira began, "It is almost impossible in this age of social media to keep anything quiet. Someone from our press office must have leaked your arrival schedule. Please accept our deepest apologies. What must you think of us?"

I placed my hand on her arm and looked into her eyes. "It's fine Akira. Please do not concern yourself. Truly. It's not a problem. We are officially big in Japan! It is an honour. We are ill prepared and that's not your fault. Like you said in the first telephone conversation with me, Angelique Santoro does not have an agent!? Perhaps, if I had one, Kelly and I would be better prepared. That's on us, not you."

"You are as kind and generous as they say you are, Angelique."

I smiled easily at her, letting her know everything was fine and I really did not want her upset at all. Looking back now, it was a wonderful experience. How many people will ever feel such love and adoration from total strangers? Plus, when you get older, we all feel less relevant, less cool and teenagers really help by making us feel irrelevant and ancient, before we even hit forty. The UK is incredibly ageist. If you lose your job in your mid-50s, get made redundant? For many, that's it. On the scrap heap you go! Who cares about your thirty-five years of experience?! You're a bad cold away from certain death or may as well be.

Kelly and I were totally clueless about the creation of a global television and social media advertising campaign and what it entailed. To make a thirty second television commercial (Which is regarded as the most effective, not too long nor too short) usually requires fifteen to twenty independent shots or clips. These are then expertly manipulated and merged seamlessly to create the desired affect and feel. At the 2022 Super Bowl, it costs an astonishing $6.5 Million for each thirty second advert run! The cost of making the advert, paying us, was relatively small versus the costs of running these adverts at prime time around the world.

Our filming was to be split over separate locations. It was decided the advert would feel fast paced and energetic by utilising five different locations. This would be highly effective at keeping the public more entertained and engaged. Impactful. Memorable. So many adjectives thrown at Kelly and I day two, in Tokyo. Day one, we were jet lagged and Sony were smart in not engaging us other than arrange lunch out in a lovely restaurant.

Kelly and I walked together after lunch just taking in the city vibes. It's like the words, hectic and vibrant were created for the people of Tokyo. All capital cities have this energy about them but perhaps Tokyo felt even more intense. Or perhaps it was first impression, so jet lagged. They say traveling East is the worse for that. Wherever we went, our two Sony security personnel came too. On the one hand it was reassuring I suppose, on the other a bit disconcerting that perhaps we needed them.

"I'll take the taller one, you get the smaller one!"

"Oh, come on! Why do I get shorty?"

Kelly and I giggled about together. Point being, we could have easily taken both our guards down in record time, but I guess they'd be handy enough if we were mobbed again. Four people is better than just two.

We had both woken up thinking about our airport arrival and over breakfast, Kelly showed me various uploaded videos of the event occurring. All the social media coverage and remarks were friendly and positive. Was weird seeing it from the teenager's viewpoint. It all happened so fast; you could see we were taken aback. A few seconds on and you could see it for what it really was. A warm welcome!

"Yesterday was mental, Sensei!"

"I know. I'm sorry we were both so ill prepared."

"Not your fault."

"Kinda is. I'm responsible for you. I'm your guardian as well as your Sensei. Perhaps, I should have an Agent. Perhaps we should."

"Every penny is going to the house deposit. If we had an agent there would be a smaller deposit so, no. I wouldn't have said yes to that anyways."

"Understood."

"Plus, I'm not being funny or anything. We got mobbed by a bunch of excitable kids. Like, my age group. It just took us by surprise. We were never in any danger."

"Yeah, that's true."

Filming was to be done at the Meiji shrine taking in the famous wishing tree. At the Shinjuku Gyoen national garden and Senso-Ji temple, then onto Yomiuriland and finally on-board a bullet train heading to Mount Fuji.

Filming began at the beautiful Meiji shrine, which was dedicated to Emperor Meiji and his wife, Empress Shoken. Construction began in 1915, was completed late in 1926 but the original structure was destroyed in WW2. Rebuilt in 1958, it is a very important religious site made even more impactful and beautiful as surrounded by 120,000 trees sat within 175 acres of unspoilt nature. The evergreens represent species found across Japan.

Kelly didn't have a passport before this trip and had never even travelled outside of London. She found the wishing tree very moving and beautiful. The Director of film production was a man called, Haruto Takahashi. He was a short, slightly built man in his early 50s. A good looking man, with dyed hair. You know you see Japanese men with that kinda Orange colour? Not sure if they are aiming for blonde and their natural dark hair doesn't take it very well or it's deliberate but I've always thought that Ginger / Orange tint really suits the men very well. He was super calm, totally chilled out. In my mind, I always just assumed the director would be intense and have this perfectionist manner which might translate into he or she being difficult to work with. I was wrong.

"Angelique? Kelly? Please come sit with me."

"You both look lovely today. I'm so excited that we have you with us for this campaign."

"Thank you, Haruto. We're happy to be here. Just tell us what you need, and we'll do our best."

"Athletes are the best to work with Angelique. This is going to be a great two weeks for sure. I have one request, and this is going to last all the time, I'm afraid."

"Go on," Kelly urged.

"Your headgear. These new headphones. Never take them off. We will have the planned filming, yes of course but assume I am always on duty, always seeking for those special non planned moments to capture on film!

"Understood."

"Thank you both so much for your understanding. It is quite possible that three seconds of this commercial production might be totally off script interaction and I must capture this. It will be where the beauty of your relationship lies."

Haruto remained constant throughout our fortnight in Japan. He was never grumpy. Never an arsehole towards Kelly and me. He knew we didn't have a clue what we were doing. We were not famous models or actresses. We were athletes, thrown into the spotlight by the universe. Quite happily, don't get me wrong but professionals? Nope. We were certainly not that.

I got the impression his team liked us tremendously because we were not acting like we were important, famous people. I mean, we were hardly Madonna or Beyonce. We were low maintenance girls in trainers and jeans until we had to change our clothing and be more glamorous for a certain scene. We did not challenge much. On a few occasions, I suggested something and the production team would listen and take on board what I was saying but usually then carried on regardless! I mean, I had ideas, but this was what they did for a living, so having said my bit, I just smiled and did as was asked of me.

Sony executives had decided that the dance remix by Ewan McVicar, "Tell Me Something Good" originally performed, of course by the amazing Chaka Khan, would be the perfect track for the under thirties to vibe off to, whilst watching the video. No argument from me. If the Instagram, TikTok generation was the target audience, it's as good a dance track as any. Akira had explained to me that the fourteen to thirty-year-olds had the largest disposable income as many still living at home and massively into new tech, gadgets and of course, music.

One evening, we managed to give our security detail the slip and worked our way to see a show at the Kabuki-Za theatre in the Ginza district. Sat in our comfy seats surrounded by two thousand happy faces all lost in the production whilst stuffing our faces with delightfully tasty food from a bento box. Kelly sat in silence throughout the entire performance. Utterly transfixed by the show, it was her first visit to a theatre.

In that moment, I realised just how privileged my upbringing had been, how much I had taken for granted growing up. I made up my mind that anything I could do to make Kelly and her family's life better in any conceivable way, I would grab. Her fascination, her smile, her life, was my joy.

CHAPTER NINETHEEN

Judge and Jury

Crown Court. Hove. East Sussex. A two-mile taxi ride for Gareth and I, which felt a lot longer that day, due to a traffic jam caused by rush hour and the school run. We still arrived half an hour early, as we had planned for all and any delays.

The building was an ugly, grey, concrete structure resembling a cardboard box. You know the kind of building kids' draw with crayon in pre-school? Yup, pretty much the same. Zero flair and style. Reminded me of communist Romania under the Ceausescu regime. It was built in 1971 to a design and I use the term design very loosely here, by Fitzroy Robinson and partners. Architects, apparently. In their defence, I can only hope they had a very tight budget and building materials were at an all-time high when they won the bid.

There were some forty protestors on "team Gareth." Perhaps

half this number again, were anti-gay sympathisers and ultimately either in support of Smitherman and Scott, believing in their proclaimed innocence, or not caring, just there to voice their views that all gay people will burn in the fiery pits of hell.

I looked at Gareth, who rolled his eyes then smiled warmly at the supporters as one put George Michael, "Outside" on high volume. They all began to dance and sing. I joined them, holding a supporter's hand and letting him lead me on a groovy waltz around the street outside the courthouse. The media were busy taking pictures and video of us. Go right ahead. This is love. Joy. Dancing. Acceptance and tolerance. A part of me was smiling, as the more we danced, the more pissed and upset Smitherman's flock of arseholes appeared. Kill 'em with kindness bitches!

"Hey, Gareth."

"Good morning, Detective Sergeant Jackson," Gareth replied, reaching over to shake Kirsty's hand.

"Hello, Jackson," I said, a little breathless.

"Hi, Angelique. That's not a sight I've ever seen outside the Crown Court before."

"Yeah, I'll bet."

"Rather lovely though."

"It is indeed. Unexpected and lovely."

"The CPS officer here yet?"

"Just spoken with her. She is doing her final prep work."

"You rate her, right?"

"She is dangerously sharp. If she has a weakness, it's she's a little nice."

"That's not great then, is it?"

"Sometimes it is a weakness, Gareth. In your case, I don't think it matters at all. She's amped up for this case as her brother is gay. Not only this, but we've given her shit tonnes of compelling evidence, which she will present to the jury better than anyone. Her gentle manner, Rachael being a genuinely lovely person, will be in our favour with all this hatred flying around."

"Let's hope so."

"How you feeling, Gareth. You ok today?"

"I'm alright, thanks. I'm glad this wretched six months of waiting is done. Just waiting and waiting, it's hard to get on living."

"Of course. It was bad pre-covid with things taking too long to get to court. It's a nightmare these days."

Gareth grunted, somewhat disinterestedly.

I get it, boy. Been a long, tedious process and here we stand on the steps of the Crown Court just a week or so from some kind of closure. Inside, as ever with me, I'm feeling utterly conflicted. On the one hand, if they get banged up, they lose, we win, that's something right? Yet, even with a perfect result and hefty jail sentences imposed on both these arseholes, what of Gareth and I? Will the universe take away his PTSD? Will my Gareth be handed back to me, memory and hurt removed, all polished up like a shiny new coin?

Day one of the trial. Kirsty wasn't on duty; she wasn't working that day but there was no way she was missing any of this trial. She would flit between sitting beside me in the public gallery and going downstairs to sit quietly behind Rachael, our CPS barrister, with her two solicitors. Silent, observant, making notes old school in her little police notebook. Twenty-eight-years old and reminded me of Sherlock Holmes or someone from another era. "My notes, my mind. Any fucks up by the defence, I'll leap on it like a tick on a dog leg."

I smiled thinking about my lover in this way. I rather suspect she was note taking on Rachael for the same reason. No one was going to mess this up. Friend or foe. Every opportunity must be seized. Winning is everything. Putting scum behind bars when proven guilty, when the graft, the evidence had been collected. It was her reward. The buzz lasted longer than retail therapy for Kirsty. It would not die the following day, as a fun shopping trip sometimes does. That said, she would never dwell on success for longer than seventy-two hours. Success was banished to some corner of her mind, to seldom think about, let alone talk about. Case closed. Next.

I'm not sure if barristers in other countries wear black robes and place white wigs on their heads. I'd only ever seen this attire on the television, and it seemed rather odd and outdated to me. That said, being physically present in a crown court, observing your barrister at work, gracefully interrogating the accused and making a mockery of the defence, whilst casually engaging the jury made me realise it was all theatre. Give this Rachael woman an Oscar!

"Mr. Smitherman, could you kindly advise the court what you were doing on 21st March 2022 please."

"Certainly. I was at home with Oliver Scott, my housemate."

"Is that so?"

"Yes, it is."

"Have you always been a dishonest person, Mr. Smitherman? You seem very comfortable telling this court lies."

"Objection! Counsel seeks to influence the jury with character defamation without evidence!"

"Sustained. The jury is to disregard that question by the prosecution. I'm warning both the defence and prosecution right now, this is not a playground for either party to play in."

"Noted your honour. I will rephrase the question," Rachael said, with an easy smile to the defence team.

"Is your car a 2022 BMW, with registration number, BT22 WEA?"

"That is correct."

"Are you able to explain why it was, that your car was located just 500 metres from the Hilton Hotel on the night of the attack in question?"

"Must be an error. I was at home."

"No, you were not at home, Mr. Smitherman. You may not be aware but it is standard practise especially on more modern, high end, luxury vehicles to have mapping GPS. In other words, if your BMW gets stolen, the police and insurance company can track its whereabouts. That's a wonderful technological advancement, isn't it? Except in your case, whereby your alibi is now non-existent."

Before the defence counsel could stand up again to object, Rachael walked over to their desk and handed the barrister a printout of what she had just claimed. Exhibit A. lovely clear photograph of Smitherman's BMW parked as she had stated within 500 metres of the attack, on the very same evening.

"Must have got my dates a little confused. I apologise to the court. I certainly wasn't trying to mislead anyone."

"That's most gracious of you. If the court now looks to the screen, I will show exhibit B. This is a still digital photograph of you and another man we will discuss later in this trial. Can you kindly confirm that this is you?"

"It is hard to say, the light is a bit tricky."

"The light is tricky you say?"

"A little, yes."

"Members of the jury, I think it is very plain indeed, there is no tricky lighting preventing us from determining that this is obviously the face of the defendant, Mr. Smitherman."

Silence from the defence.

"The court will be most interested to learn that this picture was not only taken again on the night of the attack but incredibly just 85 metres from the car park of the Hilton hotel."

"Objection! Circumstantial!" All this proves your honour, is my client got his dates muddled up. An error any of us could make!" He argued, flashing his overly white teeth towards the Jury.

"Overruled! Are we to learn from where the image was captured perhaps?" The judge said impatiently.

"From 25, Lansdowne place, your honour. A private residence with the most advanced door security cameras installed. Best on the market apparently. Certainly, the most expensive and we have the benefit observing just how crisp and clear the image taken is."

"The prosecution will now present exhibit C," Rachael said, smiling at to the jury.

"Exhibit C, now on the screen is the forensic lab report on DNA both from saliva and urine collected from the victim's clothing. You will notice with interest, members of the Jury, there is no doubt whatsoever that one of the two people which urinated and spat on the victim was Mr. Smitherman. The DNA is utterly conclusive. This is fact, which when added to exhibit A and B can only lead us to understand one thing. Mr. Smitherman is lying about being at home that night and was one of the attackers behind the Hilton hotel. Nothing in our case is circumstantial!"

Smitherman looked rattled. Rachael seized the opportunity to make him feel even more uncomfortable.

"What did you enjoy the most Mr. Smitherman? Punching and kicking a defenceless man unable to protect himself as he was already on the ground or spitting and urinating on him as he drifted in and out of consciousness?"

"I never did anything. This is a set up!"

I put my arm around Gareth, kissing his neck gently as I looked over to the defence barrister, who had closed his eyes for a moment. The reality of this case suddenly hitting home. You are defending a total piece of shit. You kiss your kids before they go to sleep and think upon this. Read them a bedtime story tonight, in a daze, speaking the words but without feeling. Your mind spinning with how you made your money this month.

It is well known to us all that defence barristers can be somewhat unpopular. We all feel at times that they must know their client is guilty. They know too much about a case, get a feeling for their client and yet they sleep peacefully in their beds at night because rightly so, everyone deserves a fair defence. A man or woman is innocent until proven guilty. I respect this and I accept this stance.

But my friends, a part of me still struggles with someone making a very comfortable living defending people like Smitherman. I have no idea how often they represent a guilty client knowingly. This guy was not representing the Sicilian mafia, but because it was my Gareth nearly murdered that night, he may as well have been.

"The prosecution has no further questions. Your witness." Rachael smirked at the defence barrister. So smart. Smitherman's response would make any normal person on the jury roll their eyes. There was no need to continue this questioning. You're fucked. The whole room knows it. It reminded me of a boxing match. When one fighter has just won the round convincingly and there is a second before they return to their respective corners. Is it arrogance? Is it confidence? What exactly does that look say?

I've always felt it expressed so many different things in a single glance. In this case, Rachael's facial expression said, "Enjoy your witness, bitch."

CHAPTER TWENTY

No. Please not this.

The decision to put Gareth on the stand was something I was never really very comfortable with. He couldn't give an accurate description of either attacker, as it was dark and the hotel car park lights were not working. Rachael had suggested the usefulness came from Gareth being able to clearly recall the words yelled at him. The bile. The hate filled language. She argued that was important because it reflected the words used online by both defendants. It demonstrated this was not just an attack on a gay man, but an attack made by men with very strong Old Testament views on homosexuality. It wasn't just a street gang being horrible to a gay man. It was targeted. Strong religious views that Gareth was a sinner, whose life was an abhorrent sin. They, by sharp contrast were soldiers of Christ doing his will. Rachael said to trust in her judgement and Kirsty had agreed with her suggesting it all fit together. The jury would hear directly from Gareth. Learn about the language used and compare it to those from Scott and Smitherman found online. It was another nail in the coffin.

"You never saw your attackers, then?"

"No. That's correct. I did not."

"You claim, you were attacked from behind? Knocked to the ground?"

"I'm not claiming anything. That's precisely what happened."

"Go on, Gareth" I thought to myself, sitting alone in the public gallery, looking down on the events unfolding beneath me.

"Yet you recall so clearly, so accurately the words shouted at you, despite slipping in and out of consciousness?"

"That is correct. I recall a lot of what was shouted at me, yes."

"Were you not very nearly placed into a medically induced coma, as there was significant swelling on your brain?

"Nearly placed you say? Yes, I was nearly put into a medically induced coma therefore I was not actually placed into one. The swelling reduced by itself, so my doctors agreed to not do this."

"What do you recall being said to you?"

"As they kicked and punched me, one of them called me a disgusting animal not worthy to breathe the same air as them. That all homosexuals are an abhorrent stain on the earth. That they were God's soldiers, put on this earth to show others such sin would not be tolerated."

"That's a lot of detail for a man with a brain injury to recall. Research suggests such memory recollections are often confused, that the mind makes things up."

"They said a lot of things, before I slipped into an unconscious state. But they did say them."

It went on like this for twenty minutes but felt like an hour or longer. I spent much of that time with my fists and jaw clenched. I thought the defence barrister was a piece of shit before Gareth took the stand. Now? It wasn't even up for debate, was it?

Rachael had done a great job, following on from the defence barrister, of allowing Gareth to say what he recalled. Rachael's mannerisms, her kindly ways, allowed him to give compelling, accurate responses to her questions. Eventually, Gareth left the stand and was seated beside our CPS team in between the two solicitors.

Both parties had brought in expert witnesses. As was often the case, the defence witness looked sharp in an expensive tailor-made suit, had a broad East Coast American accent, hair slicked back, looking stylish against a short, cropped beard. Nathaniel Melrose's impressive credentials read out loud to the court, of course, these included three books he had had published on patients' recovery to brain trauma covering everything from car accidents to motorcyclists thrown off their bikes, not wearing a helmet to violent assaults. Long and short of it was his views upon accurate memory recollection were at best patchy and sometimes complete fabrication. "The mind plays tricks on us all without extreme trauma at times," was how he summed up. In other words, we can readily get things wrong and relay information poorly or inaccurately without suffering how poor Gareth did.

Our expert witness was a public sector worker, not some fancy pants looking hot shot like the Eternity Saints had provided. They had money like the Vatican it seemed to me. She was heavy set, short and hadn't made any special effort with regards to her presentation. A trip to the hairdressers and perhaps a new jacket might have created a more professional initial impression on the jury, especially seeing what she was following on from.

All that said, she was highly credible and in my humble opinion did a cracking job of disagreeing and indeed discrediting much of what Melrose had stated to be fact. At one point, the defence barrister had said, "So, how many books have you had published, Mrs. Kingsley?"

"None."

"None, you say?" The defence counsel smiled broadly as he turned around, opening his arms to the jury.

"Yet our expert witness has had three books published on the results of various clinical tests and examinations. What do you say to that?"

"I would say, Lee Childs has written over twenty Jack Reacher novels and that Nathaniel Melrose's contribution to understanding the complexities and the effects of brain trauma on memory recollection adds up to about the same!"

The courthouse let out a combination of laughter and sniggering, me included.

"The court room will settle down!!" The judge ordered firmly.

Valerie Kingsley had spent the past thirty years working first as a brain surgeon in a top private London hospital before shifting her focus onto post trauma therapy and recovery in the NHS. She finished her time on the stand with a flourish. "I have observed, witnessed first-hand the extraordinary amount of accurate data, information untainted, from military staff suffering PTSD to pregnant women having fallen down the stairs and it is my experience the vast majority recollect a lot of information, especially a few weeks or months after the event. The fact, the defendant recalls so much and has never faltered or deviated in any way to some very specific, unusual language used leads me to believe he is a highly credible witness to his own attack."

In your face bitches!! I had desperately wanted to yell out into the silence of the courthouse.

I wanted to run to her and throw my arms around her. Her, Kirsty, and Rachael. A team of kick arse, no nonsense superwomen. I held back my tears and collected my belongings before meeting Gareth and the team downstairs. Thanking everyone for their delivery and performances, we left via the rear of the courthouse, avoiding media representatives and the general public. I just wanted to take Gareth home for a much-needed home cooked meal and cuddles on the sofa with Ralph.

Day two brought Oliver Scott to the stand. I'm not going to bore you with what happened because in all honesty it was very much like the previous day, accept there was no close-up facial picture of Scott. I had slept in Gareth's bed along with Ralph and we had all passed out within minutes of our heads hitting the pillows. Tired from the new experience being in court? Certainly. It was more than that. Our team had kicked arse and taken names on day one. If a football match? It was half time, and we were 3-0 ahead, sucking oranges.

There was no reason for the trial to last more than two to three days when the prosecution had the defence on the ropes from the very first session. Alibi shot to pieces on both defendants. DNA linked both suspects to the actual body of the victim and photographic evidence of both Smitherman and the BMW in the vicinity of the attack, same time, same date. Scott's hatred online, language used matching what Gareth had described. It was just compelling, almost overwhelming evidence against the men.

The only thing missing was DNA from Gareth's body, like blood spatter to his attackers. Clothing and shoes had been taken by Jackson's team but had not produced anything. Surprise, surprise, the defendants must have thrown away whatever they were wearing. The prosecution had no idea really what they were wearing that night. The obvious thing to do, was to take boots and shoes as trace DNA may have been found but alas there was nothing.

None of this concerned any of us. It was the icing upon our beautiful cake, not the key ingredients. After Scott had left the stand, having been chargrilled so badly by Rachael, the courthouse may well have smelled of burnt steak, the judge called recess to allow for the jury to rest and think about making their decision. It could be today, just day two of the trial or the following day.

What happened next still makes me feel physically sick,

when I let my mind linger upon it. The defence barrister and his cronies appeared excitable. They had looked down and out, like a drunk slumped up against the wall of a bar, no longer capable of standing up unassisted. Now there was renewed energy about them. That confident sneer of the defence barrister, like that of a wolf cornering its prey, knowing it was trapped. Knowing there was no escape.

Chain of Custody proves the integrity of a piece or pieces of evidence. The Chain of Custody needs to document every single transmission from the moment evidence is collected from one person to another, to establish that nobody else could have accessed or possessed that evidence without authorization. The continuity of possession of evidence and its movement and location from the point of discovery and recovery (scene of the crime) to its transport to the laboratory for examination and until the time it is allowed and admitted to court, is called the chain of custody or chain of evidence. The defence barrister approached the bench before the judge could leave. He was leaning over the desk talking excitedly to the judge, who looked taken aback before requesting Rachael join them.

The defence were pointing to something I could not see, but I saw Rachael's face as she turned back to her team and by chance looked up to the public gallery where I saw clear as day that suddenly everything was wrong. Very wrong. We had gone from swimming confidently in a calm Mediterranean ocean of blue green to drowning in the dark, freezing waters of the Baltic Sea.

I could see Kirsty standing with her hands on hips, then the next moment running her hands through her hair looking exasperated. I was stuck in the public gallery. It wasn't like I could just pop down to the courthouse. Gareth looked panicked, stood up in between the two CPS solicitors.

The jury were no longer present. They had gone off to think about how to prevent day three occurring and get back to their lives. It's not like anyone wants more time on jury duty, is it? The judge had seemingly requested the jury return immediately.

Once the jury had taken their seats and silence had been called for by the officer of the court, the Judge spoke firmly to them.

"It has been brought to the court's attention, that there is a clear breach in the chain of custody for evidence collected by the prosecution. What this means, ladies and gentlemen of the Jury is as follows. You are to go away and deliberate amongst yourselves to the very best of your ability about the innocence or guilt of the two defendants, but you are to do so without the DNA findings brought by the prosecution. In other words, members of the Jury, this case is to be decided upon with you understanding there never was DNA evidence as there is a break in the chain of custody making it inadmissible to form part of the prosecution's case against the defendants. Is this crystal clear to each of you?"

The jury muttered back somewhat astonished that they did understand what had been said and with that they went away for a second attempt at deliberation.

I ran from the public gallery, barged my way into the ladies toilet, collapsed to my knees and threw up. My head was spinning, my breathing shallow. Is this what a panic attack feels like? I grabbed the toilet seat as another wave of nausea overcame me.

Soon, I returned to the public gallery where Gareth was staring up at me, looking utterly lost. I simply stared back at him. Blank. Expressionless. I felt like I had been run over and was suffering from a concussion. I heard the words people were saying but was under water in a swimming pool and when you surface, your ears are full of water and it's just noise, without meaning.

"How does the jury find the defendant, Oliver Scott, in charge of attempted murder? Is this decision unanimous?" The Judge asked the foreperson. The person first accepted to form part of the jury.

"Not guilty."

"How does the jury find the second defendant on the charge of attempted murder and again is this unanimous?"

"It is unanimous, yes, your honour. We find defendant, Richard Smitherman not guilty."

The courthouse was suddenly full of loud and angry voices. Many like I, had sat there listening to everything these past two days and knew without doubt these men were guilty. Guilty as charged and were going free because of some technicality. Going to be free men because someone in the police forensics team has been sloppy with the chain of evidence.

Felt like I was overheating, beyond angry. I was livid. Pushing past members of the public, I ran down the stairs, as fast I was able to, barging past security to reach Gareth.

"Let's get the hell out of here!"

Kirsty and Rachael stood motionless, looking at me.

Turning my attention to Kirsty I yelled, "I never want to see or hear from you, ever again!"

Taking Gareth by the hand I led him out of the courthouse and not thinking straight, right out the main doors, directly into the arms of the media. Taylor Swift, "You Need to Calm Down" was playing loudly to the side of the courthouse. A huge swelling of Gareth's supporters perhaps over a hundred people, more than double what it was from day one, all expecting a positive outcome, were fast learning the news, that our Police and CPS had fucked it all up and guilty men were walking free.

We ignored the media, making our way towards our supporters, not knowing what else to do. You couldn't see the road for the mass of people. There was no chance of getting a taxi away from this living hell. The supporters had chosen to play "You Need to Calm Down" as a joyous, happy, gay positive anthem, just saying "Hey you guys! Hey chill out! We're not the bad guys, this is how your God made us. Stop hating on us, ok!"

With each passing second, that song seemed more and more inappropriate. No one was calming down. The anger in the air was escalating into hate on both sides. Just as our support had swelled, had at least doubled overnight, so it was true for Smitherman and Scott with a large number of members from the Eternity Saints church now in attendance, to welcome their innocent hero's home.

People were starting to jostle about, pushing forwards against the police line separating the two groups of protesters or supporters. I really didn't know what term to use for any of us at that moment. I looked up and over to the right, where this tall, heavily built man, wearing a T-Shirt saying, "Jesus Saves" had lit up a large rainbow flag and was laughing as our flag burnt high in the air.

I sprinted away from the crowd, tucked up inside the far line before reappearing just in time as the tall man leant forwards, planning another wide sweep with his burning flag. I launched myself at him. My right arm pulled back, just like an archer from the hundred years war and let my fist fly. It connected perfectly, breaking his nose but it was the second punch in the exact same spot, which opened him up like a smashed glass bottle of passata down a supermarket aisle.

I felt two police officers dragging me off him, one saying, "Remain still! Arms behind your back. You're under arrest." As his colleague cuffed me.

CHAPTER TWENTY-ONE
Lock Up

"Name and address please," requested the desk sergeant on duty.

"Angelique Santoro. Flat B, 32 Crescent Drive, Seven Dials, Brighton."

"Seems like World War three has kicked off out there, since your little stunt."

"My little stunt has very little to do with what's now happening out there. Its police incompetence being responded to Sergeant. Do yourself a favour and shut up."

"Speak to me again in that tone, Miss Santoro and they'll be adding threatening language to a police officer on top of the list of charges you're already facing."

"List of charges? I hit one man who was burning the Rainbow

flag. You are aware of the city you live in, Sergeant? You should be arresting him!"

"He has been arrested. The charges he may yet face is not for you to be concerned with."

"So, what charges might I be looking at?"

"GBH. Inciting a riot. Unlawful disturbance of the peace."

"What am I, Donald Trump? Are we on Capital Hill with a bunch of red necks shooting off guns?"

The desk sergeant ignored me and pointed to a room a few metres to my right. The arresting officers gently led me by my shoulders to the room painted a bright white yet felt claustrophobic as no windows, no natural light at all, just the dull whir of an old air conditioning system, up overhead. Once inside, my handcuffs were removed and I realised it was I to undergo fingerprint and DNA collection.

"Let the officer do his job, Ms. Santoro." The arresting officer behind me said, as his colleague took my right hand and rolled my fingers back and forth across the black ink pad on the desk in front of us. Having successfully gained a neat set of prints, it was time for the cheek swab then the removal of that arsehole's blood from my right fist, which was now crusty, having dried. I complied patiently and passively. I had no problem with these officers. They had seemingly done their jobs correctly.

In my mind, the same question kept firing around. "Who messed this up? Which idiot in their forensic lab was incapable of keeping accurate, tight control of the chain of evidence?"

I was still thinking about this and little else as I was led away to the holding cells, a short walk from the DNA processing room. The heavy steel door shut loudly, echoing down the sterile hallway as I looked about me. Metal toilet and a tiny sink away to my right and a mat not much thicker than a yoga mat on top of a concrete slab for my bed. I sat down and massaged my now swollen right hand.

I rather suspect that I will fail miserably in trying to explain to you how I felt alone in that cell, but I'll do my best. I knew a GBH charge was coming. ABH or Actual Bodily Harm would have been one punch, breaking his nose. GBH or Grievous Bodily Harm is the next level up. In my case, a very deliberate punch to the exact same place, making far worse the injury I had just given him. He would require reconstructive surgery, private, no doubt and at my expense plus his legal bills. This I found agreeable. Re-living those two punches in slow motion in my mind, smiling easily as I did so. I did it again and again. There was no remorse, nor would there ever be. You got off lightly you fuck. The look of fear and dread in his eyes, is mine alone to savour until my dying day.

"Did I just incite a riot?" What a strange question to ask of oneself, as I sat alone in a holding cell.

What exactly does that mean? Is there a scale to which I will be assessed upon? If no police officers are hurt, then I'll be in less trouble? If it's an equal number of protestors and supporters ending up in hospital, is that a good thing for me? Will it be worse if it's more pro-gay supporters or anti-gay protesters injured?

My mind was spinning now. More accurately the room had

started spinning, so I lay down and slowed my breathing, waiting patiently for the wave of nausea to pass.

"Everything ok?"

"Yeah. I'm ok."

"Just so you know, Ms. Santoro, we do a check on the hour, every hour so that and the lights never going out in these cells, you won't be getting much sleep."

"Sure. Any chance of a blanket? I'm cold."

"I'll get you one." The officer may have been in his mid to late fifties, it was hard to tell I was going more by his voice than anything as the post slot type device which he had opened did not allow me much of a view to him.

The cell door swung open a few minutes later. I automatically stood up.

"Sit down, please, Ms. Santoro. Far side of the bed please."

That same officer had returned to me. I was right on the money, late fifties was a good guess. He was overweight, his uniform looked very tight on his oversized frame, but he had kindly blue eyes. Having handed me the blanket, he stuck his head out of the cell, looked both ways then when certain no one was within earshot said, "Look. I get it. We've just let two guilty men walk free to a street party celebration from what I've heard. I'm sorry we've failed you. I really am."

I immediately welled up, my eyes watering. I bit my bottom lip, holding back my tears. He smiled gently at me and said, "Anything you need, Ms. Santoro, cup of tea or a can of coke or something, you just press the buzzer, I'm here all night."

I nodded my head towards him, still unable to speak without breaking down into tears. Such a strange sensation is it not? I know you've all been where I was at that moment. A neighbour finds out you're just back from putting your dog to sleep or you've lost a friend or family member and they check in on you that very day. You were doing ok weren't you? That look. That voice of compassion. Such pure, untainted empathy for your plight and it's like the dam just bursts or certainly wants to. Is it the sincerity within that person? Is it because you weren't expecting it? The words, Are you ok? Oh, come here you, as they embrace you.

The people I hated most whilst I sat in that cell were the police and CPS for letting us down and those guilty men, their supporters. Yet, it was here, sitting in this cold holding cell under the police station, that an officer of the law had brought me real comfort. I shook my head. Sometimes, I think I could live a thousand years and never cease to be amazed by the kindness of strangers.

Wrapping myself in the thick blanket, letting exhaustion take me, I curled up in a ball and hummed the song, "Once" by Pearl Jam, until I fell asleep.

The guilty sleep, the sleep of the dead. Well, I slept more peacefully than I had in an age. Lights on. The noise of being checked on didn't stir me. The raised voices of other people arrested, coming to join me in the cells, didn't stir me.

I had been sitting upright, huddled in the blanket, shivering for perhaps ten minutes when the door opened and that familiar officer approached me, cup of tea in one hand, tabloid newspaper, "The Sun" in the other.

"Left the teabag in the mug for you, Miss. Santoro and there's sugar here." he said, handing me two tiny sachets of white sugar.

"Today's paper?"

"Oh, yeah. That's for you too. Best you know where you're at. Your family have called the station. You've got an hour before they'll be here with your father's solicitor, ok."

"Thank you."

"Fancy a bacon sandwich? Getting myself one."

"You're a star. I'd love one, thank you."

He smiled and was gone.

Nearly spilt hot tea all over myself when I turned the paper over. Front page of a national newspaper was a picture of yours truly, hitting that homophobic arsehole. The burning rainbow flag clearly visible, as was his bloodied face. I looked like Mel Gibson roaring in Braveheart. Snarling, menacing. Fully committed to the violence I was unleashing upon that man. It was a hell of a photograph.

I was brought to a familiar looking interview room. One just across the hallway to where Gareth and I were at, for that last meeting to update our case.

"Angelique. Oh my God!" Aveline cried, as she rushed to her feet and threw her arms around me.

I said nothing but returned the love in my hug back to her. She let me go and I waited for my dad, for Giovani to stand up and greet me. Whilst his embrace was less dramatic than that of my sister, it was no less sincere. He kissed me on both cheeks whilst cupping my face.

"Are you alright, Angelique?"

"I'm fine, Dad. Sorry for this mess."

"Are you?"

"What?"

"Are you sorry for your actions?"

"No."

"Well, don't apologise to me, or anyone else for that matter."

"I wasn't planning to."

"Won't go down well with the courts, the police or the judge, showing no remorse."

"Fuck 'em then."

My dad laughed and hugged me with far greater vigor than a minute ago. You don't end up owning a successful international import-export business by tip toeing around people and not being true to yourself. I can't be sure, but I swear there was a twinkle in his eye. He wasn't the least ashamed of me, quite the opposite. His daughter had put a nasty, homophobic, hateful piece of shit in his place. Was I any different to that man by demonstrating such hatred? Was I the same in the eyes of the law, worse even? Was his burning of the gay flag symbolic of the purest hatred for people who have no choice in their sexual preferences? Perhaps, yes. But I rather suspected, I was looking at more severe punishment.

I shook hands with Malcolm Harding, my dad's solicitor. Whilst not a criminal lawyer, he was a tough, no-nonsense expert in international commercial law and had the smarts to know what to say and advise me. If someone more suitable on the criminal barrister side of things needed to be found in the future, my dad trusted Malcom to source that person.

The door swung open and in walked Detective Shaw and Detective Sergeant Kirsty Jackson.

"You've got to be fucking kidding me."

"Settle down, Ms. Santoro," Jackson said.

"I will do no such thing."

"Mr. Santoro and is it Aveline Santoro? Kindly wait in the main reception area, please."

My family did as Detective Shaw requested, leaving the room both patting my shoulder before they did so.

"Let's talk about yesterday afternoon."

"Whatever you say, Detective Sergeant Jackson."

"Did you in a premediated manner, run around the side of the crowd and then very deliberately strike not once but twice one of Smitherman and Scott's supporters?"

"No comment."

"Really? No comment?"

I glanced over to Malcolm who gave me the slightest nod of

his head.

"No comment."

"Was it the burning of the rainbow flag and all it symbolises, which made you so angry or the case against these accused men falling apart, so they walked free or both?"

"No comment."

I can't tell you how much I was hurting inside. This is the woman I had true, real, loving feelings for. The first woman since Alessia at fifteen-years-old which had meant anything to me. Not only had her and her team crushed my spirits, let Gareth and I down, as well as all gay, trans, or bi-sexual people but here she was on the attack. She was looking at me, as I was looking at her.

Staring at one another, both our eyes expressing the exact same emotion.

"How could you do this to me?"

CHAPTER TWENTY-TWO

Public Relations

"I want to be your Agent. Your Public Relations, sole point of contact."

"Not sure that's such a great idea Aveline."

"Why? Because I'm a coke head in recovery?"

"Because I love you dearly and the last thing, I would wish for you is a relapse, yeah. Is that wrong of me?"

Aveline reached over the kitchen table and grabbed my hand, just as "Crazy" by Gnarls Barkley came on the radio.

"Look, my previous company burnt me out. They knowingly overworked me, and I hung out with people doing cocaine far too much. That's not my life now. It's not who I am anymore."

"Thought you wanted to study, change your career path, do something entirely new?"

"I know, I said all that and part of me was trying to believe it, to aid my recovery but honestly, Angelique? I was meant to be an agent, to work in PR. I'm a natural."

"Ok, well, if you are sure. Absolutely certain it's not going to harm you. Fine. Thank you."

Aveline squeaked as she stood up to perform a little celebratory dance.

"Wait there, just sit tight," she exclaimed, rushing to a kitchen drawer by the cooker.

"Here you are. Already to go, then."

Aveline handed me a letter from Companies House. Santoro PR was officially registered.

"Never lacked confidence have you lil' sis?"

"It's not a Santoro trait really, is it?"

"When did you set the limited company up?"

"The night you got arrested and enjoyed the hospitality of the police in the holding cells."

I laughed.

"You need me, Angelique and I want to do this for you, for us. I owe you."

"You don't owe me anything."

"Well, it's cute that you feel that way, but I do. Mummy and dad knowing nothing of my addiction, my time away in the blue recovery centre? You lying to them about me being in the States, all that time, protecting me. I'd feel wretched if I couldn't now do good things for you. It's exactly what I'm trained for and spent a decade doing so successfully."

"Suppose you're going to want paying too, then?" I said, grinning.

"A girl must eat, Angelique! I've been living off Martin far too much. Not something I've enjoyed at all."

"Well, you didn't have much choice."

"True, but that was then, this is now."

"What the dealio, then?"

"£500 per day. My old company used to hire me out at £1200 a day. It's mates' rates for you."

"Bargain. And what do I get for your services?"

"Every phone call, email sent to you, I handle. Every company and media response is handled by me alone. I'll shield you from as much shit as I possibly can, whilst getting the world to see you precisely as I wish them to."

"And?"

"I'll secure unique business opportunities for you, seeing as you are now without income."

I'd been released from police custody just four days previously. It had taken less than twenty-four hours after my arrest for a video of the assault to go viral. Some clever tech wizards, had taken live mobile video footage and slowed it down at the precise moment I was punching, "burning flag man." Well, that's what he was being called by some people. A lot worse, by many others!

The video was in black and white, except for the burning rainbow flag and the blood from his face which was in vibrant colour. "Two Tribes" by Frankie Goes to Hollywood, accompanied the work of art. It was genius. The music. The image. The sharp contrast from black and white to colour. It was totally captivating. My mad dog facial expressions, sadly even more so.

If you didn't know who Angelique Santoro was by this point, you must have been living on the moon or didn't read the newspapers, watch TV, or have access to the internet. It was awful. The paparazzi followed me everywhere I went and had seemingly camped permanently outside our flat.

"I'm so sorry, boy."

"Don't be. I've never been prouder of you."

"I abandoned you! I left you amongst all that chaos to go after that arsehole!"

"I was with our supporters. Felt scared for a few seconds, then all the training you had given me kicked in. I'm an attack dog, right! Not just a bloody victim! Knew I could control my PTSD, if I hung back, away from the trouble and that's what I did. Ready to protect myself, to fight, but deep down, just knew I was far enough away from it all."

"You sure? We're ok? Truly?"

Gareth smiled, took a few steps to where I was standing, looking at my feet and hugged me. We stood silently. It was his turn to gently rock me to and fro.

Akira Suzuki had wasted no time calling me. It took just

two days for Sony to publicly distance themselves from yours truly. She had the decency to tell me directly herself a few hours beforehand.

"It's business, Angelique. We are a global corporate. We cannot be associated alongside an individual arrested for extreme violence, possibly inciting a riot!"

"How have sales been to date?"

"You know they've been amazing. That's not the point, is it? It's been an incredible month since the adverts went live. That's why we're so upset and disappointed in you. This could have been a long-term relationship. You've blown it. You've brought shame and embarrassment to us here in Sony, in Japan." That's all she said, before she hung up on me.

Aveline's first job as my paid PR executive, was to go through the contract with a fine-tooth comb, even more thoroughly than Caitlin had. Thank the Gods, there was no clause for me to pay back my earnings. Unsurprisingly, there was nothing stating, "If you act like a total mentalist, your contract is null and void and you must repay us everything we paid to you."

There was a clause stating, "Sony Corporation reserves the right to terminate this contract with Angelique Santoro at any time, for any reason, if we so wish." Well, it wasn't those exact words but something like that. So, I knew when I signed up, if I farted too loudly on TV, that would be it. Game over. To be honest with you my friends, I was feeling grateful and relieved I could keep the money. Pretty darn sure, moving forwards their legal experts will have something in the contract about repaying fees, if said individual were to bring their company into disrepute. I had no criminal record. I was a successful ex athlete, media personality, business owner and well-loved mentor to under privileged kids. Why would anyone think to put such a clause in their contract? Never assume anything in business or in life. Just because the forecast says it'll be glorious sunshine, doesn't mean it won't rain all day.

The following day, Aveline told me that BT Sport and Eurosport were not going to work with me moving forwards. The World Championships, to be held in Barcelona were just a few months away and I was not welcome in the commentary box. I wasn't surprised. It's all corporate bollox. Sponsors include Coca-Cola and BMW. All distancing themselves from what is seen officially as unacceptable behaviour, right?

In the five days following my release from police custody, my actions that day had split public opinion down the middle. My supporters came from all walks of life and all ages around the world. "Go Angelique!" and "He got what he deserved. You're awesome!"

Not everyone in the gay community were celebrating my actions but I'd suggest four out of five didn't appear too upset! How many gay men or women or trans people had been spat upon, abused mentally, emotionally, and physically over the last hundred years alone? A little payback, a little, "How do you like it?!" was how so many felt.

Those against my actions, seemingly the older middle classes, were expressing, "Two wrongs do not make a right!" or that "An eye for an eye, we all go blind!" That was a reasonable stance perhaps.

Others were saying, "Angelique Santoro is a disgrace! She knows the influence she has over children, over young minds and has set a dreadful example of how not to conduct yourself, regardless of the provocation."

"So, we've lost Sony and the sports channels. That's basically all your income."

"Fabulous."

"When did you last place anyone via your recruitment business, SRS?"

"Dunno. About four months ago."

"OK, so that's dead too. For now, at least. Angelique, you have no income whatsoever."

"Nor did you until two days ago. How about you tell me something I don't know?"

"Don't be snarky. I've been your agent for less than forty-eight hours and I'm already making it rain!"

I looked blankly at my sister, whilst lounging back on her sofa, hugging a cushion to my chest.

"Oh, I bet they are top drawer opportunities."

"Angelique! Are you going to be like this always from now on?"

"Sorry sis. I'm a little upset. Go ahead. I do appreciate you being on team Angelique."

"It's fine and it's Team Santoro by the way. Your wins are my wins and those hating on you, are my enemies."

I smiled warmly at Aveline. So many years not being there for one another, seemingly divided with her love for my mother and well, my dad preferring my company over hers. Nothing ever in a nasty, deliberate manner you understand, it's just family dynamics and how people are. The way we get along now has without doubt been a true highlight of the past couple few years. It took take my parents divorcing so publicly and Aveline becoming a drug addict to bring us together as one.

"What you got?"

"TV Appearances. Radio Chat shows. Mornings, afternoon, evening slots. Take your pick."

"Huh."

"Don't sound too excited."

"I'm not."

"We must put you out there. Let the world see the real Angelique Santoro. Win you more fans."

"And when they ask for my remorse?"

"You play the fucking game, Angelique!"

"Well, and therein lies the problem. You were there in the police station. You heard what I said to dad."

"What about not being sorry? Blah blah."

"Yes, precisely this."

"Well, this is PR. Public Relations. It's about turning a shit show into increased popularity and well money, shit tonnes of money."

"I don't care about the money. Sony massively overpaid me. I'm not homeless, begging on the streets."

"Oh, right, so if you had absolutely no money, were destitute, then you'd play nicely with me but since you are not, you have your what do we call this exactly? Your moral code?"

"Piss off! Moral code? It's called integrity for fucks sake, Aveline! People know me, respect me for being the real deal. I don't do false, and I won't say untruths on the television or radio because you tell me to."

Aveline scowled at me and crossed her arms defensively.

"You're going to be the very worst client I've ever had. I can just sense it!"

I flicked Aveline the bird, "Well, you've always enjoyed a challenge. Embrace this."

CHAPTER TWENTY-THREE

And it hurts with every heartbeat.

"Can you please move out of our way?!"

"Angelique, c'mon luv. Just give us a statement. The public needs to hear from you!"

"Just leave her alone. Go on, piss off, the lot of you!"

"How do you feel about the case falling apart as it did, Gareth? If Angelique doesn't want to talk, you can give us a statement!"

"We cannot afford for you to lose your temper again, Angelique. Even a mild, push away to some twat with their camera in your face and we're looking at a new assault charge. That's what they want. More news, more Santoro scandal. You'll be bloody bankrupt before you know it! Hands dug deep, head down. Always. Do not engage. Everything goes through me and

I mean everything. Do I make myself quite clear?"

I did as Aveline had instructed me. I listened to her. In other words, I kept my hands always dug deep into my pockets. I moved, head down, baseball cap pulled tight, sunglasses on, regardless of the weather. Always silently, through the gathering of journalists and Paparazzi to Nelly.

"I said piss off! You're scaring the dog now; can't you see that!?" Gareth practically spat the words at these fools.

We made good on our escape and drove straight to Aveline's villa. We found her waiting for us at the top of her drive talking calmly to a couple of better dressed, more professional looking media types than we had just experienced. They all moved out of our way, after I had given Nelly a few aggressive revs.

"I fucking hate this, boy. Our lives have turned into some crazy, media circus. When will they get bored and just leave us alone?"

"I don't know pet. It's only been a week. The internet has just blown up over this. It's relevant to the world in general, that's the issue, isn't it? World cup football in the Middle East. You know, still illegal to be openly gay there. That wasn't too long ago. Got these religious morons, running about the place trying to make abortions illegal. Guns in the one hand, bible in the other. It's like that bloody television series, "The Handmaiden – under his eye."

"I know. We're part of something far larger. Everyone has an opinion on what I did. Those with nothing to lose monetarily speaking are Team Santoro unless religious fruit bats. The corporate world, anyone which could lose money is standing neutral saying, doing nothing or openly against me, backing the law.

"Let's go play with Ralph in the back garden, yeah? Wait on Aveline. She seems engrossed in something important," Gareth suggested, checking the rear-view mirror.

We played Ralph in the middle for a good twenty minutes before Aveline found us.

"C'mon inside. I'll make us a cuppa."

We sat in the lounge, looking at the steam coming from our mugs of tea. You know that point when you want to take a sip, but you know if you do, all you'll achieve is burning your upper lip.

"Where we at, Sis?"

"Everywhere and nowhere."

"Meaning what precisely?"

"Meaning, I can't do my job very effectively, if neither of you will talk to the media."

"Look Aveline, I'm only recently back to work in a job that is a great opportunity for me, and they've been so decent ever since the attack. I can't just go blabbing my mouth. The Hilton group is like Sony, right? It's a global corporate."

"Can I speak with your head of HR? Your head of marketing strategy?"

"To what end?"

"To getting something positive out there. I can make you look good, can make the Hilton group look good."

Gareth looked at me. I said nothing, just shrugged my shoulders.

"We'll put a spin on this, and you both win, alright? We distance ourselves from Angelique's crap, make you some money, which you bloody well deserve and The Hilton will look like the greatest employer known to man."

"You want me to stand against Angelique?"

"It's not like that. You didn't hit anyone, but you are the victim of not only an attempted murder but the system failing you. I want to represent you Gareth, not as a victim but as a proud survivor, getting on with their life, showing gratitude to your employer and you know, asking for calm. That violence is not the answer."

"So, stand against Angelique, then."

"For fuck's sake! What is it with you two?"

"I can't very well go and say calm down, violence, retaliation is not the answer, when Angelique is refusing to apologize over hitting that guy. It's like, how can I do that and be loyal to my best friend. No. I'm not doing it."

I leant forwards and ruffled Gareth's hair.

"Eh, you're alright pet. You and me against the bloody world. It's just like school."

"Yes, it is and you're both still as idiotic as you were back then. Only difference is now you're twenty years older, yet clearly no wiser!"

Gareth poked me and we fell about laughing on the sofa, hitting one another with cushions.

Two days later, I was driving into London listening to Rihanna's "Umbrella." Sean had of course contacted me that fateful day my face and actions became front page news. Just like everyone else, he was just checking up on me. There was no mention of Team GB. Nine days had passed. Nine days scared and worried on top of everything else I was feeling. Parking Nelly in a spot reserved for coaches and staff, I made my way into Team GB, Jujitsu centre of excellence, through security and waited anxiously in reception.

"Sensei. We're ready for you." Steve Smith, the main man himself said, poking his head through the double doors leading to the boardroom. No stepping up close to me. No warm shaking of my hand. I stood up and swiftly followed him along the corridor, feeling nothing but dread.

Steve opened the door to the boardroom and I silently walked in, taking my seat. The only seat available. I'd never been in the boardroom with more than two or three personnel. It was full. All nine seats taken. Glancing around the room, my heartrate elevated to the point whereby I could feel the blood pulsating in my neck.

"Good morning, Angelique," Deidre Amandas said.

"Good morning, Deidre."

"You know why we've called this emergency meeting?"

"Yes, of course."

Deidre Amandas was the Team GB chairwomen. Always immaculate. She was an ex-athlete, not Jujitsu but a pole vaulter, representing Great Britain in two Olympics, winning a bronze medal back in 1984, Los Angeles. She was twice divorced and owned a finance and accounting software business, in Oxford. She was a tall, imposing woman, even sat down. I had no idea what the circumstances were leading to these divorces, but it was likely she had tired of both men and paid them to go away. She was all business and had the warmth of a great white shark.

"We find ourselves in a position none of us have ever experienced before. I think that sums up just how unprecedented this all is."

"I understand."

"Do you though, Angelique? Do you fully comprehend the mess we find ourselves in today?"

"I can't leave my flat without being chased by the Paparazzi, Deidre. I must report to the police every week as part of my bail conditions, and I've lost all sources of income. So yes, I do fully understand."

I wasn't meaning to sound confrontational but for fuck's sake, I'm not a total idiot. I may have left school at sixteen, not twenty-two as someone like her did, having successfully completed a master's degree but I don't appreciate people talking down to me as if I struggle with basic, obvious topics.

"Self, self, self." Amandas stared back at me.

"I'm sorry, what?"

"Everything you have just said back to the board. It is how your own selfish actions have affected you. Your income, your life. Not a focus on what you have done to us here at Team GB!"

"That's not fair. I live and breathe Team GB as you all know! I have since entering the squad at sixteen years old. The youngest ever athlete to be asked in. That was twenty years ago. My love and commitment to this team, to this venture cannot possibly be in question."

"Of course not, Sensei," Steve Smith agreed, sensing perhaps the chairwoman was not the best person to be taking the lead of this discussion.

"Everything you have done; we have greatly appreciated. Kelly and Marie-Claire are just two examples of young women here who have such self-belief and it is a given you are a key factor in developing such skills."

"Thank you. I appreciate you, Steve," I said, whilst giving Amandas a look which suggested she ought to take a long walk, off a short pier.

"You mentioned you've lost all income, all your commentary accounts and Sony?"

"Yes, that is correct."

"So, you fully comprehend the corporate angle of this? You understand Team GB has worked tirelessly. I have worked tirelessly to secure the likes of BMW and Coca-Cola as key sponsors?"

"Of course, Steve."

"They have made their stance over you attacking that dreadful man quite clear."

"I'm certain that they have. What about all the fans and revenue I have brought in. Is it not true? Is it not the case that my relationship with Kelly alone has created a wave of new young fans. Over half a million more people watched us against America because of me, because of Kelly and I, so we are led to believe?"

Amandas scoffed.

"You got something to say, then out with it! I've done more to make Team GB popular, visible to the public in the last twenty years than you could do if you were here for a century!"

The boardroom broke into embarrassed coughs and general murmurings.

Then comes the silence. Always the silence. No matter what I do or say in my life, there so often follows a period of silence. Is that the effect of Angelique Santoro on the world? People left stunned, upset, happy, unhappy. Never matters. There's always silence.

Steve Smith coughed lightly once more and remarked "This has to come to a vote, Sensei."

I said nothing, just took a few seconds to look each board member in their eyes.

"Those for not dismissing Angelique Santoro, please raise your hands."

Two board members including Sean, confidently put their

hands up.

Six for. Two against. Motion carried. I was out.

Steve was still talking, saying some crap about, "We will always appreciate all you have done…"

I stood up silently and left the boardroom as swiftly as my shaking legs would allow me. I couldn't stand to be in there a moment longer.

Brushing past Marie-Claire and Kelly on my way to the car park. I couldn't stop. Not now, not here and most certainly not with my girls.

CHAPTER TWENTY-FOUR

Never ever have I felt so low.

Three days, three nights lying in my bed. Alone. "Never Ever" by All Saints was playing on loop when Gareth stuck his head around the door.

"Hey, girl. Getting a bit stale in here pet. C'mon. Let's open that window, perhaps half a curtain even, get some sunshine on that pretty face."

Gareth handed me a coffee and suggested we could take a walk with Ralph. Head to the beach, clear my head a bit.

"OK, boy. If you want to."

"It's been agony seeing you like this."

I stared blankly back at him.

"You remember years ago, when we'd have some vino and watch Vampire Diaries or The Originals on the telly, eh?"

"Sure."

"It's like looking at Eleanor Salvatore after they had turned her. Later, when she switched off her humanity. When they kept her locked up in that dungeon, yeah? You know love. When she was desperate for a feed. That's what you look like."

"Nice. Kick a girl when she's already crawling in the dirt."

"This isn't you. It's like you were when Alessia dumped you back at school but like, ten times worse. I don't know what to do with you other than kick your arse."

"Appreciate you."

"All this time stuck in here, on your Jack Jones, doing God knows what to your mental health is enough girl. You've tortured yourself enough!"

"Not even begun actually."

"Stop it. Just stop it."

"Why?"

"Because it's not good for you, is why."

"I don't care."

"Fine. Well, I do. Aveline does. Sean does. Caitlin and your dad do for starters. How about Kelly? How about your Joshua?"

"I don't doubt they care."

"I get it. Switching your phone off. Just wanting to crawl into a fucking ball and die. You think I don't get how you feel?"

"Wasn't aware this was a competition or that I was seeking to be understood, boy."

"You're lucky."

I took a long, deliberately slow sip of my coffee before responding.

"Yeah. I feel it. You know. Lucky that is. Just can't contain myself with all the excitement and joy, that's filling my life."

"And there she is. My feisty little wildcat." Gareth smiled as he poked me in the ribs.

"Just fuck off, boy."

"You're lucky because Moi? Yours truly? The legend of the decks and king of the north, is your best mate."

I looked back at Gareth, expressionless.

"It's ok. No need to jump about. To feel lucky or anything. I didn't much of the time you visited me in the hospital. Couldn't wait for you to leave half the time, truth be told."

"You're such a dick."

"Point being. I'm here, I'm queer and I'm not going anywhere!"

A small smile must have escaped my lips.

"I'll take that as a win right there and cut my losses today. Finish your coffee, shower. You smell like a sewer rat."

Did as I was told. Gareth was playing Lady Gaga, "Just Dance" loudly from the living room as I got ready.

There were less Paparazzi than when it all kicked off, but still plenty of vultures around as we left with Ralph for the beach. Up until that point, I'd been so good. I took on board everything

Aveline had said to me, to her advice. To this day, I cannot tell you why I forgot everything. Why I acted how I did.

"C'mon then, boys. You've got ten seconds to get your best picture for those papers!"

I took my sunglasses off, stuck my tongue out, cocky as you like and did a perfect Winston Churchill V for victory sign with my right hand. Held this pose for a few seconds before putting my glasses back on, dipped my head and was gone from sight. Gareth was pulling on my arm, as he would Ralph's leash, when he was hell bent on chasing a cat. The Paparazzi were beside themselves, all yelling and cheering my name, like excitable boys seeing breasts for the first time.

"Oh, my God! What the fuck was that!?"

I said nothing to Gareth, just shrugged my shoulders as I interacted with Ralph, aware I'd pretty much ignored our dog these past few days.

"Aveline is going to kill you."

"I'm already dead."

Sorry my friends, I'd forgotten to tell you there had been a final nail in my coffin of hope and dignity whilst driving home after my assassination at Team GB. Rob Johnson, Brixton Council's head of youth development and leisure, called my mobile.

"Angelique?"

"Speaking."

"It's Rob Johnson from the council."

"Hello Rob. I wonder why you are suddenly calling me. Not spoken for months, have we?"

"Yeah, well, it's a shitty phone call I don't want to make," Rob said, sighing deeply. He was more cockney London than Kirsty Jackson and that's saying something.

"Just say it, Rob."

"You're getting the bullet. The Brixton Youth Jujitsu Programme is being canned."

"You total wankers."

"Don't shoot the messenger, Angelique. You know me. I'd give you a bloody medal for what you did and I drink in a boozer where I doubt a gay bloke has ever sat and enjoyed a pint! Everyone in the pub, most 'ere in the council ain't got a problem with what you did, but rules is rules."

"What rules?"

"You can't teach the kids in Brixton with a criminal record."

"I've not got a criminal record."

"C'mon luv. You're making this harder on me than it needs to be. You're getting one, ain't ya? It's black and white, your case and from what I've heard, you'll be lucky to avoid a custodial sentence."

"Wow, a messenger, a legal eagle, and a soothsayer. You are a man of hidden talents, Rob. Very well-hidden talents."

"Look. It's gutting, I know. I'm sorry, Angelique. We're writing to the parents this week to let them know, Alright?"

"Can you please put some kind of bloody empathy and the like in the wording perhaps?"

"I'll write it myself and without supporting your actions, I'll be gentle on you."

"Alright. Well then. Thanks for the call, I guess."

"Oh, one last thing before I let you go."

"What?"

"They are going to turn your weekly Jujitsu sessions into street dance. So, that's something eh?"

"Yeah. That's something, Rob," I said dismissively, hanging up.

Truth is, I like street dance. And, in fact, it's probably just as useful as self-defence in terms of keeping kids off the streets and engaging their minds in something which promotes fitness and well-being. Like my Jujitsu club, it would encourage communication, friendship, self-discipline, and teamwork. That said, I wasn't really feeling a whole lot of love for this new venture at that time.

I needed lunch with Mother and Aveline the following day like a hole in my head, but it was Mother Dearest's 62nd birthday and despite every cell in my body yelling, "Don't go, don't go!" I did of course attend. On time and looking well turned out too, I thought. Had it been her 60th birthday, when half of those in society were present, a big marquee set in the garden, all the neighbours in attendance, I rather suspect I may have been asked to stay away.

Tragedy of varying seriousness tends to let us know how many friends we actually have. Publicly embarrassing situations, such as your flamboyant, Italian husband leaving you for a plain Jane librarian, is one such example. Trouble with being a society woman is that these relationships are by and large superficial. Any support you do get is likely to be false and insincere. Nosey neighbours seeking out glorious gossip to spread about.

"Happy birthday, Mother," I said, handing her a gift.

"Thank you, Angelique. Do come in."

Neither of us attempted our typically clumsy, awkward hug. I knew what she must think of me. To even attempt a hug would be something people film, then put on You Tube under the title, "Epic Fail."

Aveline was already there with Martin. He rushed over to embrace me, whispering, "You're brave!" in my ear. He was referring to both Aveline and my mother, of course. One I had recently let down, the other I had been for my entire life, so that itself was less of an issue.

There was no-one else present. No friends or colleagues from work or one of the various good causes Mother very publicly supported. Just the four of us. Now, had I not just caused mother dearest massive public humiliation on top of the recent divorce, then perhaps the living room would have been filled with people. Not people, you'd likely enjoy a long afternoon with but people, nonetheless.

"Angelique. Kitchen now!!" Aveline yelled, grabbing me by

the wrist, leading me away from Martin and Mother.

"You switch your bloody phone off and then pull that stunt!?"

"My bad?"

"This isn't a fucking joke, Angelique."

"Last time I checked, I pay you, so perhaps you should temper your attitude towards me."

Aveline waved both her hands in my face.

"Do you even hear yourself right now? Have you lost your frickin' mind? Earth to Angelique? Hello? Real world calling. Please pick up!"

"Piss off, Sis."

Aveline stood with her hands on hips, red faced, blowing air upon her forehead.

"Ten years being a respected, leading PR consultant and I am totally at a loss with what to do with you. How is that even possible? I have literally represented some of the biggest douche bags on this planet."

"I do not doubt that."

"You won't talk to the media in a clever, controlled manner. An environment I could steer in a way which benefits you but you're entirely comfortable with yesterday's spontaneous photo shoot! You've looked like what would happen if you combined 80s Madonna with Winston Churchill. I've never been more taken aback."

"Well, are you not the queen of spinning? C'mon Rumpelstiltskin. Take this hay and spin it into the purest gold."

"Look, I've spoken with Gareth. I'm sorry about Team GB and your Brixton youth development project. I am Angelique. I am so very sorry, but you can't just go off and ignore all my advice. Please."

A tear rolled down Aveline's cheek. I closed my eyes, opened my arms as she slid into my embrace. Silence, as ever follows all and any drama involving me.

Our embrace was short lived as mother dearest, walked in, suggesting today was a birthday celebration and could we possibly try and remember that not everything was the "Angelique show!"

Lunch itself was excellent. Mother had ordered food from a Greek restaurant she liked. Just needed heating up.

"You've not touched your wine, Aveline."

"It gives me acid."

"You don't think that you might be?"

"No. I'm not pregnant mummy."

"Ah. Still taking your time on that, then."

"We are."

"Perhaps taking this career break might be the perfect time to start a family?"

Martin coughed lightly before speaking. "Aveline was under a lot of stress in that company and we're just letting her find herself, Catherine. I'm sure you understand."

I've always loved that expression.

"I'm sure you understand."

You could really be saying anything you liked from, "Why are you such a dim-witted arsehole?" to "How is it possible you think as you do. Is someone else presently using the single-family brain cell?"

"Well, I'm sure you know best, although it does seem a little odd to me that you feel Aveline's best road to recovery and well-being is to become Angelique's PR agent."

And there it was. "It's my party and I'll cry if I want to." Or in my mother's case, "It's my party and I'll poke Angelique because well, let's face it, the little bitch deserves it and a whole lot more doesn't she just!!"

"I'm finding supporting my sister very therapeutic Mummy and I'm enjoying the unique challenges it provides me."

"It's not an interview darling. You don't have to sound like you're reading off a film script or something."

I sighed deeply.

"Something you wish to add, Angelique?"

"The meal was quite lovely, and we've all managed to be civilised and enjoy that. Thank you for arranging it."

"You're all very welcome. Anything else?"

"You're not happy that Aveline is my agent?"

"Well, I think it's an odd decision bearing in mind she left her previous company due to exhaustion. I can't imagine having you as her sole client is likely helping her much."

"Why is that?"

"Well, you know dear…."

"No. I really don't, why don't you explain it to us all?"

"I'm not seeking confrontation today, Angelique. It is my birthday."

"Yes, it is. Another year goes by and nothing changes, does it?"

"Fine. Have it your way. It was bad enough having Giovani leave me so publicly for another woman and I barely recover from that before the Santoro name is again being dragged through the mud. There, you happy now?"

"Oh yeah. I'm peachy mother. Never better."

"Well, just like at school! You embarrassed me then with your antics and you're doing it again. Only now, it's fifty times worse because you are not a child anymore, Angelique."

"No. That's nothing to do with it, is it? It's because the entire world knows who Angelique Santoro is. I'm not sixteen. I'm thirty-six and again, standing up for Gareth. Standing up for gay people. People being bullied and attacked! But no. All you care about is image. Well, I'm glad. Finally, perhaps you can start caring about things that matter other than your diminishing social status."

Silence.

"Happy birthday, Mother dearest. I'm going to visit Dad."

CHAPTER TWENTY-FIVE

Another empty bottle.

Lost. Lonely, yet seldom without love or company. How does that work exactly? I've experienced sadness, a sense of loss before. I'd had my heart ripped out, haven't we all? This past month, or five weeks to be precise, since both Team GB and Brixton Council told me I wasn't welcome anymore, had been the worst period of my life.

And no, I'm not forgetting my sexual assault, Aveline's addiction requiring hospitalisation and my parent's divorce all of which happened a couple of years ago, in a single month. Looking back, that month now feels like an exotic beach holiday with waiter service as perfect cocktails are handed to you, without ever leaving your sunbed.

I had been drinking. A lot. I walked in a daze, still pissed from the empty bottle of Vodka consumed the night before, to the police station to sign on as part of my bail conditions. I was listening to The Police, "So Lonely." This was my sixth visit to the station, to do this tedious five-minute chore which usually took closer to forty-five minutes as the useless pricks made me wait around. You see, scum like me only there to sign a form saying, "No, I haven't left the country and I'm still here awaiting my time in court, for some crusty old Judge to tell me, I am the spawn of Satan, a disgrace and I'm going directly to prison," were no one's priority.

I sat there, quietly observing my surroundings, trying to stop the world from spinning. Ralph was restless. Bored and eager to go to the beach for his morning run around.

"Not meant to have dogs in here." The desk sergeant called out to me.

"And yet, here I am with my dog." I replied, throwing him a look which suggested how much more trouble could I possibly get in, by slapping your fat face?

"Leave her be, Sergeant," Kirsty Jackson said, appearing from somewhere presumably. My eyes weren't working all that well.

"Piss off."

Jackson ignored me and went behind the desk at reception, located the bail sign on form and came back to me.

"Sign it."

I took the pen from her and did something resembling my signature.

I didn't want to leave with her but before I knew what was happening, she had taken the leash from my hand and Ralph was happily following her out of the station, giving me little choice.

Jackson walked about a hundred metres from the building and stopped abruptly, handing Ralph back to me.

"Wow, thanks so much. I thought we were going to add dog theft to your list of crimes, you know, if extreme incompetence is a crime? Apparently not, as here you stand before me, free as a bird and seemingly in full-time employment. Well done, you."

Jackson looked hurt. I had ignored all her phone calls and texts since the day our case fell apart. What else was I supposed to do? Write or call her back and say, "Hey Kirsty! It's fine. Look, don't worry about anything, don't lose sleep over it. These things happen! Can't be helped! We gave it the old college try; it wasn't meant to be!"

"You look like shit and smell even worse."

"No."

"No. No." I said, pointing my finger in her face. "You don't get to do that to me. You are not a person who has any rights to address me in that way," My legs felt unsteady beneath me, my vision still hazy.

It's hard to tell somebody off properly when your body and face are not behaving themselves. You know how you want to come across and be received but damn it, the level of intoxication I was still under, meant it was simply a bridge too far.

"I'm sorry."

"We're all sorry. Well, actually I'm not and you can see how brilliantly that's worked out for me."

"Let me buy you a coffee. We need to talk."

"Talk!?" I yelled, making a few passers-by stop and stare.

"Piss off. All of you. Jog the fuck on."

"Being drunk isn't a good look on you."

"Oh really? There I was thinking perhaps being like this would help me secure some new income. Perhaps, I can be the face of a new clothing line. You know the ones with T-shirts having fun slogans on the front? Like, FCUK IT. Clever play on words by French Connection. Maybe, I should get Aveline to write to them, let them know I'm available."

"C'mon. Come with me."

I was exhausted. I'd barely eaten in days and what I had was crappy takeaway food. My body was malnourished, especially when compared to how well it was usually taken care of. My skin, dry and spotty. My beautiful plump lips cracked and sore.

Kirsty put her arm around my shoulder, supporting me as we entered a local coffee shop which thankfully was quiet, nearly empty, so at least I didn't have to go through yet another morning of strangers staring and pointing at me, nudging their friend or partner, "Isn't that Angelique Santoro?!"

Kirsty ordered two Americanos, with an extra shot in each and we took a table, farthest away from the entrance.

"I want to explain, if you'll allow me, Angelique?"

I looked blankly back at Jackson.

"Fine. Go on then."

"I'm not making excuses. I take full, total responsibility for those shits walking free. It's my team. It's on me."

"What even happened?"

"All bullshit. Chain of evidence wasn't broken. There was however found to be a two-hour window, in all the weeks and months we had evidence where in theory the clothing might have been tampered with. Evidence of the suspects DNA could have been planted. Obviously, even if that was the case, it would have had to have been planted by someone within the force, so it's bollox. It's a technicality and the world knows they did it."

"Huh."

"I've suspended the forensic officer for messing up but ultimately, it's my fault. It's my case and I failed you. It starts and ends with me."

"Can I be honest with you now?"

"Of course."

"You look like shit too."

"I've not slept very well since the case collapsed. It would be bad enough if just an ordinary case but it was you and Gareth. I've just felt so awful. Then, like moments later, you exploded at that flag protestor. Fuck, I wish you hadn't done that."

"Why? Does it make you feel even more guilty? Had we won? I'd have not struck him because we'd have been in the pub drinking champagne. My life turning to shit, is directly on you Kirsty."

"That's not fair, Angelique."

"Isn't it?"

"Your team messing up, was the catalyst for everything that followed. Perhaps, I shouldn't have smacked that arsehole but why did I? Why was I so furious that I lost my frickin' mind? Because I believed in you. I believed in the law, the system. You all failed me. Failed Gareth and you failed all gay, bi-sexual, and trans people. So, ultimately? You failed yourself Kirsty."

A few days later, I had woken up sober for a change but felt like shit. Your body does not reward you for abusing it. If you think leaving it alone for two or three days is sufficient time for it to heal and make it well again, you're even more deluded than I was. I felt toxic. I was toxic. In my body, heart, mind and soul, I was becoming more and more rotten.

In the odd moment of crystal-clear thought, I was an eagle, soaring high over the world with the insight of a Shaman. When people start talking to you in this way, help them. The trouble is, they don't want help or rather they desperately do but they are too lost, too confused and muddled in their own minds, trapped in the depths of hatred and ill feeling, that they cannot accept it.

Gareth had been amazing, as had Caitlin and Aveline. Kelly and Marie-Claire called me often and even though I usually didn't pick up, I would listen to their loving voicemails later. There was a lot of love for me. My rock, my universe however, became Joshua. I arrived at his home that day to find him waiting in the driveway for me. He never used to do this but it had become our thing. I'm not sure when it became normal but more often than not, I'd find him there, cup of tea in hand, patiently waiting for the familiar sound of Nelly dropping down through the gears, the exhaust burbling away.

"Cup of builders?"

"Yes, please."

I followed Joshua into his home and settled myself on the sofa. A couple of minutes later he joined me with tea and some fruitcake his mother had made for him.

The record crackled as it found itself and the greatest hits of Simon & Garfunkel began.

"Not heard this album in an age."

"I know right? I was digging around the other day, just not sure what I felt like. You know when you're in a nothing kind of mood? Played it and just thought to myself, there's never a bad time for these two."

"Yeah. Would have been great to see them live in New York, just before they were famous."

Joshua nodded his head. I felt this way about so many artists from AC/DC to Elvis to Otis Reading to The Cult and U2.

"How's Melanie?"

"Wouldn't know."

"Really? You dumped her? Why?"

"Perhaps, she dumped me?"

"Did she?"

"No. We kinda agreed it wasn't working."

"How so?"

Joshua sighed and looked at me.

"Really, Angelique? Do I have to spell it out for you?"

"I've not been super good at anything lately, Joshua. Trying to read your mind and hers, is likely to take a lot of effort and ultimately be unsuccessful."

"Melanie said I was seldom present, even when just the two of us."

"Right, ok. Understood. Yeah, us girls quite like men to be present, especially if we made the effort to dress up, look nice and drive to their place."

"Of course. Rightly so."

"But you weren't?" I said, trying to sound casual. This fishing expedition of mine was hardly subtle but I really didn't have the energy or the skills at this point in my life to do any better.

"Bridge Over Troubled Water" had just began. Joshua singled for me to come lay in his arms. I did so happily. Snuggled right into his muscular, warm body. We lay perfectly still. Silently listening to the song. By the time the track had ended, I was weeping. Joshua's neck wet from my tears.

"I love you, Joshua" I whispered in his ear.

"What took you so long?"

I wiped my eyes and gazed into his.

"Aren't you meant to say it back to me or something?"

"Been saying it daily, since the first time I met you, Angelique.

Just without words."

"Tell me."

"Dry your eyes. I'm not going anywhere."

"Tell me."

"I love you, Angelique. Je t'aime."

CHAPTER TWENTY-SIX

A lot can change in a week.

There are two types of dogs. One you can kick constantly and eventually it will die. Then, there is the other type of dog, which will take a few kicks from your boots before turning around and savaging you. I'm the second type.

Eight days had passed since Joshua told me he loved me. Life was much improved as a result. Drinking far less, not waking up still drunk or with a head pounding so much, I usually threw up and even that did little to make me feel any better.

Angelique Santoro was back.

Heart FM was playing, "Love is All Around" by Wet Wet Wet, as I drove over to Aveline's villa. I was feeling lucky. Did I deserve Joshua's love? I mean, had I done so many lovely, sweet things for him that he had to fall deeply in love with me? Hardly! Let's face the truth. We're getting good at that aren't we? I'd pushed him away on many occasions. Never made him a top priority in my crazy, messed up life and yet he never faltered in how he felt about me. How is that even possible? Melanie looked like a great option, but he'd sent her away. Remained incredibly patient and stuck to me, like glue.

"Angelique!"

"Hey, Aveline" I said, exiting Nelly, gracefully.

"Oh, my God. You're sober."

"I am indeed."

"Amazing!!" Aveline squeaked, embracing me so hard, I could barely breathe.

"Easy, lil' sis."

"So, you and Joshua sitting in a tree, KISSING."

"Cute."

"Gareth told me. I hope you don't mind."

"Not at all. It's a good thing. I love him too."

"Come inside. I'm like super excited. We have options."

This past month can't have been easy on Aveline. How exactly do you create business opportunities for your kick arse older sister who refused point blank to do interviews or appearances? How do you create opportunity for someone shutting themselves off from the world? Angry, lashing out and seldom sober?

Now that I was sober, I felt guilty. No, not because I was being difficult. I was paying Aveline well to do her job, but I likely added more stress and that could have potentially triggered a relapse. Anyways, as it happened, my selfish, self-indulgent crap had not impacted negatively upon her. In fact, quite the opposite. She told me she knew I'd snap out of myself and planned accordingly.

"Have a few sunbeds in the next week, please."

"What?"

"You know. Those things which make you look less like a zombie and more like hot, olive-skinned Angelique Santoro?"

"Why?"

"Because we have a meeting!"

"OK, so we're doing meetings, now? You've booked me in for something, without talking to me first."

"Yes. Absolutely, I have. Been a busy bee, doing my job. You know that thing I do and bill you £500 per day for, whilst you've been a drunken wretch."

"I'm listening."

"Have you heard of Notorious energy drinks?"

"Nope."

"OK, so like their CEO and founder, is a man called Charles Brightstarr. Incredibly successful, more money than sense and wants to take on Red Bull, Monster and Relentless. He wants to become the number one energy drink brand."

"Isn't the word notorious, typically a negative vibe, like the opposite of reputable?"

"It can be neutral, simply meaning very well-known but yes,

the Krays were notorious London gangsters. It's often used in an edgy kind of a way. But my dear Angelique, I hate to state the obvious but notorious is what you've become."

"Fuck it. I like it. Notorious Angelique Santoro. Put that in your pipe and smoke it, Team GB!"

"Glorious. I was hoping this was how you were going to react."

"No. You've nailed it lil' sis. I love it. Let's embrace what happened and stand tall. I still feel no remorse nor will I ever, so if notorious sticks to me like wet mud to a wall, so be it."

"Oh, my God. It's like, my sister is back!!"

"I'm back alright. Sorry for worrying you."

"No, it's fine. Like super cool. You're a client. You're all such dicks."

"Mother will lose her shit over this."

"She will."

"And you're ok with that?"

"I am, yes. I feel you've been treated very poorly over everything. Had a rubbish couple of years in so many ways. When life gives you big fat, juicy Amalfi lemons, you'd best get busy making lemonade!"

We laughed and embraced one another, neither of us in any rush to end the hug.

"Anything else bubbling?"

"There is one thing, I'm exploring but it's still in the

discussion phase. I take it, I have your blessing as per Notorious drinks to interact and feel out opportunities for you?"

"I trust you, Aveline. If I don't like it, we won't be doing it, so go for it. Just keep on, keeping on."

"Excellent response. I shall indeed carry on then and please don't forget the sunbeds. Charles thinks you've been visiting our grandparents in Amalfi. It's been glorious there lately; you need to look tanned and chilled out when we meet him."

"Jeez girl, you lie so easily."

"I think what you meant to say was, wow Aveline, that's incredible how you pushed the meeting back ten days without arousing suspicion as to why."

"Because I was a drunken mess?"

"Yes. Absolutely. I was hoping another week wallowing in your own pathetic shit might be long enough."

"Understood. Sunbeds it is then."

The very next day, I drove over to see Joshua. Greatest Hits radio was playing the biggest songs from the 90s. Volume way up, I was bouncing and singing along to the epic track, "It's Like That" by Run-D.M.C, featuring Jason Nevins. Driving fast. Throwing Nelly about, giggling to myself every time the rear end stepped out, power sliding through those flowing country roads.

I like giggling to myself. I'd not done it in the past couple of months, but it felt more like six. Funny the things we notice or miss about ourselves once we turn the page, is it not? Suddenly become so aware we've been out of step, out of character to the point daily things we used to do, which amused us, we've not even realised we'd stopped doing them. I think mental health is incredibly fragile. You don't need to be on meds or go to the doctors, be prescribed something. Heck, you don't need to be "officially ill" to be struggling within yourself. How many of us are dulling our emotions, our true feelings with drink or drugs? Prescription meds not actually prescribed but sourced through a dealer? What human beings can readily do to themselves, in terms of causing real harm, is limitless.

Joshua was in the garage polishing up his Ducati when I pulled up. The garage door was open and all I could see was his perky bum as he was on his knees reaching in to clean the wheels.

"Be with you in a minute. Just finishing up."

"Oh, you take your sweet time whilst I take mine, Joshua."

"You perving?"

"I most certainly am. Could find me a camping chair and just settle in with a cold beer."

Joshua stopped what he was doing, sat back over his knees, and looked over his shoulder.

"Just a dirty slut, aren't you really? I mean, deep down?"

"Not even deep down."

"Not my fault you look so fine, Sir Josh-UA."

"Gotta say you look and sound like yourself. That's great."

"I'll grab us a couple of cold ones' and you can tell me about your day."

He said nothing, just smiled before going back to the bike.

Joshua had made love to me, not fucked me this past week. Soft, gentle, tender. So much kissing. You know when you were with your first love as a teenager? Perhaps, the parents are around and whilst you're intimate to a point you know, clothing remains on. You're not having sex with them a few rooms away! Well, I certainly wasn't. That week, I was fifteen again. I loved every second of it. So many kisses planted on my face, my neck. Hands through my hair, in such a way, I knew what I meant to him without a single word spoken. When you've been though a lot, those feelings are amplified.

The internet café I liked was situated in central Brighton. The nearest car park was a total rip off, but I used it anyway that day. I had found a balance. If I was with Joshua and needed to get my research done, I would say Gareth needed me and vice versa. Did you know that locating where CCTV cameras are positioned is within the public domain? I know right? That shocked me as well, but the information is just a few clicks away.

I had learned through the court those two days sat there observing silently, that Smitherman and Scott had given the same address. The cousins lived together. How lovely! How sweet! Such a close, loving family dynamic. Convenient for them, their work in the church perhaps. More significantly, it was wonderfully convenient for me.

I tried not to scratch my head too often, to avoid drawing attention to myself. The red wig and horn-rimmed glasses were always in the boot of my car. There, whenever I required them. The fact I was now famous or notorious or whatever the fuck I was, meant not being recognised going out and about had become critical. Never entered my home or left it wearing my disguise. The paparazzi, whilst a bunch of arseholes were not stupid, nor predictable and could hide behind cars and bins. I was careful to ensure there was never a picture of me in the wig.

They lived in a large, semi-detached three-bedroom house on Arnold Street. Number 34. It was the last in a line of expensive properties just off Queens Park Road. In other words, they had just one direct neighbour. Preferable to being mid terrace or indeed in a block of flats with neighbours all around. Queens Park in the Hanover district was for the posh or successful only.

Some of you reading this are British, many won't be, so those of you not from our overpopulated island, I will explain why this is significant. The British people can be and often are emotionally shut down. Putting our heads in the sand and pretending the shit which has just happened, in fact didn't really happen at all and yes, we will stop what we are doing for a nice cup of tea around 4pm on any given day. Now, what you might not know is that in this area, neighbours are not really neighbours. If you are living in a cheaper, more densely populated area, you may know your neighbours quite well. You are perhaps more down to earth and well, so are they. The fact you live in such proximity, not unlike rats behind a fancy restaurant means saying, Hello! How are you today? are likely to be experiences you frequently have and of course from here some kind of friendship may develop. Now, in sharp contrast, when you live in a property which costs between £1 million and £3 million in the UK, you not only have less neighbours, but you also have large garden walls, garages, and private land such as a driveway for your expensive Mercedes or Range Rover. A lot of British people keep themselves to themselves. "An Englishman's home is his castle" is a term you may have heard. It is true. So, you have geography keeping the neighbours at arm's length and you have the natural Britishness to not get involved and pretend things are not happening or whatever it is, you are quite sure, "It will be ok."

I was banking on this. I was confident these two obnoxious arseholes, especially Smitherman, did not have a close relationship with his neighbours. Scott was socially awkward and just weird looking so I hoped he would keep himself to himself.

My research was complete. Knew exactly where they lived, how to get to their house and return safely to mine, without ever being seen on CCTV. I smiled to myself as I logged out, muttering, "See you soon boys."

CHAPTER TWENTY-SEVEN

Part 1

WOW!!

It was just two days until the meeting with Notorious energy drinks. Been somewhat preoccupied with it. Over the years running SRS, I had met so many smart businesspeople, that a meeting about partnering up was nothing new but this one had me on edge. It's reasonable I felt this way. Having lost all sources of income, had my life turned upside down and inside out, I was eager to have a positive outcome and to share this energy with my sister. Aveline had worked tirelessly promoting and protecting me and I wanted her to have a win, not just me.

"Wear a dress. Be elegant, classy this evening," Joshua had said.

"Where are you taking me?"

"Can't say. Just trust me."

"Fine. I shall dress up for you and I very much look forwards to it."

"Gareth is fine staying alone tonight?"

"He's going to a friend for dinner. Taking Ralph. He said he may stay over."

"Ah. Understood. That kind of friend!"

"His PTSD, his night terrors seem to be less severe as of late."

"They are, yes. I'd not feel comfortable leaving him home alone frequently but a couple of nights a week, I think he's happy to wind down from work, have some peace and the flat to himself."

"Great. Right then. I'll see you at my place at 8pm."

"See you then!" I said, hanging up. Joshua was not typically a man who sprung surprises upon people. I'd suggest that's not really his thing. Well, to date, he'd never been this coy about an event, always upfront. Women by and large like to know where we are going to dress appropriately. Being underdressed or even worse overdressed doesn't feel great.

A classy, little silk black dress to the knee, I judged to be correct for the evening. I drove Nelly in trainers as always, placing my heels on the passenger seat.

I arrived at Joshua's home at 7:30. Traffic was clear, and it had taken me less time to get ready than I thought. Wasn't going to sit on the sofa, clock watching whilst getting covered in

Ralph's dog hair.

"You're early."

"Does that matter?"

"No, I suppose not. Come on in. Champagne?"

"Are we celebrating?"

"Possibly."

Joshua was wearing a lovely blue tailored suit, white shirt, without a tie, two buttons undone. The look completed with expensive looking Italian, brown leather shoes.

"You look rather lovely, Joshua."

"Thank you. As do you."

We clinked our glasses together, said cheers and enjoyed that crisp, chilled champagne together.

Half an hour later and two glasses consumed, I was feeling relaxed and giggly. I noticed Joshua looking at his watch for the second time since my arrival.

"When is the taxi getting here?"

"Oh, it's not."

"So why are we both dressed up if not going anywhere?"

Joshua smiled lovingly at me, went to a drawer in the living room and returned handing me a mask. One which covers half your face not your mouth. French or Italian looking. Expensive. Elegant. Not something you pay £3 for in a fancy-dress costume shop. An item which would evoke thrilling memories and be worn many times.

I put the mask on.

"Only you can rock elegant and beautiful all at once with an air of total minx, Angelique."

"What's her name?" I enquired, whilst looking at myself in the hall mirror.

"Sorry? You've lost me."

"What's the name of the girl whose coming to your place tonight?"

"You assume it's a woman?"

I laughed, as I put my hands on my hips studying my boyfriend. I suppose this is what one would call him.

"Oh, Joshua! What have you done!?"

My eyes must have been sparkling like a diamond caught in perfect light. They always did when a huge grin took over my face.

There was a confident, bold, four knocks upon the front door.

I looked over to Joshua thinking no ordinary man knocks that confidently upon a stranger's door for the first time. Joshua smiled easily at me, shrugging his shoulders.

"You might want to get that."

I was dying to say something quirky, something fun or coy or well anything so this moment might be relived in the future and I'd come across all cool and alive. My mouth opened and shut without a single word escaping. This is real life not a movie my friends.

I opened the door, and a small gasp escaped my mouth.

"Hello, Angelique. I'm Eros."

Eros stood at least nine inches taller than Joshua. Making him about six foot, seven-inches tall. Shoulders so broad, he had to turn his frame slightly to enter the hallway. Ruggedly handsome, dark skinned, with deep brown eyes and black, shoulder length hair. The closest thing on this earth to this hunk was Jason Momoa, playing Khal Drogo, in Game of Thrones.

"Nice to meet you Eros. Aren't you beautiful."

He laughed and I felt a total idiot. I was just stunned. It was impossible for anything to come out of my mouth and not make me appear foolish. Like some silly schoolgirl with a crush on their best friend's dad. Just such a shock! One minute laughing around with Joshua, feeling the alcohol flow into my bloodstream and now, I had Drogo for real, standing before me. Towering over me. Don't forget, I'm only five-foot, four-inches tall.

"Eros, you made it!" Joshua cried out, as the two men shook hands.

"It was an easy journey, no delays even."

"Come into the kitchen. I see you've brought a bottle of your famous Vodka."

"I promised I would."

"Champagne and Vodka mix up. This could get messy," I suggested, finally finding my voice.

"All we are missing is music!" cried Eros.

"Angelique will see to that, let's go to the kitchen and prepare the drinks."

The boys left me standing alone in the living room, coming back to myself. "Cheeky Angelique it is then!" I muttered under my breath. I shook my head thinking of Joshua. How many men do you know who would go to seek out a stunning hunk of man to join him and his girlfriend or wife? I am not talking about men who are cuckhold here. Nor bi-sexual guys. Straight guys want a hot bi-sexual or bi-curious girl in their bed. To feel like a stud, to have two women at once.

To be straight and be like Joshua? Wow. You'll be hunting high and low to achieve such a thing. Most guys are insecure about their performance deep down so to invite a man nine inches taller than you into your universe. Confidence. A man so at ease with himself. A man so confident in what he feels towards his partner and knowing she is utterly besotted with him. Knowing no man could ever threaten them. To me, this is a very special love. I am not yours. Not a possession. Never try and control me. I'll leave you in a heartbeat. Love me properly. Show me I am yours alone, where your heart is concerned, and I'll light up your darkest night like a shooting star.

Having selected Pink Floyd, "Brick in the Wall." I walked over to the kitchen to join the men.

This large bottle of Vodka was taking centre stage. Peach Vodka.

"This is what Eros does, Angelique. He owns a Vodka production company."

"Ha! You make me sound important; it is just a small concern, Angelique."

"Wonderful. Looks inviting," I said, looking him up and down.

"Who do you own the company with?"

"My wife. Well, soon to be an ex-wife. We are great friends not very good husband and wife."

"Sorry to hear that. It happens of course."

"It's fine. We are in discussion with some investors. It's possible our little vodka company might be a lot larger in the future," Eros suggested, before asking where the toilet was and leaving Joshua and I alone for the first time.

Joshua was reading my mind.

"Keep the mask on."

"Playing with fire here, Joshua!? What if he uses us then goes to the papers?"

"Relax. I met him a week ago, checked him out. Look, he doesn't even know who Angelique Santoro is. He's utterly engrossed in this business taking off and sorting out a divorce amicably with his wife. They have two young kids; he wants full access to them. I don't believe he would go to the papers even if he could. His flying under the radar is essential to his own well-being. It's cool but yeah, keep the mask on. You look hot in it."

"OK. Cool. I trust you. Of course, you did your homework. Good boy," I said, patting Joshua on the top of his head, like a puppy.

We were giggling and larking about when Eros returned.

"You two are a truly, wonderful couple. There is no jealousy between you. What you have is a very pure love. I can see this so clearly. I'm a little jealous if I am honest. My wife would see things that were not there at times and the slightest flirting would cause arguments that lasted a week!"

"Thank you, Eros. Sweet of you to say. What nationality are you?"

"I am Greek on my mother's side and Iranian on my father's."

"My wife is full on pure Greek hence the jealousy is not her fault. All Greek women are created like this!!"

We all laughed as Eros filled large shot glasses. Each glass held two shots.

"Please. Enjoy the peach Vodka," he said, passing a glass to us.

It was quite lovely. Subtle peach flavours, not harsh or overpowering nor sickly sweet.

"You deserve a thriving business, Eros. That really is special."

"Thank you, Joshua. You are too kind."

"Still forty percent proof?"

"Oh yes, Angelique. We make Vodka taste good. We do not tame the Vodka."

"Oh, my days! You could get messy on this."

"This is true!" Eros put his head back and laughed.

He reminded me of a warrior king from a fantasy film.

There was something so overpowering about this man. When he laughed it was more a roar, his deep voice filled the room.

I left the boys chatting having finished my Vodka. I returned to the living room, looking through the dance vinyl records delighting myself when I sourced, “Missing” by Everything but the Girl, remixed by DJ, Todd Terry.

Casually I walked back to the kitchen, deliberately letting my hips sway in an aggerated manner, knowing the men were watching my every move. I picked up Joshua’s hand and kissed it, whilst locking eyes with him before turning around and reaching up to kiss Eros.

CHAPTER TWENTY-SEVEN

Part 2

WOW!!

Eros kissed me back with the lustful passion of a man, who needed a release, a distraction from his everyday life. Fine by me. I'll be whatever you want me to be. The Gods blessed this man with such genetics, I suspect he could make any woman weak at the knees by just smiling at them. Why have I always found mixed raced people so hot? Yes, the mixing of blood from different parts of the world can create very beautiful people. But, as ever with me, this is far too simplistic.

As I kissed him, losing myself in this passionate embrace, I couldn't help thinking, "so your dad is Iranian, your mother Greek? Did they have to endure racism to be together? Did their love have to shine and power through darkness? You shouldn't be together! Did his parents suffer for their love for one another? The idea that they did and stuck two fingers up to the world and that Eros was the product of their unbeatable love, made me horny. The idea they didn't care and fucked like wildcats on heat, made me kiss him back even harder."

I turned around to kiss Joshua. Running my hands through his gorgeous blonde locks, feeling my pussy getting wetter with each passing moment. After a few minutes of kissing each man in turn, I pulled away to catch my breath.

"Stand beside Eros."

Joshua did as he was asked.

Reaching forwards, I felt both cocks twitch involuntarily beneath my touch.

"Don't move. Remain silent."

I moved closer, keeping my hands on those hardening cocks. Standing on my tippy toes to reach high enough to rest my head on Eros's chest. Stroking his big, hard cock, whilst listening to the pounding of his heart. I looked deep into his eyes, remained silent and repeated my seduction, doing the same thing with Joshua.

He grabbed both my wrists, squeezing so hard he hurt me. I smiled back at him.

"Something you wish to say, Sir Joshua?"

"Take Eros in your mouth. I want to feel how wet you'll get doing that."

"You wanna lick my pussy, whilst I suck this stranger's cock? Is that what you want?"

"Yes."

Eros was the perfect guest, the perfect everything. He laughed. A grin so wide covered his face said everything to me.

I hitched my silk dress up and over my hips, put my hands on Joshua's head and pushed him to his knees. Looking down to lock eyes with the love of my life, as he pulled my satin, black lace thong to one side, opened his mouth, letting his tongue glide effortlessly over my wet sex. His gaze never left mine until I pulled his head harder into me.

One advantage of Eros being so tall? All I had to do was bend a little at my waist and that cock of his was right there in front of my open mouth. Don't like long, thin cocks. Don't really like long cocks at all in fact. I'm quite short so anything over eight inches just whacks my cervix and hurts. Eros had the most perfect cock. Like two coke cans joined together! But prettier, of course!! Perhaps 7 inches long and so thick, so girthy, I had to relax my jaw to take him. "This cock is staying in my pussy, not going up my arse tonight," I thought to myself, as I strained to take his massive cock further into my mouth. Both hands on Eros's hips, supporting myself as Joshua's tongue dipped in and out of my pussy. Licking me all over, before taking his sweet time sucking my clit. I wasn't wet. I was drenched.

Finally, my jaw muscles stretched and relaxed enough to take Eros deep into my mouth, letting that hard, pulsating cock hit the back of my throat, releasing him just before I started gagging. Using all that spit to further lube up his already beautiful, glistening helmet.

"Alexa. Play Dirty, Christina Aguilera."

As the tune started, I began to ride Joshua's face harder. Faster. Grinding my wet sex into his pretty face. Feeling my first orgasm approaching at pace, I held onto the back of Joshua's head, pulling him further into me, releasing Eros's cock from my mouth, gasping for air.

"Fuck, I'm Cumming!"

Joshua grabbed my arse cheek with one hand, the other arm wrapped tightly around my thigh, preventing me from going anywhere.

"Hold her tight, Joshua. Hold her! Make her cum again!"

Eros grabbed the back of my neck, forcing my mouth back onto his cock and held me there as Joshua's tongue worked me, like his life depended on it. Cumming harder than my first orgasm, unable to speak, to even mutter a single word, as my mouth, my throat was full.

I pushed myself away from Eros first, then Joshua. Leaning up against the kitchen worktop, panting, my legs shaking, feeling my wet juices moving down my thigh, before sticking to my skin like glue.

Still breathless, wiping the saliva from the corner of my mouth.

"Follow me. Now. Both of you!"

The men did as I commanded and followed me. I could sense they were perving at my full, round arse cheeks, nudging one another, chuckling like a couple of naughty schoolboys about to find themselves in detention.

Reaching the sofa, I crawled cat like across it, arching my back, letting my breasts drag along the leather cushions. Face down. Chest down. Submissive.

“Johnny up, Eros. Fuck her hard.”

“Angelique. I’m going to face fuck you, whilst you try and take that monster cock.”

“Fucking use me, Joshua. Use me, yeah.”

Some women are submissive, some are dominant. Men are the same. I love that Joshua is so like me. I am very happy to dominate other girls, as I did Kirsty and then when with hot men, flit between the different mind-sets. There are times, I just want to be used like a stupid, dirty slut. A totally submissive, fuck toy. Just use me. Don’t ask for my permission, just do it.

I was so wet, and it still wasn’t enough. His cock just so thick. I couldn’t take him.

“You’re hurting me, Eros. Spit on the Johnny please!”

Joshua ran to the bedroom, grabbed some lube, and smiled at the handsome giant struggling to enter his girlfriend. God, I love this man. Not a hint of jealousy or possessiveness. Such a rare find. Just wanted me to get off longer, better than I had in my life and take satisfaction that it was he and he alone which created this unique night of passion shared. The best footballers in the world do not score the goals my friends, they set them up. The striker just taps it into the back of the net. In American football, it is the star quarterback who throws the perfect spiral pass which is caught and run in for a glorious touchdown. He makes it rain. Joshua made the heavens open that night.

Eros lubed his cock up generously I assume, as he entered me without further pain. But oh, my days, he stretched me to my limit. I could barely breathe. It was as if he stole my vocal cords, my breath and anything else he wanted. As he pushed deeper into my pussy, Joshua grabbed the back of my head and pulled me towards him. I just had time to open my mouth before his hard cock came in and he started to face fuck me in time with Eros. Slow, deep, trusts from both men. Like synchronized swimmers at the Olympics. Just together, in perfect step with one another, yet total strangers before half an hour ago. I felt like the luckiest woman alive in that moment. Sensory overload. Seeing stars, bright colours. God, he was so big, felt so magnificent stretching me wider than I've ever known.

"Christ, she's so tight!"

"Like a vice around your cock?"

"Like a virgin or something, Joshua!"

I tried to join the men laughing together but there was no way. Powerful men, holding you firmly at both ends is so submissive, it's like it would be wrong to try and join them. Just shut up and be used.

Joshua removed his rock-hard cock from my mouth and got on his knees to kiss me. We kissed passionately before he pulled away smiling at me, looking over my shoulder to Eros.

"Fuck her faster now Eros. C'mon man, step it up!"

I gasped out loud as Eros did as Joshua commanded of him.

Joshua gently cupped my face.

"Open your eyes, Angelique. Look at me."

I opened my eyes to see Joshua's easy smile and a cheeky wink.

"He's stretching you wide, hmmm?"

"Oh, my God Joshua, he's amazing!" Gasping for air, trying to talk to my boyfriend but failing to achieve anything further.

Joshua laughed as my eyes rolled and left me to try and keep myself alive by taking regular breaths.

I felt Joshua kissing down my back, one hand locked into my hair holding me firm, as his other hand was grabbing, massaging my arse. Next thing I knew a wet finger was drawing pictures, circling around my arsehole, teasing me. The finger suddenly stopped, only to return significantly wetter covered in saliva. Joshua eased that wet finger into my arsehole, inch by inch until knuckle deep. I moaned as he started finger fucking me in perfect time with Eros's thrusts. Feeling that finger massage along that huge cock through the thin membrane separating my pussy from my bumhole was heaven.

"You like that, Angelique?" Eros asked.

"I fucking love it."

Joshua didn't need any further encouragement and eased a second lubed finger to join the first circling inside me. Massaging, stretching within my arsehole sending me over the edge. I shuddered as my orgasm ripped through my body just as Joshua went deeper yet pulling back on my hair as he did so.

"Fuck her harder, Eros."

I heard no response from the man mountain, he just grabbed hold of my hips with those huge hands and thrusted harder, faster into my wet sex as Joshua kept those two fingers buried deep into my arsehole. My eyes rolling, hair soaked in sweat, I cried out as I came again.

"Stop. Please stop!"

"Eros, come here, let me kiss you." I gasped, flopping onto my back.

He held his huge structure up on his well-muscled arms and kissed me. I could feel warm sweat dripping from his body onto mine. Licked his chest, tasting his salty skin as we lay together, his tongue licking along my neck, taking my sweat along with it.

"Water?"

Joshua had seemingly vanished, gulped down a glass of water in the kitchen and returned to kindly give us a glass each.

"Thank you so much!"

"Most welcome, you deserve a little refreshment, Eros!"

We went to the kitchen to return the glasses and have a cheeky double Vodka, keep the party on track, keep fueling the lust. Whilst Eros was doing the honours with his prized peach Vodka, I asked Alexa to play "Sexyback" by Justin Timberlake.

The minute or two away from the sofa was sufficient for us all to catch our breath, enjoy some refreshment but not long enough for two studs such as Eros and Joshua to lose more than an inch from being fully erect.

"I want to ride you whilst Joshua fucks my arse."

Looking each man in the eye as I spoke, they both squeezed my hands at the same time and chuckled mischievously at one another. Do men ever actually grow up!? Obviously, that's a rhetorical question my friends.

Eros took a step towards me, placed his huge hands around my arse cheeks and hoisted me into the air. I wrapped my thighs around his waist, my arms around his neck and kissed him. You want to know the definition of a perfect boyfriend? It's a straight man which recognises a task requires his assistance and does so without hesitation. In other words, he took Eros's cock and guided him into me.

I'm a 65kgs athlete. I'm not 50kgs. I'm densely muscled, especially in my legs and bum. Eros walked back to the living room as if he had such a tiny woman in his arms. Each step he took, meant his cock reached deeper into my wet pussy. Owning me. I couldn't have gotten away from him if I'd wanted to. Locked up. Trapped in his embrace, like prey in the grasp of a python.

Joshua threw the sofa cushions onto the living room floor and Eros lay down, with my body still entwined to his. I started riding this gorgeous man, this perfect thick cock stretching me like never before, entering me so deeply, as I ground my clit upon him. I felt Joshua moving in close behind me, kissing the back of my neck as his swollen helmet nudged gently away at my arsehole.

"Put it in. I want it."

"You want me to fuck your arse?"

"Please. I'm begging you. Do it."

Nothing is hotter for me than commanding a man or men what to do with my body, accept the glorious submission of the physical act, having done so. Hmmm, just so hot. The mind body connect. Telling them what to do, then relinquishing all my power. Allowing myself to become a rag doll. Allowing myself to be taken. To be used and abused. To become that cheap fuck toy by my own design.

Joshua entered me confidently, one long slow stroke and he was into me, balls deep. No messing around. He had already excited me, helped me cum a few minutes earlier opening my arse up with his two fingers. I was ready for his cock. My head started spinning, my eyes struggling to focus, I just had to close them, relax my body, and try to breathe freely. Two fingers had made me feel incredibly full with Eros's cock stretching my pussy to the maximum and now Joshua's big cock opening my arsehole just as much. I thought I was going to pass out at one point. No pain. Just incredible, overwhelming tightness and pleasure all at once, was overwhelming.

Joshua ruined me, fucking my arse like a pussy as Eros lifted his hips from the floor to enter me more deeply. Both men thrusting into me with such passion, such vigor, I couldn't take it a moment longer and gave in as my orgasm tore through my body leaving it lifeless, listless, slumped upon Eros.

"Get up, Angelique."

"What?!"

Joshua took his cock from my arse and repeated himself.

"Get up."

I stumbled to my feet, unsteady on my legs, looking at my man, puzzled, still trying to breathe normally.

"What do you want from me?"

"I want to watch Eros cum in your face."

"Yeah. I want that."

Eros stood over me and started to wank himself off, as Joshua held my arms behind my back.

"Fucking cum for me please!"

Eros's thighs started to shake, a little at first then more visibly as he reached climax. He groaned. A deep guttural moan, as his cum leapt from his pulsating cock into my open mouth, across my face and mask.

Eros collapsed into a nearby armchair.

Joshua busied himself taking all the cum from around my face and mask, letting me lick Eros off his fingers.

"All of it."

"Of course. Tastes sweet." If a man eats a good diet, especially fruits such as pineapple and oranges girls, he tastes good. Make a little mental note of that. Can thank me if we ever meet.

Whilst our man mountain recovered, Joshua pulled me down to join him on the floor, turned me around so we were spooning and eased his cock into my pussy. Wrapping his arm around my inner thigh, so he could gain access to my clit. Real men watch lesbian porn. OK, I'll rephrase that. My man does, with me. Watching, studying how girls make each other cum. How they touch one another and use their fingers and tongues should be mandatory sex education in schools! Would save a whole lot of girls who grow up to become women married to men who think foreplay is a foreign language. Rubbing my clit clockwise, then anticlockwise, up and down mixing it up, so before long, I didn't know what he was doing. It was all lustful pleasure, his touch in perfect harmony to his beautiful, hard cock thrusting into me.

Just as Eros stood up, his limp cock starting to show signs of life again, Joshua took his cock from my pussy and re-entered my arse.

"Fuck yes."

"You want me to double-dip you?"

"Yes! Oh my God, yes!"

Watching Eros stroke himself in time to Joshua's thrusting was a delightful sight. That thick cock, reborn, growing so swiftly. I couldn't take my eyes off it. Part of me was wondering just how on earth I took him inside of me. Lying on my side looking up at him, it was like looking up at a scaffolding rig being erected.

"Eros. I want you to tell Joshua when to change holes."

"Fuck, that's hot."

"Let him do this for me yeah, Joshua?"

"As you wish, my life."

"Change!"

Joshua did as he was instructed and removed his cock from my arsehole and eased himself back, balls deep into my pussy and quickened his pace.

"Fuck! That is amazing" I cried out.

Eros had moved himself in front on me, sat on his knees he pushed his cock into my mouth. I took him as deep as I could then released him, licking his helmet, spitting on his tip, using my fingers to rub, to massage my saliva around his swollen shaft. He was transfixed watching Joshua take me.

Then he'd suddenly look into my eyes and I'd lose myself getting fucked so beautifully whilst gazing back into his deep brown eyes. I need intimacy even in such an encounter. Losing yourself in a hot stranger's eyes whilst he controls your lover's every move is mind blowing. It is sensory overload. It is that river crossing where love meets lust, and they are not enemies but friends. The two emotions are not mutually exclusive from one another as we are taught in the bible or at school. Lust is good. Love is good. Let them meet and become one.

"Change!"

Joshua took his cock from my pussy and entered my arsehole, just as Eros took over from him in taking ownership for my clitoral stimulation. His tongue darting like a firefly in the evening dust. Licking my clit, sucking that bud as I took him back into my mouth.

Eros took his cock from my mouth and started teasing me, using his fingers over my clit as he asked, "You want that cock in your arse a little longer?"

"I do, yes."

Eros laughed. "Joshua! When I count back from ten to zero you change!"

Eros started to count down, that deep, booming voice of his filling the air.

"Ten, nine, eight, seven, six, five……four…. three"

I started moaning with anticipation.

"Two, one! Put your cock back into her pussy."

Again, Joshua did as he was asked by Eros, re-entering me in a single thrust, making my head spin. I was seeing stars, unable to speak as Eros put that huge cock back into mouth, still rubbing with my clit. It's one thing having your man do things to you, right?! I mean, I still can't predict what's going to happen next because any good lover is unselfish and mixes patterns and rhythm up to enhance your pleasure, right? With a total stranger, you have no clue as to what they will do next! It's a head fuck. A gloriously hot mess up.

"Fuck me harder!"

Joshua grabbed me by my hair and yanked me back onto his shaft. Grabbing my hair and pulling on it with each thrust of his hips.

"I'm fucking Cumming," I cried out.

"Yeah, cum with me, cum with me, baby!"

My abs tensed up, nearly cramping in pain, my whole body was convulsing as I felt Joshua lose himself to me. Four pumps from his pulsating, twitching helmet as I felt him cum deep inside me, setting me off again. Eros held me tightly around the back of my neck, pulling my mouth onto his cock as he too lost himself to me, his sweet cum hitting the back of my throat.

CHAPTER TWENTY-EIGHT
Charles Brightstarr

Charles Brightstarr was the founder of Notorious Limited. His brand covered everything from the new energy drink to owning a successful record label, hotels and various luxury products including the very best leather goods sold out of the coolest shops in places such as Paris, Milan, London, and Dubai.

He came from privilege. Had gone to Eton, was old school pals with our disgraced ex-Prime Minister, Boris Johnson. He was a 24-carat arsehole. Ruthless, aggressive, menacing and a very shrewd businessman. Brightstarr inherited a small fortune when his father passed from cancer some eight years previously and trebled it within just five years. Standing six-foot three-inches tall, brown, wavy public schoolboy hair down to his shoulders, strong jawline and being athletically built, did nothing but support his arrogant stance.

"Notorious Angelique Santoro!" he exclaimed, extending his hand to me.

"Been called far worse," I replied, shaking his hand.

"Haven't we all, eh."

Aveline presented herself.

"Of course. The queen of PR herself. Pleasure to meet you, Aveline. Your reputation precedes you, just not quite as much as your sister."

We sat in beautifully crafted armchairs with leather soft as kitten fur. The office was on the 28th floor of The Shard. One of London's most famous and tallest skyscrapers, near London Bridge. Even sitting down, the views across the city were spectacular through huge glass windows.

"A view of London comes with a serious price tag."

"I can only imagine Mr. Brightstarr."

"Fuck the formalities, Angelique! Call me Charles for Christ's sake."

"Quite the view Charles."

"Yes, it's something alright. I'm a very busy man, even if you're not a very busy woman these days. Shall we crack on?"

A nice little dig at my life. Is this how you do business? Charming and easy going but every other sentence laced with poison?

"Angelique will be busy soon enough."

Charles laughed at Aveline.

"Is that right? Got dropped by Sony faster than a bullet train. Soon as that fight scene went viral!"

"You're not the only person wise enough to want to tap into Angelique's growing popularity."

"I'll bet, I'm the only successful global brand you're having a meeting with this week, Aveline."

"That is correct. The reason for that however is you've always been ahead of the curve. I bet if other companies knew we were sitting here with you right now, they'd be thinking about doing the same."

"Flattery. I was warned about you."

"Not flattery. It is a fact. Every business venture you've gone into was because you saw an opening before others. If you feel happier to call it flattery, that's up to you."

BrightStarr sat back in his recliner, steepled his fingers and remained silent for a while. When he spoke, it was as if his mind had visualised the next year with or without Angelique Santoro in it.

"It's a risk going with you two."

"You like risks. Gets you off."

Charles slapped his hand on the aluminum desk and sprung to his feet.

"Yes! It does. I wish at times it didn't but you're right, Aveline. Gives me a fucking hard on being controversial. I can't stand whimsy, gutless people. Take a fucking risk. What's life without risk? I married a girl with ties to the Russian mafia and I'm still here, despite numerous threats by her people to cut my balls off!"

"You probably deserved it," I said, finding my voice.

"I probably did, Angelique."

"I like the Santoro sisters. Perhaps we may do some business together."

Charles pressed a button on his telephone. "Joy, please bring in the sample drinks."

Moments later, the door opened and a breathtakingly beautiful woman dressed in an elegant, emerald green suit walked in, holding a silver tray with four cans. Joy put the tray down and left silently.

"Four cans, four different flavours. Help yourselves."

Aveline reached forwards, selected a can which appealed to her and handed me a different one.

"The artwork, graphics still a work in progress but you can see what we're going for."

The cans were all in bright colours. Surprisingly artistic and bold.

"Go on, go on! Take a sip for fuck's sake."

Aveline and I opened the cans and each took a sip.

"Well?"

I took another sip. Aveline followed suit.

"Surprisingly good," I replied.

"Yeah, mine's actually really refreshing, not sickly sweet."

"Brilliant!" Charles yelled, as he slammed the desk again, his eyes wide.

"Ask me why it tastes good. Go on. Ask me."

I shrugged my shoulders.

"Because compared to Monster energy drinks or that putrid Red Bull shite, it is good. Read the ingredients on the back."

Essentially, all Notorious energy drinks are natural, taurine free and the sugars in the drink are there naturally from fructose not processed white sugar like you get in those sachets in a coffee shop.

"The buzz comes from Guarana?"

"Correct Angelique. The highest-grade Guarana has five times more caffeine than coffee beans. BUT because of its' antioxidant properties, unlike caffeine alone, it's actually pretty good for you. In moderation of course."

"I like Guarana. I used to take it half an hour before a contest. Sharpens you right up."

"Exactly! But notice we have blended it with Sage and Siberian Ginseng, so this is not only an energy drink but has a heap of antioxidants. We believe if you were to drink a can a day, you would only experience positive mental alertness and increased well-being."

"And if you drank three cans a day?"

"Well, you'd probably be twitching like a junkie needing a fix, Aveline."

Brightstarr paused, put both hands in his suit trouser pockets before continuing.

“Sorry. That was insensitive of me. How is your recovery?”

“Sorry. My what?!”

He eased himself back into his recliner, put his feet up on the desk in front of him.

“One thing you need to know about me, ladies. I know everything. I do not get into bed with any potential business partners without learning all there is to know about them.”

“My recovery is none of your business. I’d like to know how you could even possibly know about it. It is not in the public domain.”

“Don’t take that tone with me, Aveline. Seriously. It won’t win you favours around here. Your cocaine addiction is not widely known but it is known when you dig about. I have the best investigators at my disposal. I do not invest millions without knowing what or who I’m dealing with.”

“Touch the devil and you can’t let go,” I muttered under my breath.

“Sorry, you say something, Angelique?”

“Nothing important.”

“Your past is interesting too, Angelique. What is it now? twenty-one years ago since you got suspended from school for protecting Gareth. For beating up the school bully. History does like to repeat itself, eh?”

I grabbed Aveline’s wrist before she could say anything.

"Do you usually aim to upset, disarm, generally unsettle new business partners? Is this a tactic you find works well or is it just because you're an arsehole?"

Aveline turned to smile at me as Charles rocked back in his chair and laughed.

"You see! This is why I like you two. Both as fiery as I am!"

I was thinking, "You're a first-class douche bag and I do not like you at all but let's see what you got."

"We've another meeting to attend so shall we get down to it?"

Charles ignored Aveline, went back to his desk phone and buzzed Joy again. "Joy. Could you be a doll and ask Jenny to join us please?"

Charles stood up, put his hands back in his pockets, turned his back on us and looked out over London from his eagle's nest. He didn't move a muscle when Jenny entered the room, stood silently, still like a statue leaving Jenny to introduce herself.

"Jenny Jenkins. Global Head of Advertising. Pleased to meet you both."

Jenny was casually dressed in black jeans, designer boots and a brown cashmere jumper, her hair dyed blonde, although I think from her eyebrows and eye lashes, she would have been a mousy brown naturally.

She rested her bum on the desk, like she owned the place and made her proposal.

"You've got beautiful hair, Angelique."

"Thank you."

"It's got to go."

"Sorry?"

"Your hair. It's going. We want you in a cute but edgy pixie cut and we're going to dye your hair the colour of a rainbow."

I looked at Aveline who was grinning.

"What are you grinning at?"

"I like it."

"That's cause it's not happening to you."

I looked at Jenny. "Go on, I'm listening."

"Right Angelique. It's like this. The whole video of you attacking that wanker was perfect. Just because all the business opportunities you had are gone doesn't mean there isn't massive public support for you. You're kind of like a Robin Hood folk character right now."

"Robin Hood?"

"Yes, precisely. Loved or hated, depending upon your stance but the hair is just too upper middle class and civilised for the vibe we want."

"OK."

"Right, so picture this. We've got The Prodigy, "Firestarter" blaring out, flashing images, close ups of your face, all twisted and angry then like with a group of acrobats, street performers and fire eaters. After a short clip of you guys having a chill in the park, glorious sunshine all around, drinking the Notorious drink, then doing crazy parkour shit, leaping from buildings. Sexy, edgy. The police are chasing you all, as the advert ends. High energy, frantic."

Aveline squeaked.

"Genius; I love this!"

"My idea," Charles offered.

"Hardly," Jenny replied.

"Alright, well the police chase at the end was."

"Fine. The last bit was Charles's idea. Take a bow," Jenny said sarcastically.

The prick did precisely this. God, he's the biggest twat waffle this side of the Atlantic. Real money makes you a total arse wipe, it really does.

"Oh, and I want you with a nose stud. We'll fix that up. Real emerald to match your eyes."

Finally, a suggestion I was happy about. Nose studs are cute.

"Not loving the pixie cut."

"Get into character Angelique. Promoting a new global product is product placement. We want the fourteen to thirty market, and this will get them. The rainbow pixie cut is reminding everyone who you are and that you stand unapologetic for your actions that day."

"You sure about that?"

Jenny looked angry.

"Did you know when you hit the flag man in the face you

would break his nose?

"Yes."

"Did you know when you launched the second, almost vicious attack on him he would likely require reconstructive surgery?"

"Pretty much."

"Right then. You know fighting, I know product launch. How about you stick to what you know and leave the rest to me and my team?"

"Angelique is just a little surprised that's all. She's totally onboard with everything isn't that, right?"

I smiled easily back to Aveline, then turned to Jenny.

"Fine. Let's do this. I like the rainbow bit; I'll get used to the hairstyle."

"You're a beautiful woman Angelique. You can wear your hair any which way we want, and you'll remain beautiful."

"How about you get Sam Smith driving a limo or massive SUV to pick up our naughty street kids. You know the police chasing them, they turn a corner, and they all jump into a vehicle driven by him. Massive gay icon, mega pop star?"

Charles turned around and looked at Aveline, then Jenny.

"Amazing idea, Aveline! Jenny make the call to Sam's people, see if he'd be interested in working with Notorious Angelique Santoro."

I smiled at my sister. Love that she had some input into this project.

Jenny knew it was time for her to leave and did so, saying she hoped to see us again soon.

"I'm going to stand here looking at this view and Aveline you are going to get up and sit at my desk. You are going to pick up that gold pen and write down a number. You and Angelique will then leave. We will be in touch."

Aveline got up, moved around his desk and casually flopped into his chair. I could see Charles was itching to turn around, but he didn't. He remained with his back to us. Aveline wrote a number down and moved towards the door singling for me to follow. The goodbye was the number Aveline left on his desk.

We remained silent until a good few metres away from The Shard.

"What number did you write down?"

"£2,000,000"

"Two million pounds!? Are you insane, Aveline? He is the only person that is offering us anything now."

"Whatever figure I give him, he'll cut it in half so go in high and we can settle on a cool million."

I had never really seen my sister before. Not in any kind of professional manner. She was so cool, confident and bullish. She knew these types and knew it was a game you play to win.

We boarded the train back to Brighton, holding hands as the train pulled away from Victoria station. I stroked Aveline's hair as she rested her head on my shoulder. Within minutes she was fast asleep as my mind shifted to Smitherman and Scott.

CHAPTER TWENTY-NINE

Knock Knock.

I don't like the term, "Stalker." Makes me feel creepy. I preferred, "Watcher." Just a person which merely had an interest in two individuals.

I'll admit my interest in Smitherman and Scott was neither passive nor kindly and I certainly wasn't watching them out of any concern for their well-being. So many evenings lying to either Gareth or Joshua, coupled with getting soaking wet and cold was only pouring petrol onto my fire of hatred which burned deep within me.

Three weeks had passed since our meeting at the HQ of Notorious. Aveline negotiated the contract terms with the tenacity of a Pitbull off its leash, tugging on a rope. She did not secure the "cool million" but close enough at £900,000. Seemed a lot of money for someone now infamous for messing up the face of some homophobic, flag waving cunt. They had just finished my rainbow-coloured pixie cut; perfect emerald green nose stud sourced for the hole they had put in my nostril. I was running out of time. My life was soon to be owned by Charles Brightstarr and Notorious drinks. It was time for action.

Most people are creatures of habit. Thankfully, Scott and Smitherman were too. After a few weeks stalking, I'm sorry, I mean watching, it was clear to me that the best evening to pop over and say, "Hello, gentlemen," was a Thursday evening. After evening prayer group held at their church on Lewis Road, they usually went to the Lion and Lobster pub, a half mile walk, heading towards Brighton city centre. From here, the men would walk home together, sometimes singing songs such as, "Onward Christian Soldiers." By 10 pm they would be home, not drunk, but a few drinks in their bloodstream. Precisely where I wanted them.

Had arranged for Gareth and I to get a Thai takeaway, settle in for the evening watching a film with some good French red wine. I deliberately selected a film we had both watched before, albeit a few years ago. We finished eating around 8pm and I had gone to the kitchen to open the second bottle of vino. I placed exactly three grams of GHB into Gareth's wine and stirred it. GHB is a party drug, sadly often used by scumbags to date rape their victims. It acts as a serious depressant to the central nervous system, making people pass out swiftly, especially when consumed with alcohol. I had been very careful measuring the amount of the drug and ensuring he had consumed no more than 2 glasses of wine. I kept one eye on the movie and one eye on Gareth. Thirty minutes later he was sleeping peacefully. Placing him into the recovery position and covering him in a warm winter blanket, I left him and Ralph on the sofa and went to the bathroom.

I had gone through this evening in my mind, most nights, ever since my stay in the police cells. Unless Joshua made love to me with the performance of a leading porn star, and then cuddled me to sleep, it usually invaded my sleep. The same dream. The semi-detached house where they lived. The neighbourhood. The CCTV cameras. The celebration of their "victory" outside the courthouse. Hitting the flag man, usually in slow motion. Night after night, the same, recurring dreams. Waking up feeling angry, full of hate. I'd had enough of these images, these feelings, which did not go away. They did not dry up like pavements after heavy rain once the sun came out. My pavement stayed wet. Full of deep puddles, which would soak your shoes.

I tapped around my breasts with elastic bandages, taking me from a D cup to more like a B. Using high grade theatre make-up, I turned my pretty face into that of a demon. Black and red with red contact lenses sourced from a fancy-dress shop. In my bedroom, I dressed myself. Black motorcycle catsuit which would serve perfectly as my under garments, to allow total freedom of movement whilst keeping my skin and any DNA on my person. Military spec combat trousers, steel capped boots and a black hoodie completed my outfit. I returned one last time to the bathroom to cover my face in Vaseline. Placed a polo swimming cap over my head and picked up the Dainese racing gloves. Super lightweight gloves, with carbon fibre protection over the knuckles and moved back into the living room. Silently checked Gareth's pulse and put my ear to his mouth. He was out cold, snoring peacefully.

Cycled to Smitherman's house, hoodie up, head down, avoiding all CCTV cameras and since now aware of how effective private doorbell security cameras can be, made a point to not get too close to any posh houses whereby they might have these and outdoor lighting in place. The streets were quiet, my journey uneventful. I left the stolen bicycle 50 metres away from their house around the back of a recently bankrupt fish and chip shop. Another failed business. So many businesses boarded up. So many people struggling, ever since Covid fucking 19 hit the world.

Checked my watch. 9:45pm. Too early. "That's ok, Angelique. Go pre contest, fight mode, girl." Taking long, deep breaths, I began to meditate. Some minutes later, returning to planet earth, I felt light as a feather, my fuel cells full to the brim. In my head, my heart, my body, I was twenty-eight years old about to fight in the final of the European Championships. Always knew I would be victorious that night. It was never in doubt. I leant backwards, opening my chest to the dark night sky and threw my arms open wide. It was game time.

10:20pm, crouching down by the rubbish bins, playing Metallica, "Enter Sandman."

Knocked three times upon their door having taken a final look around the street, ensuring there was no movement. The hallway light came on, the door opened a couple seconds later.

I took one long stride forwards, entered the house, punching Smitherman hard to his throat, shortening, collapsing his windpipe in the process. He gasped, stumbled backwards, bringing both hands up to his neck, leaving his torso fully exposed. I took full advantage of his weakened, exposed state, double tapping him to the chest. Two perfectly executed punches, the second cracking his sternum. He would have cried out in pain if he could but had no voice.

Smitherman collapsed to the floor. I squatted over him, staring into his eyes. Motionless. Silent. Then it happened. Pure fear, pure terror in his eyes as he lost control of his bladder. The intense smell of urine filling my nostrils. I smiled at him, remained motionless glaring into his eyes. The American military would likely describe this attack as "shock and awe."

Stood up swiftly, just in time, as the skinny frame of Scott was hurtling down the stairs towards me, carrying a baseball bat.

"I fear no demon!" he yelled, as he reached the bottom of the stairs swinging hard. He missed me by a couple of inches, his bat smacking into the wall. I punched him to the gut, taking his bluster from him. He recovered well enough to take another lunge at me. Flailing wildly, smashing a vase full of flowers, sending water and china across the room. I reached around, took hold of the dining room mirror, removed it from the wall and swung at him. The mirror hit him hard across his face and temple, knocking him unconscious before he hit the floor. That annoyed me. I wanted to experience the same feeling, the same sensation I had a moment ago with Smitherman.

"Too much fucking noise, Angelique" I muttered to myself.

Even typically British middle-class neighbours, might think to knock upon the door or more likely, call the police.

It was time to finish what I had always had in my mind to do. To leave now, with this last task not undertaken, would bother me for the rest of my life.

I took the unconscious right hand of Scott between both of mine and twisted violently up and around, breaking it immediately. He came to and would have screamed the house down, but I had planned for such a response and before a sound could leave his mouth, I put him in a chokehold and held him there until his body fell limp in my arms.

You're doing so well, Scott. Just behave a while longer and I'll leave you be.

I repeated the action with his left wrist. This time he remained unconscious. Could hear Smitherman groaning, struggling to get to his feet, so I moved at pace back into the hallway, grabbed the back of his head and smashed it against the wall.

"Nighty Night, you homophobic cunt."

Stamped on both his hands multiple times with my military grade boots not stopping until I was certain his fingers if not his hands were broken or badly fractured.

Why were their hands so important to me, you ask? It's not as simple as because these were the hands which nearly killed my Gareth. You should know me well enough by now to understand me. To understand that is only part of it. My actions that night would mean for the next few months at least, both men would have to have others wiping their arses. Cutting their food into bite sized portions and feeding them. Washing, dressing them.

Judge me. Don't judge me. Couldn't care less what you think of me. I'm not them. Could have left them for dead. I could have ended their lives. Yet I didn't. That was never the game plan.

Humiliation and pain. That was always the plan. That and an awfully slow recovery with a nice touch of PTSD for the pair of you.

I threw a crumbled piece of paper onto the floor beside Smitherman. The writing upon it, simply read,

"An eye for an eye."

CHAPTER THIRTY

Homeward Bound.

Left their property via the back door just in case the noises caused by my actions had brought neighbours into the street. I clambered over the garden wall and crouched down in the darkness in between the recycling bins. Silence. I waited another ten seconds before sprinting back to the fish and chip shop, getting on the bike and cycling away as fast as I could, my heart pumping, buzzing, high as a kite with the overwhelming flood of adrenaline and dopamine coursing through my veins. The blood pumping hard in my jugular.

Other than making more noise than planned, the event itself was a resounding success. Gold star, Angelique, take a bow, girl. As I peddled away with all my might, I reassured myself this was not a kind and caring local community. It was unlikely the neighbours would have forced entry to check upon them, even if it were. Might have someone called the police? No way of knowing. What mattered now was successfully implementing part two of my plan. Thankfully, it was a clear sky that night, no chance of rain as I approached the allotments, over the hill by the side of Brighton Racecourse.

There were perhaps sixty or seventy individual allotments on this site. I'd looked for cameras and security lighting around the sheds in daylight but never found any evidence such things were being used. The sheds typically contained simple gardening tools, such as folks and shovels, fertiliser. Nothing of value to a junkie seeking to steal anything and sell it on.

The main gate to the site was locked but as there was no barbed wire along the top, it was a simple task to climb over it and find myself with my small torch in hand, trying to locate the shed I had selected. A little further away from the others, it had drawn me in looking unloved, unused, with weeds growing in the soil where flowers or vegetables ought to have been. Perhaps the owner had died, and no one knew about this plot or they had lost interest but still paid the monthly direct debit to the council.

Located the old oil drum behind the shed, grateful it remained as I had left it. Full of dry kindling wood and a can of petrol. I had placed plastic sheeting over the drum in case it rained, as the last task that day before leaving the site a week previously. I wasted no time in getting down to my underwear, having emptied the petrol over the wood and setting it alight. Fed my items of clothing into this fire pit, one at a time slowly, being certain it was fully ablaze before adding the next item. My rucksack containing clean gym gear was where I left it under an old, rusted wheelbarrow. Dressing myself as swiftly as possible, I went back, climbed the fence and was on my way.

I smiled to myself as "Think" by Aretha Franklin started up. Freedom. Peace of mind. No more restless nights waking up angry, furious at our incompetent police and court system. No longer feeling justice had not been served. Karma was taking her sweet time giving us any kind of payback, so I had decided to help her out as she was clearly busy elsewhere. "So many arseholes, so little time. I get it Miss Karma. This one is on me."

Walked the last mile back to my flat having discarded the stolen bicycle. It seemed rather over the top to wipe the bike clean of my fingerprints but that's what happens when you've watched too many CSI Vegas television shows. They show you the smallest bit of DNA or whatever can be used to lock you up. My hood was up on hoodie number two I was wearing that night, but I kept my head down and out of the streetlights, walking in the shadows as best I could.

My biggest fear approaching my home was a neighbour who might have been in our local pub calling out to me recognising my body shape, my walk, whatever or a dog walker out late taking his or her dog for a nighttime wee. Again, the Gods were siding on team Angelique. I did not see anyone and felt confident no one saw me.

Back in the flat, the first thing was to check upon Gareth. My heart had been pounding all the way home not just because of the assault on Smitherman and Scott but what if I had given Gareth too much GHB? What if I hurt him or worse killed him?! I knew this was nonsense, as not only did Gareth regularly take various party drugs with friends so had a certain tolerance, but I had also been super careful to give him enough to knock him out, nowhere near what would be considered a dangerous dose. Regardless, I had had a mini panic attack during that walk home.

He was fine. Fast asleep. Breathing was normal. Heartrate normal.

I got into the shower and scrubbed my face time and again until my skin was red and sore. That theatre make up is a son of a bitch to remove people, let me tell you. How professional entertainers wear this, then take it off nightly, I do not know. Once was bad enough for me! Studied myself in the mirror, turning my face this way and that, under my chin, everywhere. I only left the bathroom once confident there was no makeup left on me.

Some of you are perhaps wondering why I had covered my face in Vaseline before leaving the flat? The reason was three-fold my friends. Firstly, it gave a crazy, melted face look to my demon which somehow was even more disturbing to look upon. The second and main reason however was in case one of the men had managed to reach out and scratch me, claw at my face. They would have successfully got Vaseline under their fingernails not my skin, not my DNA. Lastly, it would make an even harder to prove picture in court that the offender was yours truly. The picture would come out blurry because my face was blurry to begin with!

"Hey, Joshua. Hope you had a nice, chilled evening. We had Thai food from that restaurant you said was good. It was divine. Great Thai food is hard to beat! So good, thanks for the tip. We watched, The Irishman dragged on a bit for me. I'll see you soon. Big love. A. xx"

I had left my mobile in the house. If anyone were to question my whereabouts. I had Gareth as my alibi and my phone signal never left the living room. This text to Joshua was made before midnight from this very living room. The phone company can tell the police these things in a few minutes if that. The Irishman is a film which drags on too long. Three hours long. Total snore fest my friends. Should have made it two hours quite frankly. I chose the film because it would give me long enough to do what I had to and return whilst it was still playing. Even Netflix and TV companies could prove the show was being streamed live at the time of the attack.

I snuggled in with Gareth, under the blanket, giving Ralph a bit of love and tried to calm my breathing. No chance of me getting any sleep tonight. There were only two questions in my mind at that time. When was there going to be a loud knock upon our door and would it be Detective Sergeant, Kirsty Jackson doing the knocking?

Acknowledgements

To my **Life Partner** whose belief in my writing, my characters and storytelling has never wavered. To the ultimate cheerleader, I salute you, always, forever.

To **Linda Jeffreys** for her proof reading and eagle eyes. Your love for Angelique gave me so much energy!

Nikki Lamers (Romance Author and Editor). I cannot thank you enough Nikki for such a thorough job as my Editor.

"The Mafia Thirteen". You know who you are. The love and support I have had from you all, ever since Diary of a Contemporary Woman was released two years ago.

"Angelique" is the result of my increased self-belief and confidence. Do not underestimate your part in my development.

To **Mhairi, Jess and Brad**. Reading each chapter as soon as it was completed, bristling with energy for more. Encouraging, full of life, love and support for me, for Angelique. Thanks so much.

To **Mum and Dad** for proof reading and letting me know what worked and suggestions when it didn't flow or feel quite right.

Lastly and most importantly, to anyone who has suffered abuse, had their lives made a misery, be it at school, in the workplace or just out in the street for being true to yourself. Crying yourself to sleep at night, guilty of nothing other than being true to yourself.

You are the inspiration behind Gareth and Angelique, this book is for you. They are my gift to you. Stay strong, never be ashamed of who you are. True beauty lies in having the confidence, the conviction to be exactly who you were meant to be. Fuck the haters.

Printed in Great Britain
by Amazon

27429050R00189